GOOD
BAD
MOTHER

GOOD BAD MOTHER

ANYA MORA

bookouture

Published by Bookouture in 2025

An imprint of Storyfire Ltd.
Carmelite House
50 Victoria Embankment
London EC4Y 0DZ

www.bookouture.com

The authorised representative in the EEA is Hachette Ireland
8 Castlecourt Centre
Dublin 15 D15 XTP3
Ireland
(email: info@hbgi.ie)

Copyright © Anya Mora, 2025

Anya Mora has asserted her right to be identified as the author of this work.

All rights reserved. No part of this publication may be reproduced, stored in any retrieval system, or transmitted, in any form or by any means, electronic, mechanical, photocopying, recording or otherwise, without the prior written permission of the publishers.

ISBN: 978-1-83618-450-8
eBook ISBN: 978-1-83618-449-2

This book is a work of fiction. Names, characters, businesses, organizations, places and events other than those clearly in the public domain, are either the product of the author's imagination or are used fictitiously. Any resemblance to actual persons, living or dead, events or locales is entirely coincidental.

*For my sister, Alessandra,
Thanks for always reminding me I'm a good mom—especially
when I need it the most!*

PROLOGUE

The crib is empty.

For a second, my body goes completely numb, the air sucked from my lungs. *No.*

I rush toward it, but there are no blankets to throw back. I look around the empty room in a desperate attempt to make sense of what I'm seeing. But she's gone.

Clover. My baby girl is gone.

I stagger back, my vision swimming as a scream lodges in my throat. This can't be real. My breath comes in ragged gasps, my chest burning as I try to think—try to piece together what's happening. Where is she?

I back up, my hands trembling. That's when I notice the smell. Smoke.

Thick and acrid, it clings to the air, curling around me like a warning. I turn toward the hallway. My mind spins and my body moves before I can think. *My house is on fire.*

I bolt down the stairs, smoke growing denser with every step. The heat hits me as soon as I reach the bottom—a wave of it, thick and smothering. Flames flicker at the edge of my beautiful living room. Tendrils of fire climb the walls, spreading faster than I can process.

My eyes sting. My lungs burn as I cough, stumbling backward. The fire is crawling fast, it is unstoppable.

I reel, choking on the smoke. *Clover*. I have to find her. Frantically I scan the room, desperate for my baby girl. My one true love. I have to find my baby.

The flames lick at the walls, consuming everything in their path. The house—the perfect life I built to replace the horrors of the past—is turning to ashes right before my eyes. My perfect nursery. My perfect family. All of it is going up in smoke.

I stumble toward the front door, my heart racing, but the heat is unbearable now. The fire spreads too fast. I can't breathe. I have to get out.

Tears stream down my face, mixing with the smoke, as I choke back a sob. I have to find Clover.

My last thought is that this fire is no accident. It is revenge. My past has finally caught up to me. Someone wants me to pay for what I did.

And then everything goes black.

ONE

AMELIA

Eight weeks earlier

If my husband knew the truth, he would leave me.

Which is why I have to make sure he'll never discover my secrets. They're too precious. Or rather, this life I've built with him is too precious. I truly love him. And now that we have our daughter, Clover, I can't mess any of it up.

Our two-month-old is finally asleep in my arms. After crying for the last hour, it's a relief that she's quieted. I wonder if the reason she's been so upset is because she can sense I'm a nervous wreck today.

Her long lashes are as fair as her hair, her skin smooth, her cheeks rosy. There's a little pink bow clip in her wispy red hair. She's wearing an ivory-colored cotton dress, with a pair of hand-crocheted booties on her feet. She is fed and sleeping, and while I feel scatterbrained, I think I've done everything possible to have her ready for what's about to happen.

This family photo shoot from hell.

I push down my worry as my husband, Timothy, walks over, a grin on his face, the diaper bag on his shoulder. Timothy always commands a room. At six-foot-three, he is a strikingly handsome man with sun-kissed blonde hair and deep blue eyes. His tall muscular build and warm smile radiate effortless confidence. Fitting for February's chill, he's wearing a tailored navy wool coat over a charcoal cashmere sweater.

"Amelia," he says gently, sitting next to me on the settee in his parents' grand foyer. "Are you hiding from everyone?"

I've been avoiding the living room. It isn't that there is anything wrong with it. It is a beautiful space, same as every other aspect of their mansion. The estate is wrapped in luxury and decorated tastefully in homage to the Pacific Northwest, where we live, with a rustic live-edge wooden coffee table crafted from reclaimed timber, showcasing the beauty of the region's forests. Floor-to-ceiling windows with thick natural linen drapes frame breathtaking views of evergreens reaching for the sky. But I'm not ready to walk into where the photo shoot is going to be taking place. Once I step foot into that room, there will be no turning back.

I know the photo will be taken in front of the stately fireplace, a mounted elk hanging above the mantel, flanked by impressive floor-to-ceiling bookshelves of leather-bound books. Opposite the fireplace hangs a portrait of Timothy and his younger sister, Lydia, when they were children, standing near their lakeside home in Eastern Washington.

"Not hiding, exactly," I whisper to my husband, forcing a soft smile, wanting to be amiable. Wanting to be loved. "I just wanted to make sure Clover was sleeping before I brought her in. I know your parents don't like it when she fusses. And she is always on the verge of tears these days." My breath catches in my throat. "Maybe I should call the pediatrician. I'm scared I'm not doing enough. That I'm not giving her what she needs..."

Timothy frowns, sitting next to me, his arm draping around my shoulder. "Darling, you are a wonderful mother, and a picture-perfect wife." He kisses my ear and I feel myself relax. He does that to me—calms my entire nervous system. I didn't know being with the right person could do that. But Timothy's touch always seems to bring with it a sense of peace.

I just wish I weren't simultaneously lying to the man.

He swept me off my feet and married me, not unlike a fairy tale. I have repaid him by giving him an entirely fabricated version of myself.

"Be easy on yourself, Amelia. Clover is a baby, of course she cries," he adds.

I smile tightly, knowing he isn't privy to most of it. And that is how I want it. I don't want to bother or burden him with Clover's needs. I need to be useful, so he doesn't regret marrying me.

So I make sure he sleeps through the night while I am up nursing our baby and rocking her back to sleep. And he is gone all day with his business projects, which means he usually comes home to a washed, fed and sleeping baby. He misses her crying in my arms, her inconsistent sleep schedule, her dozens of diaper changes.

"And my parents don't mind if our baby needs a bit of extra attention. They love Clover," he insists. "And they love *you*."

I give him a wry smile. "I can maybe buy that they love Clover, but *me*? Let's not get crazy."

Timothy and I both know how disappointed his parents were to hear of our spontaneous engagement. Later, they learned we were already pregnant when he got down on one knee. That was a tough pill for them to swallow. I am nothing like the daughter-in-law they envisioned for themselves. I think they're desperate to replace me with a more sophisticated woman.

Maybe his sister, Lydia, will find a more suitable partner. Although with her free spirit, I'm not sure they will get what they are hoping from her either.

"Well, I love *both* my girls tremendously," Timothy flatters. "Can I help with anything? I think the photographer is ready."

My heart pounds at his words and I press Clover closer to my chest, as if she were my protector, not the other way around. I wish I had an excuse to run back to our home next door. To exit this situation all together.

"And just let me know if you want me to take her during the photo shoot," he adds. "I know you've said you wanted to hold her in the family photo, but in case you change your mind, I'm here."

He's always so thoughtful. One step ahead. The kind of husband who women dream about. The kind of man who knows how to make more than a packet of ramen when their wife is away. The kind of man who can get his hands dirty, but not in a way that ever feels dangerous. I don't think he'd ever hurt me, which is why the idea of me hurting him breaks my heart. Which is why I want to do everything I can to make his life as easy as possible.

But I can't do *this*.

"Thanks, sweetheart." I smile at him, trying to keep my voice steady. "But, Timothy, I don't want to take the pictures. I don't know why everyone is so insistent on it." I rock Clover as a way to soothe my own anxious heart.

"I know you don't like being in pictures, but this means a lot to my parents. The fact that they're writing an article about our family in *American Journal* is a big deal."

"I know," I say, my heart racing. "And you should all be so proud. You've built an incredible family business, but I'm not the family. I don't need to be in the picture."

Timothy's brows knit together, immediately displeased. "Amelia, you're my wife, the mother of my child. Of course, you are part of this family."

I press my lips together. "I don't like getting my photo taken," I repeat for the tenth time this week.

"Which is something I think you should get over," Timothy remarks, leaning in close, kissing my cheek firmly. "You're the most beautiful woman I've ever laid eyes on. And, God, your smile, the way your eyes sparkle... you light up a room. I *want* you in this photo, at my side. You are part of the Sterling legacy, and so is Clover."

My stomach twists with dread, realizing I'm cornered. This is a no-win situation for me. The last thing I want is to hurt Timothy, and I know the bigger fuss I make about this, the more I'll be questioned as to why I'm being so resistant. It doesn't make any sense why I would be this difficult about a family photograph. But I have to think beyond this moment.

My mouth is dry as I search for words. "Remember why we had a small wedding? I don't like attention..."

Timothy exhales, his patience wearing thin. "I know. And it's something I love about you. You are low key, which is refreshing after a lifetime of being around people who love to be the center of attention. But this time it isn't about you. No offense," he adds, carefully choosing his words. "It's about my parents. They've done so much for us."

I nod, recognizing that if I don't just go with the flow on this point, there will be a divide that will begin to grow. And that's the last thing I want to happen. But the risk for me is high. This photograph could completely collapse this house of cards I'm living in.

I take Timothy's hand in mine, Clover nestled in the crook of my other arm, and I play the only card I know I have left. "All right," I say, "but can I look down at the baby and not at the camera?"

Timothy's eyes glaze over, a look of annoyance veering on disgust appearing on his chiseled face. His words are tight. "I don't want you to be uncomfortable, Amelia. But you need to do this properly." He wraps an arm around my shoulder, his fingers gripping me hard, as if keeping me in place.

He holds me tightly at his side, close enough to hurt, as we walk into the living room, Clover still sleeping peacefully. Timothy's father and mother, Alexander and Isabelle, and Lydia, are waiting for me. When I enter, they smile, then stand, as if on cue.

It is only then I look around and see the scope of what is happening. Studio lights have been set up, and there are several people here from *American Journal*. In the corner of the living room, there is a hair and makeup station, a clothing rack filled with designer items for wardrobe changes, and several photography assistants checking bulbs and flashes.

There are a dozen people in this room, and it seems overwhelming. I don't know what I was expecting, but when I put on a light blue linen dress this morning, I figured that would be good enough for the photo shoot. Now a woman is here, explaining to us what we will be wearing for the first photo. Timothy's eyes catch mine. Unease washes over me as I absorb the flintiness in his eyes that offers a silent warning for me to be on my best behavior in front of his family.

A look that says thank you, a look that says I love you.

A look that says *behave*.

Lydia walks toward me, her slender figure sashaying with a glass of sparkling wine, her tiny dog, Petunia, at her heels. "Down this, Amelia. It will calm you. You look like a nervous wreck."

My cheeks flush, insecurity washing over me. Lydia is intimidating any day, but right now, photo shoot ready, she is downright frightening in her perfection.

I take the flute from her. "Do I look that terrible?"

She smirks, her glossy lips full, her teeth bright. She's equally iridescent when she is all done up, like she is at this moment, or when she is in the saddle on her prize-winning horse, Priscilla. "You look like you did on your wedding day. A bit..." She frowns. "*Frightened*."

My stomach lurches as the sweet wine slides down my throat. I'm doing the one thing I vowed I would never do. Have my photo taken by a stranger. Because if my picture is out there, it means someone could find it. Someone could see my face.

I look over at my mother-in-law, Isabelle, and her eyes catch mine—a dark glimmer of annoyance fills me with dread. My resistance for this photo shoot is certainly not helping my standing with my husband's family.

Isabelle steps toward us and offers her children and husband a generous smile, not even glancing at me. It isn't surprising. Today, her pleasure is found in her perfect family. I am irrelevant in any way that matters. A front-page story featuring her family's achievements is the pinnacle of everything Isabelle has ever dreamed of achieving.

"I think we're ready to begin," she tells the photographer.

My blood runs cold.

Because as soon as this article is released, anyone can see my face.

And remember.

Remember who I am and what I've done.

TWO
AMELIA

One month later

It's early morning and I'm attempting to get a bit more sleep, having just finished giving Clover her early-morning bottle. Back in my bed, I pull up the duvet, desperate for rest.

But just as I'm drifting off, I hear a text message come in and reach for my phone. I look at the lock screen, frowning. Timothy never texts after he's left for work.

He's sent a link.

My stomach clenches with dread.

It has been a month since the photo shoot, and I knew this day was coming, but I was hoping some miracle could erase it all from happening. I click the link to the *American Journal* article.

My eyes widen as I take in the photograph.

The photos show us in the living room at the Sterling estate. My husband's elegant parents stand side by side, not a hair out of place nor a crease in their clothes. His mother, Isabelle, is tall and slender, impeccable in her sage-green slacks and blouse. Alexander, the patriarch, has ruddy skin and radiates warmth—

as if his wealth is all simple good luck. Their daughter Lydia looks glamorous in her slinky cream-colored slip dress and confident smile, holding her dog, Petunia, under one arm. Timothy, in a tailored navy suit, is dashingly handsome, with a hand on my back, looking straight at the camera. Everyone is blonde and blue-eyed, poised as if they were American royalty.

And then there is me.

Tears fill my eyes as I take in my worst nightmare. There is no hiding that I am right there, in the middle of this family photo. Foolishly, I had clung to a fantasy that the photographer would have decided to focus on Clover, or even on the attractive Sterling family—but there I am, more visible than I have ever been in my life.

My bright red hair stands out, as do the freckles kissing nearly every inch of my skin. The baby in my arms has a mop of red curls of her own. As beautiful as the Sterlings are, my daughter and I stick out because we look different.

Typically, I would be described as cute over sexy any day. Except in this photo, I am *voluptuous*. My cheeks redden as I register just how shapely I look. My choice of wearing a linen dress was immediately vetoed by the photo shoot's stylist. She insisted I wear a forest-green wrap dress that shows off every curve and my new, fuller breasts.

My pulse racing, I begin reading the article, my eyes dancing for clues to where we live or personal details about me and Clover.

> *The Sterlings have made a life for themselves a ferry boat ride from Seattle, Washington. The luxurious Cutter's Island has more millionaires per capita than any other city on the West Coast. Their real estate business, Sterling Enterprise, made them overnight millionaires two decades ago, and now with a net worth over eight figures, their empire continues to expand.*
>
> *This time it is twofold, with real estate expansion and with*

their newest family member, Clover. Born two months ago, mother Amelia, wife of Timothy, comments, "She is a delight, and I feel so grateful for the warmth the Sterlings have shown me since joining their family. What a blessing to be surrounded by so much love."

My stomach churns and I run to the en suite bathroom. I retch over the toilet, my throat burning as the fear sets in.

This perfect life I have somehow been fortunate to find is all going to fall apart. There is no escaping that. I vomit again, crouching on the marble-tiled bathroom floor, my feet ice cold, my mind reeling with panic. *I can't lose this life*, I think, as my pulse races. *I can't lose Timothy or Clover.*

Panting, I swallow hard. The familiar cry of my daughter sounds through the baby monitor, and wiping my mouth on the towel, I wash my hands quickly before walking down the hall of our renovated farmhouse. I agreed to live in this exclusive island community, just a stone's throw from my in-laws, but insisted we purchase a house that feels like a home. The sort of home I wish I had grown up in.

But if someone puts the pieces together of who I say I am, and who I really am, will I be able to stay and raise my daughter here? The house may be perfect, but how long will it last before it all crumbles down around me?

I quicken my pace down the hall to Clover's nursery, suddenly needing to feel my daughter in my arms.

Clover starts crying even more loudly as I lean over her crib. She sees me and her eyes brighten, locking on mine, her cries telling a story I wish I understood.

Does she question if I am good enough to be a mother too? It is a question I ask myself every single day.

I lift Clover from the pale pink sheet she was sleeping on and bring her close to my chest.

"There you are, sweet girl. Mama has you," I murmur.

I do have her. And I won't let her go.

As I carry her to the changing table and set her down, all I can think about is the article, the cover photo, feeling certain that there are more photos featured in the pages of the glossy magazine I haven't even seen yet. One paragraph in, I already feel as if my perfect world is on the verge of collapse.

Is this how the life I built for myself comes to a crashing halt? I am not at all prepared to lose it all. Not when happiness has finally found me after so many years of looking for it.

My hands shaking, I reach for a diaper. I run my hand over Clover's belly, soothing her with a song as I look out the window. Beyond our home is a smattering of apple trees. Right now, all the branches are empty, the leaves gone. It is February and the green buds of new fruit have yet to arrive. Surrounding the perimeter of the trees are several raised garden beds where I had planned to plant seeds this spring. It will be my first summer here, and when we moved in I had high hopes for the sweet little family we created.

Timothy always calls me "refreshing" and "old-fashioned"— I prefer a slow lifestyle to the hustle culture he is used to. He smiled indulgently when I told him my dream was to have a home with a big front porch, where we could drink coffee in the morning as the sun came up. The sort of home where we sat around a table eating dinner with veggies I grew and bread I baked.

We are opposites in so many ways.

Before we got together, Timothy lived in a high-rise condo in the heart of Seattle, with granite counters and stainless steel everything. I lived in a studio apartment over someone's dilapidated garage, with vintage lace tablecloths covering the single pane windows and a hot plate instead of a modern appliance.

We found a middle ground with this place next door to his parents—all the charm of an older house, with a renovation that updated it to Timothy's standards. Central heating and air for starters. Yes, we have wide-plank wood floors throughout, but they are reclaimed wood from an English estate, shipped over, along with the fireplace and mantel, which were extracted from a historic home, just for us.

It all felt too good to be true.

But now, with my face exposed and the possibility of anyone coming after me, I wonder if it was a cruel joke I played on myself. Who am I to have this much fortune after so much damage?

Maybe I should flee now before I am found out.

I could run away. There is cash in the safe in our bedroom closet. A thick stack of bills that would allow me and Clover to get far from here. Somewhere we could disappear and start over again.

I change Clover's diaper swiftly, not wanting her to have a new reason to be upset with me. When I expressed my concerns with the pediatrician last month, he told me it is all a learning curve, for both baby and mom. I was relieved to hear Clover doesn't seem to be exhibiting any sort of health-related issue, but why does she have to cry so much?

Once she's in a clean diaper, I slip her cotton onesie back on, cooing as I place a sock on each foot, my mind, though, on the past.

My mistake last time was not running far enough. Back then I was young and scared and foolish, a part of me hoping that it was all a terrible dream. Never did I expect to meet someone who truly loved me, and who wanted to share a life with me. If I hadn't met Timothy and gotten pregnant, maybe I could have stayed invisible forever...

Beyond our apple trees and our neighborhood is the great expanse of Puget Sound. The water dark and blue, big enough to carry me and Clover to a different life. I could board a ferry, with my daughter and a suitcase, a wad of money in the diaper bag. Once on the other side of the water, Clover and I could keep going.

Leaving without an explanation wouldn't be so easy this time, though. The Sterling family would stop at nothing to get their granddaughter back. And how could I do that to Timothy, after everything he has done for me?

As I look out the window, bouncing Clover in my arms, I see a car slow as it passes my house. It crawls past my driveway. Immediately, I tense.

Has the past already found me?

THREE
AMELIA

Since I saw that car creep past my driveway, I haven't been able to slow my panicked heartbeat. Sleep-deprived and in desperate need of a shower, I set those obstacles behind me as I focus on what matters: Protecting my daughter.

Down in the kitchen, with Clover in my arms, I pour a cup of coffee with shaking hands, wanting a dose of energy while I formulate a plan. I need to leave right now, start over while I still have the chance.

My phone buzzes as I take my first sip, and I wonder if it's Timothy. Has he already been tipped off that I'm not who I say I am?

My hands tremble as I see it isn't my husband, followed by relief when I see it isn't my past coming to haunt me.

I groan in despair. It's my present. I wonder if that will be just as dangerous.

Tabitha is texting now, wanting to know if I've seen the article. She's my only friend, on the island or otherwise, and her friendship has been a lifeline since Timothy and I moved out of downtown Seattle, where we met, and relocated across the Sound to the windswept oasis of Cutter's Island.

After Timothy and I discovered we were pregnant and subsequently got married, he suggested we move closer to his family. Since I have no family he knows about, it made sense. We wanted to raise our daughter in a small community, not the bustling madness of a large metropolitan city.

Shortly after moving to Cutter's Island, Tabitha and I met at the obstetrician's office. We were both six months pregnant and navigating our impending motherhood for the first time. Realizing we lived in the same neighborhood, and that we were roughly the same age, we became fast friends.

Now she is texting me a screenshot of the magazine cover. Standing in the kitchen, I lean against the butcher block counter, bracing myself for whatever comes next. I open her message.

You look gorgeous! And your boobs! Dang, girl!

I chew my bottom lip. I know she means it as a compliment. My chest is bigger now I'm nursing Clover. But it only feels like more attention. Which is the opposite of what I want.

Right now, I need to disappear.

The thought pulses in my mind, relentless and clear, as I drop the phone onto the wooden kitchen counter without replying. My heart slams against my ribs, faster and faster, every beat a warning. I try to breathe, but it's like there's no air left in the room. I glance down at Clover in my arms, her tiny body bundled up, her innocent eyes gazing at me, unaware of the storm inside.

"It's okay, sweet pea," I whisper, my voice cracking as I walk upstairs to my bedroom and set her in the center of the bed. I try to believe it. "Mama's got you."

But deep down, I'm not sure I've got anything under control.

I place Clover in a bouncy seat in my bedroom, and then

swing open the closet doors, the cold metal of the handle grounding me for just a second. The vast walk-in closet looms before me, filled with reminders of the life I've been living. Rows of designer clothes, elegant coats, shoes lined up perfectly—all things Timothy's mother insisted I wear to "fit the image." The image of being a Sterling.

But none of this is mine.

I drop to my knees, rummaging through the back of the closet where things I never use are stuffed. The darkness feels thick, oppressive. I pull out a large suitcase from behind a stack of boxes, the same suitcase Timothy and I took to Hawaii last year. That trip feels like it happened to someone else. Another version of me, a woman who wasn't scared, who believed she could start over. A woman who thought she was safe.

I haul the suitcase into the bedroom. One should be enough, I think. It has to be because I can't take much—not if I'm running on foot with a baby. My throat tightens as I push the suitcase open, my movements frantic. My mind whirls with fragments of escape plans, none of them fully formed.

How far can I get?

How long can I stay off the grid before someone notices?

I glance at the hanging clothes—silk blouses, tailored dresses and designer coats. I don't need any of those. I need leggings, hoodies—clothes that let me disappear, become invisible. Black, simple, unnoticeable. The kind of clothes I wore when I was hiding before. The kind of clothes I never thought I'd need again.

The tears come hard and fast, but I keep moving. My vision blurs, but I don't stop. I can't. I wipe my face with the back of my hand, my heart clenching with the same sick dread that's been building for days. I can't breathe properly. My sobs are choking me. And I can't *think*. It feels like I'm drowning in memories, being dragged back to a place I never wanted to return to.

For ten years, I've stayed hidden. Head down, invisible. Seattle gave me space—a two-hour buffer between me and the past. Between me and the town of Bellport. But when I met Timothy, I let myself believe I was safe. I let myself believe I could be someone new. Someone free.

But I was wrong. How could I have been so stupid?

The sound of Clover's soft whimper pulls me from my spiraling thoughts. I stand up from the floor, my legs shaky, and scoop her into my arms. Her tiny fingers grip my shirt, and I hold her close, her tiny body pressing against me, keeping me tethered to the moment.

"It's all gonna be okay," I whisper, but I can't keep the tremor out of my voice. "I promise, Mama's got you."

But as I stand there, cradling her, I realize I don't know if I can keep that promise.

I turn back to the suitcase, my free hand moving on autopilot as I shove in clothes. My mind is already racing ahead —calculating, planning, failing. The ferry terminal has cameras everywhere. There's no way to get off the island without being seen. And the moment I'm caught on camera, he'll know.

They'll know.

The panic hits me again, a fresh wave so strong I nearly collapse. I drop the clothes, stagger back, clutching Clover tighter with both hands. I can feel my pulse throbbing in my throat. I'm being watched. I *know* it. This place, this island, it's a trap. There's no escape. Not like this. Not with the cameras. Not with *them* tracking my every move.

I spend the next few hours in a daze, pacing the bedroom, the walls pressing in on me. Every few minutes, I stop and stare at the suitcase—half packed, half abandoned. I can't decide. I can't think straight.

Eventually, I shove the suitcase back into the closet, burying it beneath shoes and boxes, as if hiding it could erase the decision I almost made. As if pretending it didn't happen could make my panic disappear. But the panic doesn't go away. It lingers, sharp and relentless, gnawing at me from the inside.

I lift Clover again, holding her so tightly she stirs, her tiny cry snapping me back to reality. I press my lips to her head, rocking her gently, trying to calm both of us. The tears spill over again, hot against my cold skin.

"I'm sorry, baby," I whisper, my voice barely audible. "Mama's trying. She's trying so hard."

But I don't know how to fix this. I don't know how to make it stop.

I stare at the closet door, the suitcase buried beneath the facade of the life I thought I could have, the life I can't seem to hold on to. Every fiber of my being screams at me to run, to disappear again, to protect Clover from whatever's coming. But I can't.

I'm trapped. In this house. On this island. In this life I no longer control.

Suddenly, I'm desperate for air. I walk outside to check the mailbox. I don't even know why I do it. I'm simply going through the motions, pretending like everything's fine when it's anything but. My mind is buzzing with half-formed plans, all of them collapsing before I can commit to one. I breathe in deeply, but the afternoon air is thick, damp, as if the world knows I'm about to break down.

I jerk open the mailbox with more force than necessary, my heart still racing from the panicked energy surging through me. Bills, ads, useless flyers, all clutched in my trembling hands. And then—

A letter.

It's different from the others. Plain white envelope, no return address, no stamp. Just my name, scrawled across the front in jagged handwriting as if it has been hand-delivered. The lettering is dark, pressed into the paper like it was written hard, in a hurry. My heart pounds, a cold sweat breaking out along the back of my neck. I stare at the letter, my breath catching in my throat.

A thousand thoughts collide in my mind at once, none of them good. My fingers curl around the envelope, the paper crinkling slightly in my grip. Something about it feels off—wrong in a way that I can't shake. My chest tightens, and I glance down the street. It's quiet. Too quiet. I can't see anyone, but my eyes dart around. The thought of being watched makes me paranoid, like someone could be there right now, ready to strike.

Someone left this for me.

My legs feel weak, and I stumble back toward the house, clutching the letter like it might slip out of my hands at any moment. The front door feels too far away, like I'm moving in slow motion. My heart pounds in my ears, my mind buzzing with every worst-case scenario.

Who sent it?

Inside, the air is too still, too cold. Clover is in the bassinet in the living room. She's quiet for now, but I can't shake the feeling that something is coming, that everything is about to come apart at the seams. My eyes dart back to the letter, still clutched in my hand. It somehow grows heavier with each moment that passes.

I should open it. I need to know what's inside.

But I don't. I can't.

Instead, I stand frozen in the middle of the room, the letter gripped tightly in my hand, as if opening it would make everything real. Too real. Like once I read it, there will be no going back. The walls of the house seem to close in around me, shrinking, pressing in on all sides.

Running away suddenly feels naive. Foolish. Like a plan for someone who still has options. And I don't.

The room spins, and for a moment I forget to breathe. The

envelope sits in my palm, the corners crinkling under the pressure of my grip as I tear it open.

Someone knows.

FOUR

AMELIA

My nerves are raw, stretched thin as I stand at the stove, my hand gripping the wooden spoon like it's the only thing keeping me upright.

The soup bubbles softly, filling the kitchen with the scent of herbs and broth, but I can't bring myself to taste it. My mind is elsewhere, consumed by the letter. By what I read. By the knowledge that everything has shifted, and nothing will ever be the same.

I try to focus on the task at hand. Dinner. That's what I'm supposed to be doing—cooking a meal, preparing for Timothy to walk through the door like any other evening. That's what he expects. It's what I've trained myself to expect too. But tonight, everything feels wrong.

My hand shakes slightly as I stir the soup, the rhythmic motion barely enough to keep my thoughts in line. I swallow, trying to ignore the tightness in my chest, the way my pulse won't slow down no matter how hard I try to focus on something—anything—else.

I glance at the clock. He'll be home soon. I need to keep it together. *What else am I good for?*

The thought presses down on me, unrelenting. If I can't give him this—this image of the perfect family, the perfect wife—then what do I have left? My value in this house, in this life, is measured by how well I perform, by how seamlessly I fit into the role Timothy and his family expect me to play. The dutiful wife. The loving mother. The ever-polished Sterling.

I stir the soup again, slower this time, feeling the spoon drag across the bottom of the pot. The kitchen is warm, cozy even, with its butcher block counters and wide windows that let the last light of the day filter through. It's the kind of space you'd see in a Nancy Meyers movie—one of those kitchens where people gather around with glasses of wine, laughing while dinner simmers on the stove, lives perfect and uncomplicated.

But that life, that version of reality, is nothing more than a fantasy for me. A foolish, fragile fantasy. One that shatters the second I think about the letter.

I grip the spoon tighter, my knuckles white. The paper had been so light in my hands, but the words... the words had a gravity I wasn't prepared to carry. Even now, hours later, they cling to me, sinking deeper into my chest with every passing second. The pit in my stomach grows, gnawing at me, whispering that no matter how hard I try to make this life work, the past will never stay buried.

Someone knows.

I blink back the sudden sting of tears, focusing on the sound of the soup bubbling, the clink of the spoon against the pot. Anything to drown out the thoughts racing through my head. I glance over at Clover, resting in her baby swing. She's too young to understand, too innocent to know what's happening.

But she will. Eventually, she will.

My heart tightens, and I force myself to keep moving, keep stirring, keep pretending. I've gotten so good at it over the years —pretending, that is. Smiling when I don't feel like it, laughing when I want to cry, smoothing over the cracks in my life so no one can see how close everything is to falling apart. I've perfected the art of disappearing into the role I'm supposed to play, but now... now I'm not sure how much longer I can keep up the act.

The letter.

I can still see it in my mind, the ragged handwriting, the way my name looked so out of place on that envelope. The way my hands trembled as I opened it, knowing—*knowing*—that whatever was inside would change everything.

And it did.

I shake my head now, trying to clear the thoughts, trying to hold myself together. I can't fall apart. Not now. Not yet. I have to keep going. Timothy will be home soon, and I need to have dinner ready. I need to smile when he walks through the door, ask him about his day, pretend like everything is normal. Because if I don't... if I show him even a glimpse of the panic clawing at my insides, he'll know something's wrong.

When Timothy walks through the front door ten minutes later, he greets me with a kiss and a hug, whispering in my ear, "We made our periodical debut today, my love."

Stepping back from the embrace, I plaster a fake smile on my face. "Right," I exhale, "the article came out."

"You don't sound happy." Timothy sets a copy of the magazine on the kitchen table.

There it is. In all its glossy, front-page glory. I want to grab the magazine and shove it in the recycling can. Or set it on fire over the stove. Rip it into tiny shreds and throw them out the window. Anything to erase it from all our memories. Timothy is all smiles, and I am nothing but tense.

Before I gave birth to Clover, I had this vision of Timothy walking through the door after work, a loaf of sourdough bread warm from the oven resting on a cutting board, a fresh green salad tossed in a bowl that we received as a wedding gift from one of Timothy's relatives. The lights would be dimmed down low. In the swing a few feet from me, Clover would be sleeping, her late afternoon nap timed perfectly with my dinner prep. A life of ease.

My reality doesn't match that vision.

The soup simmering on the stove is from a can. The bread in the oven came from a foil bag at the grocery store. And sure, Clover is sleeping right now, but only because she spent the last two hours wailing while fighting her much-needed nap.

Domestic bliss, this is not. The envelope in my back jeans pocket may be out of Timothy's view, but it is the only thing I can see right now.

Technically, if we threw out the magazine and note, I would appear to have everything I've ever wanted right in this room. It should be as perfect as perfect can be.

I wish I could be happy and join in this moment with Timothy by popping a bottle of champagne and toasting our little moment of fame. But everything within me is tense. It feels like at any moment an already precarious ball could drop, upending the life I want.

Grinning, he flips through *American Journal*. "So, did you see the copy? I texted you about it earlier, but you never replied."

"I had a long day," I tell him honestly. I look over his shoulder as he flips through the magazine. I grip the back of a barstool as I take in the photo. I want to rip it from his hands but instead I force myself to answer more fully. "Clover was fussy and I was trying to get rest whenever she did."

He sets his briefcase on the kitchen island and pulls off his coat, hanging it on the back of a high-back chair at the counter. "Can I make you a cocktail?" he asks. "To celebrate?"

I lick my lips anxiously, wanting to push away my sense of dread and be here with him, in this moment. "I'll have whatever you're having," I tell him, tempted to ask for a double of something strong. Honestly, maybe a drink will help calm my nerves.

He smiles, walking over to the bar cabinet in the corner of the dining room. He pulls out two highball glasses and a bottle of bourbon that's fancy. Like all the other bottles of bourbon, and all the wine. Same as all the silverware and appliances and knives and everything in this house. This home is perfectly curated. There's nothing left to desire. Everything I have ever wanted is already here, purchased and paid for.

I wish I could enjoy it, but instead, at this moment I can only consider that perfect scrawl, the way my name was written on the front of the envelope delivered to our home earlier this afternoon. Innocuous, but damning.

Turning my attention back to the soup, I put the burner on low and pull out the garlic bread from the oven. This store-bought loaf is a far cry from the bread I used to imagine making for my husband, and the dough I kneaded at the bakery where I worked before I met Timothy.

It feels like a lifetime ago, but I loved those mornings in the back of the shop, working in the early dawn, alone, without anyone watching me or asking questions.

It was lonely, but it felt safe.

Then I met Timothy, and he was a breath of fresh air. It seemed as if he was from another world, and his other world was so far from my old life that I never feared the two might merge.

But now the article is out. And I'm back to wishing I were invisible.

With Timothy's back to me, I squeeze my eyes shut, aching with the unknown. Who wrote that letter? Who found me? Who wants me to lose everything?

A few minutes later, Timothy walks toward me with two Manhattans, handing one to me.

"Cheers," he laughs, and we clink glasses, both of us taking a sip. It's strong, and I wince. He chuckles. "Sorry, I can finish what you don't."

"No, it's good," I say, indulging in a long sip of the cocktail, hoping it will take the edge off the day. The glass feels cold against my lips, but it does little to calm the storm brewing inside me. "Dinner's ready. It's kale and white bean soup with Italian sausage."

I don't tell him it was prepackaged, and I don't have to—Timothy wouldn't care either way. He's too focused on the scene I've created: the dinner on the stove, the drinks in our hands, Clover sleeping peacefully nearby. To him, this is all part of the life we've built. The life I pretend is flawless.

He looks over at the cutting board, where I've set the loaf of bread. "And I see you've been baking," he says, a smile spreading across his face. "I don't think you know how happy that makes me. It reminds me of the day we met."

His words hit me, pulling me back into the memory. It was a year ago, but it feels like a lifetime. I force a smile, even though it hurts a little.

I was exhausted that day, working a double shift at the bakery. Flour dusted my apron, clung to my hair and smudged my hands. My auburn hair had been tied back with a handkerchief, and I was wearing clogs that had seen better days. No makeup, just the barest version of myself, thrown together because I had been up since 3 a.m., kneading dough and stacking trays.

And then Timothy walked in.

He was polished. Impeccable. The door chimed when he entered, and it felt like the world shifted for just a second. I looked up, expecting to see just another customer, someone wanting a baguette or a croissant. But when our eyes met, there was something different. His gaze didn't just skim over me like everyone else's did—he looked at me, *really* looked at me.

He walked up to the counter, all suit and tie, with his

leather briefcase and shined shoes. He dressed as if he belonged in a boardroom, not in the little bakery, but there he was. And the way he took me in—it was like he had found exactly what he was looking for.

"You're beautiful," he had said, his voice rough, his eyes scanning my face like he was trying to memorize it. "I could see you from outside the window. And I had to meet you."

I had felt my cheeks burn under his gaze, and not just because of the heat from the ovens. I wasn't used to being noticed. Not like that. I reached up, instinctively brushing a hand across my cheek, embarrassed that my face—something I never gave much thought to and had been hiding for so long—was the reason this man had stopped in. "Is that so?" I'd said, trying to sound casual, but my voice wavered.

I remember his eyes danced with amusement, and he had leaned against the counter. "Those freckles, and your hair. That red—it's hard to miss. Kind of like you walked straight out of a painting." He'd given me a small confident smile, the kind that made me wonder how many times he'd said lines like this before.

I felt flustered, caught off guard. I'd been invisible for so long, and here was this man who seemed to see everything about me in one glance. "Don't you have somewhere to take that baguette?" I asked, nodding toward the bread in his hand, trying to deflect his attention.

But he didn't bite. Instead, he gave me a slow easy grin and said, "No. I saw you through the window and decided I needed a reason to stop in."

There was something in the way he said it that made my heart skip. It wasn't just a line. He meant it. His words hung in the air between us, and for the first time in years, I felt... visible. *Seen.* I wasn't just the tired bakery girl behind the counter. I was someone. Someone he had noticed.

"Amelia," I'd said, introducing myself, because what else

could I do? His confidence was disarming, but I liked it. I liked the way he looked at me like I was the most interesting thing in the room.

He smiled again, his hand reaching out. "Timothy," he replied.

That night, we went out to dinner at a Michelin-starred restaurant. I felt out of place in my secondhand dress, sitting across from him in his tailored suit, but I wanted to fit into his world. Seattle's Space Needle loomed above us as we dined, the lights of the city twinkling in the background. The French cuisine was incredible, but I barely tasted it. I was too busy trying to keep up with him, with his stories, with his charm. By the end of the night, he kissed me like he already knew I was his. Like he could pull me into his world and make me forget I ever had a past to hide.

I was drawn to him. His confidence, his ease, the way he made me feel seen in a way no one else had. But I knew, even then, that I was hiding. That there were parts of me I'd never let him see.

Now, we're standing in our perfect kitchen, our daughter sleeping nearby, and that moment in the bakery feels like a distant dream. Back then, I was a girl trying to escape my past, desperate to be seen by someone, anyone. Now, I'm standing here, wrapped in the life I built with Timothy, but there's a gulf between us—a secret so big it could swallow us both whole.

I glance over at him, watching the way he moves so effortlessly in this world he created, the world I've been pulled into. He thinks I'm still that girl from the bakery, the one who enchanted him with freckles and auburn hair, flour dusted on her cheeks, who let him believe she was uncomplicated, free.

But that girl never really existed. I'm not the woman he thinks I am.

The letter in my pocket drags me down, its words lodged in

my mind. And when Timothy finds out, when he finally sees the truth, what happens then?

My heart aches with the strain of lies, with the deceit I've carried. It's too much, but I would spend my life concealing the baggage if it meant keeping my daughter safe and my family intact.

For a decade I have been able to push my lies aside and compartmentalize the past from the present. But it's hard to do on a day like this, when a magazine is released with my photograph on the cover. A magazine that has been distributed all across the country.

And even though the people I don't want to see it live only a few hours from Cutter's Island, it doesn't change the fact that anyone could see me and remember.

Timothy grabs two bowls from the cabinet and hands them to me. As I ladle the soup, he speaks. "Well, I thought you looked gorgeous in the photographs. That's what I was calling earlier to tell you."

I laugh, reaching for two spoons from the silverware drawer and carrying them to the table. "Tabitha texted and said the same thing." I looked down at my chest. "I know my boobs are bigger since I've had Clover, but I didn't realize that was going to be the angle of the camera." My cheeks feel hot as I say it.

"You're *blushing*," he teases, reaching for my hand and kissing me again. "Amelia, do you have any idea how cute you are?"

I roll my eyes. "Stop, Timothy."

"No," he jokes, patting my butt playfully. "You are perfect. And those photos, God, I can't believe you're my wife."

I bite nervously at my lips, wishing it was just that simple, knowing nothing has ever been quite that easy for me. Wishing that this perfect moment was the entirety of the story, the full picture of my life.

Timothy has no idea that there's a small white envelope in my back pocket. An envelope linking my past to my present.

Timothy's voice fills the room, but I barely hear it. He's talking about work, something about an upcoming project, but his words blur into the background. I nod, stir my soup, force a smile, but I can't feel anything. Not really. Not when the letter is pressing down on me, heavier than anything I can handle.

I take another sip of my drink, hoping it will calm the nerves still buzzing under my skin, but it's no use. Nothing can take the edge off what's hanging over me now. I've read the letter—those words are burned into my brain—and no amount of pretending will erase them.

"I'll be right back," I say, standing abruptly, not waiting for his reply. I can't sit here another second. The air feels too thin, like it is being squeezed out of me. I feel faint at the thought of what I am being forced to face. Timothy glances at me, curiosity flickering in his eyes, but he doesn't ask. He never does.

I walk down the hall, my pulse quickening with every step, the sound of his voice fading away behind me. The house is quiet, the only sound the soft creak of the floor beneath my feet. I close the bathroom door behind me, my breath coming in shallow gasps, the cold tile floor grounding me as I lean against the wall.

For a moment, I just stand there, staring at my reflection in the mirror. My face is pale, my eyes wide. I hardly recognize the person staring back at me. The woman I've become. The woman who has lived a lie for so long she's forgotten how to be anything else.

I pull the letter from my pocket, the paper crinkling in my hands as I unfold it once again. There is no reason I need to reread it. I already know what it says. I've read it enough times to have the words seared into my brain, into my bones. But still, I look at it, just to remind myself that this nightmare is real.

The letter is a single line, and a simple question, but it cuts deeper than anything I've ever faced. I trace the tight cursive with my finger, the handwriting unfamiliar, but the message clear. Someone knows. Someone has seen through the carefully constructed lie I've built, and now they're asking the question I've spent years avoiding.

I stare down at the six words that will undo my life.

How can you live with yourself?

FIVE

Then

Mom always does this, disappearing for hours on end, not telling us where she's going and leaving us in charge of the baby.

Don't get me wrong, my baby sister is cute. I mean, as cute as a two-year-old can be. She cries a lot and needs our attention constantly. Honestly, I get that. She's a baby, but I'm thirteen.

This is *my* summer vacation.

I shouldn't be spending it sitting in an apartment with no air conditioning and my annoying sisters. What I should be doing is going to the community pool. That's where everyone hangs out. That's where *I* want to be. Becoming someone who matters.

"Do you know when Mom's getting back?" my sister asks as she kneels in front of the baby.

"She didn't say. My guess is she's down at Blue Street Bar," I reply. "I'm gonna go down to the corner store and get us some ice cream."

"Do you have money for that?" she asks.

I shrug. "Yeah, I have some," I lie, thinking I was just going to steal a pack of ice cream bars. I slip on my flip-flops. "Don't do anything stupid," I tell her before kicking open the front door.

I take the stairs two at a time, heading down to the parking lot, desperate to get out of that hellhole. I feel free for the first time all day.

Walking into the corner store, I keep my head down. I open the freezer section, grab a box of popsicles and shove them under my tank top.

Instead of going straight home, I walk in the other direction, opening the box of popsicles and undoing the wrapper on one of them. It's hot outside, the middle of July. Summer is going to last forever and I'm already sick of it. I start walking home, taking my time.

That's when I hear it, the sirens.

I watch as a police car, an ambulance and a fire truck zoom down the road.

The road I walked down to get here. I turn, curious, my pace quickening.

The emergency vehicles are parked outside our complex.

And that's when I see my sister. Sobbing, hysterical.

"I just turned around!" she's screaming at the paramedic who has a stretcher.

On that stretcher is our baby sister.

Lifeless.

SIX
AMELIA

As Clover's cries cut through the pediatrician's waiting room like a knife, every glance from the other parents feels like a blow. I try rocking her, bouncing her, cooing softly, but nothing works. My arms feel weak from holding her, and my head pounds with the echo of her unrelenting screams.

She's been like this for days—every day a relentless storm of tears I can't calm. The other parents, with their quiet babies, don't understand. Their sympathetic looks only make me feel more alone.

The nurse calls our name, and I gather Clover, her shrieks ringing in my ears. The hallway to the exam room seems too long, the pastel-painted animals on the walls taunting me. I settle Clover on the examination table, her tiny fists still clenched, her face red with frustration. I feel every beat of my heart in my throat. *What if something's wrong with her?*

Dr. Reynolds enters, all warmth and calm, and I want to scream at how out of place he seems in my panic. "How's Clover doing?" he asks, too casually.

"She won't stop crying," I say, the words spilling out before I can stop them. "It's been like this for days. I've tried everything. I don't know what I'm doing wrong…"

He examines her, running through the usual checks while I hold my breath. His hands are steady. But I feel like I'm shaking apart.

"She's perfectly healthy," he says, smiling. "It's probably just a phase—a growth spurt, maybe. She'll grow out of it."

Grow out of it? His words feel empty, like a lifeline that slips through my fingers. He can't see what I see—how her cries break me, every failed attempt to soothe her proof that I'm a bad mother.

"What if I'm not doing something right?" I ask, my voice barely a whisper.

Dr. Reynolds meets my eyes with that look I've come to despise—pity, like I'm just another worried, overreacting mother. "You're doing everything right. You're a good mother."

A good mother.

If I were, I'd know how to stop her tears. I wouldn't be living a lie, and I wouldn't be lying to her father every minute of every day. I nod mechanically, forcing a smile, but inside, doubt digs deeper.

I thank him and leave, Clover still fussing softly against my chest.

The drive home is stifling. I glance at Clover in the rearview mirror, finally asleep, but the relief doesn't come. It's like her crying is still ringing in my ears.

What if I'm missing something?

I pull into the driveway and my eyes drift across the street to the Sterling estate, wondering if my in-laws are watching me. I carry Clover inside, feeling like a failure. Her body is limp with sleep now, and I gently lay her in her crib. I stand there, watching her breathe, waiting for the guilt to fade, but it lingers like a shadow over everything.

Deep down, I can't shake the fear. What if I'm not overthinking it? What if I'm failing her—and everything else too?

I don't deserve any of this—a beautiful daughter, a beautiful home, a beautiful life—not after what I've done.

Not with the secrets I've kept.

Clover's nap is short-lived. An hour later, I am back to bouncing her in my arms.

"Clover, please just go to sleep," I whisper pleadingly into her hair.

I love my daughter, I do, but sometimes I wonder if her fussiness is payback, some sort of karmic retribution for what I did. As I rock her against my chest, I can't help but think about the letter.

I buried it in my dresser drawer, terrified. Knowing someone has discovered who I really am has left me in an anxious sweat for the past week. I haven't been able to sleep or eat. I can barely keep a thought together long enough to complete a task. Something as simple as doing the laundry has become insurmountable. No wonder Clover has been so upset. She must sense my fear. And if she senses it, what must Timothy think?

I'm deep in thought when the doorbell rings. Instantly, I grip Clover close to my chest protectively. I'm not expecting anyone and Timothy always uses his key. My heart starts to race, and Clover's cries only grow louder. Holding my breath, I inch toward the peephole in the door.

But it isn't a ghost from my past—it's a threat from the present.

Lydia, my sister-in-law. I take a deep breath and pull open the front door, feigning a smile. Lydia is only two years younger than me, but it feels like our worlds are lifetimes apart. Timothy is our only common ground. Although we are dissimilar in so many ways, she does go out of her way to dote on Clover, always gifting her frilly dresses or new stuffed animals when she drops by the house for an impromptu happy hour with her brother on our back porch. Since I have no family to speak of, I try to appreciate that Clover has an auntie.

She's holding a bouquet of tulips and a paper bag from the local grocery store.

"Oh, did I wake up the baby?" Lydia asks in her singsong voice, frowning.

Who rings the doorbell when they know there's a two-month-old living inside the house?

I exhale, keeping calm. Fighting a grimace, I smile, "No, she was fussing already. I don't know what it is. She's constantly cranky at the moment."

Lydia walks inside my home and it's then I see that her little dog is on a leash trailing behind her.

"You don't mind if Petunia comes in, do you?" she asks.

I shake my head, knowing it doesn't matter. The dog goes with her everywhere. It was even in the photo on the cover of that magazine, for goodness' sake. Breathing, I urge myself to relax. I am on edge from a string of sleepless nights.

"I haven't had a chance to talk with you in ages," Lydia purrs. "The magazine article came out a week ago and we haven't even had a chance to debrief."

I give her a tight smile as we walk through the house toward the kitchen.

"Brought you flowers," she beams over her shoulder. "Want me to put them in a vase for you?"

"No, I got it," I say. Lydia eyes the screaming Clover in my arms and I relent. "Um, sure," I say. "The vases are in the cupboard next to the refrigerator."

She walks over and pulls one out. "It's so cute how you like to live in this... *little* house."

Cute?

Clover screams in my arms, her tiny fists flailing against my chest. I rock her gently, trying to calm her, but my own irritation flares. The word grates against my nerves. My jaw tightens as I bounce my daughter, feeling the tension rise with each of her cries. I bite down on the sharp retort forming on my tongue and force a smile instead, letting out a breathy laugh that doesn't quite reach my eyes.

"Yeah, *cute*."

I unbutton my blouse to offer Clover milk. Clover refuses to latch on and I feel myself growing frustrated. She lets out a sharp cry. I close my eyes, not knowing what she needs. I lift up the cup of my bra and move her to my other arm, offering her the other side, desperate for her to just fall asleep.

"Is she always so cranky?" Lydia asks.

I shrug. "I guess she's a little fussy, but Timothy thinks it's because I'm fussy too."

"*Are* you fussy?" Lydia squints her eyes, taking me in. "I've never seen you and Timothy even have an argument."

"I guess fussy can mean different things. I'm still a little on edge lately, anxious."

"Are you okay?" Lydia asks.

I shake my head. "Yes, I'm just..." I shake my head. *Exhausted? At my wit's end?* "Tired."

Carrying my daughter, I walk over to the couch and sit down in among the fluffy down-filled cushions. I close my eyes for a moment, not in the mood for company, especially company that is judging me.

"Well, I brought *you* some treats this time," Lydia tells me, unpacking the grocery bag. "I know I usually bring something for the baby, but I was at the store and I saw these nice bottles of wine and I thought maybe that's what Amelia needs right now. You haven't been returning my calls or my texts. I'm trying to not take it personally," she laughs. "Afternoon apéritif?" she asks, pulling out two wineglasses from the cupboard, holding one in each of her slender hands.

At this point, I have no option but to say yes. "Sure," I mumble.

She uncorks a bottle of white wine and carries the glasses over to the coffee table before returning to the kitchen. "I also brought us some fruit and cheese and this *delicious* looking prosciutto. And I just can't believe how beautiful these apricots are. Don't they look *divine*?"

"They do," I say unenthusiastically as she makes a little fruit and cheese plate.

I'm thankful that she feels comfortable in my kitchen at least, walking around as if she owns the place, because I am in no mood to host.

She sets the food down on the coffee table and then sits next to me on the couch. "I really don't know how you do it. I can't imagine having a child without a full-time nanny and a housekeeper. But honestly? You look a little bit of a mess."

"Geez," I say. "Not pulling any punches, are you?"

She nods, her glossy blonde hair swishing as she does. "Timothy told me you didn't want to do the magazine."

My blood runs cold at the mention of the article. I keep my face neutral, but a knot tightens in my stomach. *Why bring up the article now?* I force a smile, my mind racing. Is she fishing for something, or does she already have the answers?

"It's not that," I lie, trying to regain control. I can't shake the feeling that there's more behind Lydia's comment. "It's just adjusting to motherhood, you know?" Suspicion simmers beneath my words, but I keep my voice even. I can't let her see what's really going on. Clover squirms in my arms, her cries rising again, and Lydia's eyes on me make my skin prickle. "Right now, I'm just focused on taking care of Clover," I say, shifting her a little, hoping the conversation ends there.

"None of this has to be hard," Lydia smiles. "Look at me. My life is literally the easiest thing ever. I go where I want, when I want. Travel when I want, see who I want. I don't have to suffer. That's one of the perks of being a Sterling. Neither do *you*." She rolls her eyes. "And neither does my brother, for that matter, though he insists on it—but I'm sure he has his reasons for working so hard, especially now that Celeste is back in town."

My stomach twists. This is why she's really come. I can feel it.

"Who's Celeste?"

Lydia frowns. "Celeste Salsberg. Her mom, Eleanor, lives across the street. Surely you know that?"

I shake my head, trying to mask my unease. "Mrs. Salsberg? I've met her a few times. She's not very friendly."

Lydia laughs. "Well, of course not. She's not friendly to *you*. She wanted Celeste to marry Timothy."

I blink. "And who's Celeste again?"

"Mrs. Salsberg's daughter. Timothy's ex-girlfriend of five years. We all thought she was the one for him." She stares at me. "Come on, surely you know all of this?"

I shake my head slowly, but my mind is already spiraling. *Why is Lydia here?* First, she mentions the article I didn't want to do. Now, she's dredging up Timothy's past. Lydia shows up in the middle of the afternoon with food, flowers and wine— what is she after?

"I didn't even know Mrs. Salsberg had a daughter, let alone that she was Timothy's ex," I say, trying to keep my voice level. "If she hates me for that, it's not my fault."

"Yeah," Lydia remarks casually, but something feels off. "Celeste is living there most of the time now."

I freeze. "Really?"

Timothy's ex-girlfriend lives across the street?

"She's working on Cutter's Island as an interior designer. She's working closely with Timothy now," Lydia adds casually.

I nod, my stomach knotting.

Clover fusses, and I bounce her gently, heart pounding as I think about the letter. I had thought it was someone from my past, but could it be Lydia? Or Celeste?

"Wait, so why were you stopping by again?" I ask her, shaking my head in an attempt to clear it.

Lydia takes another sip of wine. "I haven't had a chance to talk about the article and I feel like you were avoiding me. Were you offended by what I said?"

"Offended?" I ask her, confused.

She throws her head back, laughing. "Oh my God, are you *kidding* me? You didn't even notice?"

"Notice what?" I ask. I don't tell Lydia this, but I've been mostly consumed with the fact my face is on the cover of the magazine, and the fact the journalist decided to announce to the world that we live on Cutter's Island.

"Well," Lydia sighs, "I'm really sorry. I think you're a great sister-in-law, and when I said it was a surprise that Timothy married you so quickly, I didn't mean it as a slight."

I nod, registering the comment. I do remember it now that she mentions it. She'd been asked by the interviewer how she liked being an aunt and she'd made a comment that she loved Clover and that, while she was surprised by her brother's choice of wife, she adored me too. It wasn't exactly flattering, but to be fair, I figured it was pretty honest.

That is a quality I admire in anybody, considering how often I lie.

"Well, I was sure you hated me," she confesses. "And then I looked on social media and people were tearing me apart, saying I am a *terrible* sister-in-law. I mean, sure, there are comments that you're a gold digger too, but—"

I cut her off with a lie. "I don't care about comments online."

The truth is I have read all the posts I can find. In the

middle of the night, when I should be sleeping, I find myself scrolling on my phone, reading comment after comment, trying to find a thread that links my past to my present—anxiously looking to see if someone who knows who I really am has found me.

Lydia laughs. "Oh my God, are you *joking*? Reading them is all Mom and I have been doing for *days*."

"What are you reading exactly?" I ask, worry creeping up inside me.

"All the blog snark and the social media posts," she says casually. "People think you're pretty hot, by the way. *Traditionally sexy*. You know, your boobs look incredible, so I don't blame them."

I shake my head again. "I don't go on social media ever. I don't even have those apps. I just prefer to—"

"I know, I know," Lydia interrupts, her smile tight. "You're so *sweet* and *simple*, and that's why Timothy loves you. You're not like the other girls."

My stomach tightens, but I force a smile. "I... appreciate that," I say, trying to keep my voice light, though my thoughts are spiraling. A knot forms in my chest. I need to read any newly posted comments.

Clover squirms in my arms, her fussing the perfect excuse. "I think she needs to rest," I say, glancing down at her. "I should get her down for a nap."

Lydia doesn't seem to register that I want her to go. She sits on the couch, not at all in a hurry. "You're *not* like the other girls. At least not like any of the other girls Timothy dated before you. Certainly not like Celeste."

"Okay, enough about Celeste." I hear my voice rise and I struggle to calm myself. "I don't care about Timothy's past. I care about my present with him."

Lydia stands and I wonder if she is annoyed at me, or if it's something more.

"All right," Lydia sighs. "I get it. You're practically perfect in every way. No wonder Timothy loves you. You refuse to gossip, won't talk about his ex and—"

I cut her off. "I'm not *perfect*, Lydia. I'm just doing my best to keep my head above water, and honestly, I'm calling a nanny service this afternoon. You're right—I need help. I'm not trying to be a martyr. I'm figuring it out as I go, and it's a lot. I don't have a mom I can call for support. Okay?"

"Sorry," Lydia mutters, shaking her head. "I'm not trying to fight with you. I just—"

"What? You want me to feel bad? I can't. I've spent too much of my life being sad. Right now, I'm *happy*." I emphasize the last word just as Clover lets out another cry. "I mean, I'd be happier if Clover wasn't so colicky. But honestly, she's healthy, she's... alive."

Tears prick my eyes, and I blink them back.

"I'm sorry." Lydia hesitates, her tone softening. "I wasn't trying to start anything or upset you. I just... honestly, I don't know. I guess I did want to gossip about Celeste Salsberg. I'm here if you want to be friends."

I nod, but her apology sounds practiced, rehearsed. I force a smile, but inside, the doubt lingers. *She doesn't mean it. She's just saying what she thinks I want to hear.*

She walks to the front door, and I close it behind her firmly, exhaling as I bolt the door shut. Clover finally stops wailing. I look at my little girl, wondering what she makes of all this. *She's a baby—she can't understand.* But as I gaze into her eyes, I get the strange feeling that maybe, somehow, she knows.

I press her gently to my chest as her breathing evens out. Climbing the stairs, I take each step carefully. When we reach her nursery, I rock her for a few moments more, holding on a little longer than usual, before laying her in the crib. As if hearing my silent prayer, she stays asleep.

I sit in the rocking chair, not wanting to be far from her.

The exhaustion from the tormenting truth of my life has wrecked me to my core.

Why would Timothy have told Lydia my fears about the photo shoot? And why did no one mention Timothy's ex-girlfriend's mother living right across the street? The knot in my stomach tightens as I glance out the window.

Just before I drift into a fitful sleep, I'm sure I see Mrs. Salsberg watching me before her shadow slips behind the curtain.

SEVEN

AMELIA

In the morning, I push Clover's stroller down the driveway, the cold damp February air settling around me.

The Pacific Northwest in winter is always this way—gray skies, mist clinging to everything. But today, it feels oppressive. The island community, once a sanctuary, now feels like a cage. Every house here is perfect, every lawn pristine, but there's always a sense that someone's watching.

I stop at the end of the driveway, glancing at Timothy's parents' house next door. Theirs is one of the grandest on the street, with its towering windows and sweeping view of the water. It was comforting at first, having them so close, but now it feels intolerable. *Are they watching too?*

As I wait for Tabitha, my mind drifts back to last night.

Timothy came home late, his footsteps quiet as he made his way to the bedroom. He took off his watch, placing it neatly in the leather tray on his dresser. That's just who he is—thoughtful, composed, always in control.

"Your sister stopped by today," I said, my voice calm, though my mind was racing. I remember wrapping my arms around his waist, trying to ground myself in his presence, to remind myself that this was my life now—Timothy, our family, this house.

"Oh yeah? What did Lydia have to say this time?" he'd asked, his tone light, but something in his eyes had flickered.

"She mentioned the neighbors," I'd said carefully. "Celeste in particular."

His body tensed, but only for a moment. He's good at hiding his reactions, it's something I've always admired. "Celeste? Why would she bring her up?"

I stepped away then, walking into the en suite bathroom to splash cold water on my face. Her name had felt sharp on my tongue, like it didn't belong in our home, but there it was. "It just feels like everyone else knew, except me," I had replied, rubbing the towel across my face.

Timothy appeared in the doorway then, leaning against the frame. His expression had been neutral, but his voice carried a gravity I couldn't ignore. "Amelia, you loved this house. I didn't tell you because Celeste wasn't living here when we moved in, and I didn't want to ruin what we were building. This place—it's your dream."

He'd stepped closer, taking my hand, his grip almost too firm. "Why drag the past into it when we're creating something new?" His words made sense, but the way he said it—like he was closing a door to something I wasn't meant to see—left a chill in my chest.

Now, standing in my driveway, I glance at the mailbox. Feeling a strange pull. I open it, and there it is—another envelope, the same careful curved handwriting. No return address.

My heart races as I tear it open.

You think you're safe, but I know who you are.

I quickly shove the letter into my pocket, glancing toward Timothy's parents' house. The tall windows reflect the gray sky, but behind them, I know his mother, Isabelle, could be watching. She always has an eye on things, especially when it comes to me. *Does she know?*

I look across the street and catch Mrs. Salsberg peering from behind her curtains. Her eyes meet mine, cold and unwavering. The moment I see her I know I didn't imagine it last night, she *was* watching me. I feel a shiver run down my spine.

Tabitha arrives moments later, waving as she approaches with her son, Johnny, in his stroller. She's smiling, but there's a heaviness in her eyes.

"I'm not ready to go back to work," she frets when she reaches me. We've become best friends, and I appreciate that she isn't even bothering with small talk. "I thought I'd have it all figured out by now, but I don't. I just don't want to leave Johnny with a sitter."

"Do you have to?" I ask, trying to be present as we start to walk, but my head is somewhere else.

"I don't know," she sighs. "I've worked so hard to get where I am with my career, but now... I can't imagine not being with him." She glances down at her son, then back at me, her voice quiet. "What if I can't do both?"

"You'll figure it out," I say, but my mind is unfocused, the brutal truth of the letter weighing heavily in my pocket.

Our strollers' wheels click rhythmically over the pavement as Tabitha and I walk toward Main Street on Cutter's Island. The air is damp, a light mist clinging to everything, but the cool February breeze feels good against my skin. Normally, these walks calm me, but today I can't shake the tension sitting deep in my chest. The letter, the one telling me someone knows my secret, keeps replaying in my mind.

"Are you sure you're okay?" Tabitha asks, glancing over at me. Johnny is fast asleep in his stroller beside Clover, who's thankfully quiet for once.

I nod, forcing a smile. "Yeah, just... tired. You know how it is."

Tabitha doesn't push me, though I can tell she wants to. She's been my only real friend since moving here, and I don't want to shut her out. But how do I explain the growing panic, the feeling that my past is creeping closer?

We're nearing the small market on the Main Street of Cutter's Island, and that's when I spot her.

Celeste.

She's stepping out of the market, holding a coffee in one hand, her phone pressed to her ear with the other. Though we've never met, I know it's her. Even though I promised myself I wouldn't, I couldn't resist Googling her last night when I should have been sleeping. Long glossy dark hair, a perfectly tailored camel coat and an air of confidence that makes her stand out. She's laughing at something, completely at ease in her surroundings.

I freeze, my grip tightening on Clover's stroller. It's like my brain can't quite process her presence. She's real. She's *here*. Timothy's ex-girlfriend, the woman his family wanted him to marry, living just across the street from us.

Tabitha follows my gaze and leans in slightly. "Who is that...?"

I nod, my throat tight. "That's her. Celeste." Cringing, I add, "I looked her up on social media after Lydia left."

Tabitha raises an eyebrow, glancing back at me. "Wow. She's, uh... *exactly* how I'd imagine."

I swallow hard, trying to tear my eyes away from Celeste, but I can't. She's the embodiment of everything I'm afraid of— someone who fits perfectly into Timothy's world, someone I'll never be. I don't want to feel threatened, but seeing her here, so effortlessly poised, makes me feel even more out of place than I already do.

Celeste's heels click against the pavement as she walks past us, her phone conversation still going. She doesn't even glance in our direction as her perfume washes over me.

Tabitha gives me a sympathetic look. "She didn't even notice us."

"That's fine," I say, my voice tight. "I'm fine with that."

But the knot in my stomach tells me otherwise. "I need to eat. Something sugary, I think."

"To the bakery section we go," Tabitha laughs, shrugging off my fear.

We step into the market, the warm air inside offering a brief reprieve from the chill, but I can't stop thinking about Celeste. Just knowing she's here, that we're bound to run into each other again, makes my skin crawl.

"I wouldn't worry about her," Tabitha says, her voice low as we head to the bakery section. "Timothy loves you. You have Clover. She's in his past, remember."

"I know," I sigh, but the words feel hollow.

Because Timothy's past isn't just some distant memory. It's *here*, walking down the same streets, living right across from us. I glance down at Clover, who's stirring in her stroller.

Tabitha reaches for a few raspberry Danishes, placing them in a paper bag. "Honestly, she looks a bit full of herself. You're nothing like that."

I nod, trying to push the image of Celeste out of my mind, but it lingers. I keep picturing the way she walked, so sure of herself, so comfortable. Like she belonged here. And me? I'm still trying to figure out how to stay invisible. To avoid being found.

I push the stroller down the aisle, my heart pounding despite Tabitha's calm reassurances. Timothy chose me, but what if Celeste doesn't see it that way? What if she's still a part of his life, just waiting for a way back in?

As we head to the checkout, I force myself to breathe. Celeste is just another person. I shouldn't care.

But as we leave the store and step back into the cool misty air, I can't help but glance down the street to where Celeste had disappeared into the fog. The uneasy feeling stays with me.

Tabitha bumps my shoulder lightly. "Let it go, Amelia. She's got nothing on you."

I smile, but it's forced. As much as I want to believe that, I can't help but feel like Celeste is more of a threat than I want to admit.

We walk in silence for a moment, the fog thickening around us, muffling our steps as we both eat the pastries with one hand on the strollers. The neighborhood feels eerily quiet, the mist swallowing the sounds of the island. A car pulls into a driveway in the distance, and I can't shake the feeling that eyes are following us. Watching me. Waiting.

Tabitha looks over at me, her brow furrowed. "Are you sure you're okay?" she asks again.

I force a laugh, but it comes out strained. "Yeah, just a lot on my mind."

Tabitha gives me a sympathetic look. "You were checking the mail when I came up to the driveway. Anything good to distract you?" she asks, trying to lighten the mood. "I got a flyer for a food delivery service I might try."

My breath catches. My mood isn't due only to Celeste. It is the letter, seared into my memory. "Just junk," I say, my voice tight. *More lies.*

The neighborhood looms behind us, silent and still. But I know better. A cold shiver runs through me, my skin prickling with dread. Behind the windows and the perfect facades, they're all watching. They know something.

They know who I really am.

EIGHT

Then

Blue lights flash as I approach the house. The sound of sirens cuts through the quiet, but it's distant, like background noise. Everything feels slow, like I'm moving through water. And as I approach the apartment, I know that everything has changed. The past shimmers like a haze as I take in the reality of the present.

I see my sister first. She's standing near the steps, shaking, her face streaked with tears. She looks so small.

I walk toward her, just watching the scene unfold. When I reach her, she collapses into my arms, her sobs rattling through her body.

"I didn't mean to," she chokes out, her voice raw and panicked. "It just—it happened so fast. I didn't *mean* for it to happen."

Her words tumble out in a rush, but they don't register. Not yet. The air feels thick, like it's pressing down on me from all sides. I force myself to glance over her shoulder at the stretcher, at the flashing lights, at the figures moving back and forth. Something inside me twists.

"It's okay," I say, my voice steady. "It wasn't your fault."

But I know. Deep down, I know what really happened.

The noise surrounds us—officers talking, medics moving around—but it's like I'm underwater. Everything muffled. Distant. My sister is clinging to me, her sobs quieting into hiccups, but she's still shaking, still gasping for air.

"I wasn't paying attention," she whispers, her words barely audible. "I didn't think—I didn't think she could open the door."

I glance over at her, my face blank. "You need to calm down," I say, my voice firm but not unkind.

She looks at me. Her wide eyes fill with guilt and fear. "W-What if th-they ask me what happened?" she stammers.

"They won't," I whisper. My tone is flat. "You turned around and she was gone. That's all you tell them."

She nods, like she's trying to believe it, but her hands are still shaking. Her breath is still catching in her throat.

I turn back toward the house, glimpsing the officers huddled together, speaking into their radios. They're asking about our mother, but I already know the answer. She's not here. She's never here.

My sister tightens her grip on my arm, her voice barely a whisper. "What do we do now?"

I glance down at her, then back toward the flashing lights. "You don't do anything," I say softly. "Just stay quiet."

Mom's screams cut through the air before we see her. She's running toward the house, wild-eyed, face twisted with panic. I don't flinch, but my sister presses closer to me, her breath hitching in her throat.

Mom throws herself over the stretcher, sobbing, her voice broken, desperate. "*My baby... my baby...*"

I don't look. I can't. Instead, I focus on my other sister, who's trembling beside me, her face pale. "We can't tell her," I whisper, leaning in close to her ear. "She'll hate you if she finds out."

My sister's breath catches again, and she looks at me, her eyes wide. "But I didn't mean to—"

"I know," I say softly, but firmly. "But we have to stick together. Just keep quiet."

Hours later, the house is quiet. The flashing lights and the officers are gone, but the reality of the day consumes us. We're upstairs now, in the small dark bedroom.

My sister sits on the edge of her bed, staring blankly ahead. She's still trembling, her breath shallow. I lean against the doorframe, watching her.

"I didn't think..." she whispers, her voice hoarse. "I didn't think it would end like this."

"You weren't paying attention," I say, my voice cold this time.

She turns to me, her eyes filling with tears again. "I didn't know she could get herself out the door."

I shrug, watching her carefully. "It doesn't matter now. It happened."

She breaks down again, her sobs wracking her body, but I stay where I am. Detached. Unmoved.

"How am I supposed to live with this?" she asks, her voice breaking, her words muffled by tears.

I stare at her for a moment, then turn my gaze to the window, where the darkness presses in from outside.

"You'll figure it out," I say quietly, emotionless.

NINE
AMELIA

The next day, I'm searching the kitchen counter, lifting a stack of flyers and setting it back down with a frustrated sigh. My laptop is missing—I hate to blame mommy brain, but I feel like I am in a fog. I need to check if the nanny service has sent an update, but I can't do that if I can't find the laptop.

I glance at the clock. Fifteen minutes until I'm supposed to meet Tabitha for our walk. Normally, I'd shrug it off and wait to look until later, but something about today feels different. I want Timothy to think I'm on top of things.

Since my laptop is nowhere to be found, I head toward Timothy's home office. He's out, and I figure it'll be easy enough to use his desktop just to check the emails. No big deal.

His office is tidy as always, every paper, every pen in its place. I settle into his chair, the leather creaking softly as I sit down. His desktop hums to life. The screen glows softly in the dim room. Just a quick check, I remind myself, my fingers hovering over the keyboard.

But then, as the home screen comes up, an email notification catches my eye.

I hesitate. I shouldn't. This has nothing to do with me. But the subject line is impossible to ignore:

Condo Deal—Celeste.

The knot in my stomach tightens. I click on the email, my hands trembling slightly.

Timothy,

Celeste showed me the final designs for the interior of the condo project. Let's aim to finalize everything by the end of the month. Keep me posted on her progress. Everything is looking incredible!

Best,

Gordon

I pull away from the desk, the air in the room suddenly feeling too thick. Just as I'm about to close the email, I see another notification pop up on the corner of the screen—a message from Lydia.

Just saw Celeste at Pilates. She looks so happy.

I feel the blood drain from my face. She's not just living across the street—she's integrated into his professional and personal life. *What else hasn't he told me?*

Trying not to panic, I quickly log in to my email account and read the update from the nanny service. I have to remind myself I wasn't trying to spy on my husband—I was trying to get help with Clover. But nothing I can say now will dim the ache in my chest. Timothy's ex is still undeniably wrapped up in his life.

I quickly close the email and log out of his desktop, my

hands shaking. I can't confront him—not yet. I need more time to figure this out.

The sound of Clover stirring in the other room pulls me out of my spiraling thoughts. I glance at the clock. I'm supposed to meet Tabitha in five minutes.

I push myself up from the desk, trying to focus on anything other than the sinking feeling in my stomach. Grabbing my coat, I head for the door, forcing a smile as I hear Clover cooing softly.

"Just a walk," I whisper to myself. "We'll clear our heads. Figure it out later."

As I leave the house, I glance across the street, where Celeste's mom's house stands. The windows glow in the late afternoon light. Celeste could be in there right now and I wouldn't even know.

The thought sends a chill down my spine.

I grip the stroller handle so tightly my knuckles turn white.

Tabitha is talking, and I should be listening—after all, hanging out with her usually calms me. She reminds me I'm not completely alone in figuring out motherhood. But today, it's different. My nerves are wound tight, and every word she utters spins them even tighter.

The narrow road we're walking on winds through Cutter's Island, where everything feels pristine, almost too perfect. Each estate stands tall and immaculate, a symbol of wealth and power. The Pacific Northwest air is thick with the smell of saltwater and pine, but there's also a feeling of isolation—not the comforting kind. On the island, you don't disappear; you're *seen*. Neighbors notice every move, every visitor. There's no escaping the gaze of this tight-knit community.

Nowhere to hide.

We pass by Timothy's parents' estate, the towering gates and massive glass windows giving it a fortress-like presence. Their home overlooks the harbor, all sharp lines and grandeur.

It's beautiful, but it feels oppressive, like I'm always being watched. Isabelle is probably inside, sipping her tea, waiting for me to trip up.

The thought makes my skin prickle. I don't want to run into Isabelle, not today. Her smile never quite reaches her eyes, and every time she looks at me, it's as if she's searching for cracks.

"The thing is," Tabitha wonders aloud, pushing her stroller alongside mine, "Keith still thinks I'm going back to work. But I just don't know how I'm going to tell him I'm not ready."

I nod at the right moment, but my mind keeps drifting back to the letters. It's hard to shake the feeling that someone's watching me. Someone knows. And I can't figure out who. I glance at the estate again, wondering if Isabelle's prying eyes are just waiting to catch something.

"Do you think Keith will be opposed to the idea of you staying home?" I ask gently, trying to focus on Tabitha. I need a distraction from my own fears, after all.

"Maybe," she considers aloud as we approach the coffee shop. We push through the door, the comforting scent of espresso washing over us. I breathe it in, thankful to be tucked away from the island's watchful eyes, even if only for a little while.

As we order our drinks, I tell Tabitha what I've been up to. "I called the nanny service," I admit, keeping my voice light. "The one Timothy wanted me to hire."

"Oh yeah? What'd they say?"

"They're going to give me a few recommendations in the next few days. I guess I have to fill out an application or something, to give them information about us and what we're looking for."

Tabitha raises an eyebrow. "That's good, right?"

I nod, but I'm lying. The truth is, I'm terrified of what the service might uncover. What if they look into *me*? What if they find out there's nothing from before I turned eighteen? That my name isn't real? My identity is a fragile, made-up thing. How long until it all falls apart?

We take a seat, our drinks and pastries in hand. For a moment, the warmth of the coffee shop soothes me. But the thought of the nanny service finding out who I am lingers, like a dark cloud overhead.

"Honestly, I never imagined I'd want to stay home," Tabitha expresses, bringing me back into the conversation. "It's weird how the idea of motherhood is different from the reality."

"What do you mean?" I ask. We've found a corner table, the babies quiet for now, and the café's cozy interior invites lingering. It's rustic but modern, with reclaimed wood accents and big windows letting in natural light. The kind of place where everyone seems perfectly put together—except me.

"Well, I thought it would be harder than it is. At least, for now. While Johnny's little, I'm enjoying every minute." Tabitha's face softens. "You know?"

I try to smile, but inside, her words twist like a knife. I want to know what that feels like, but I can't. Motherhood isn't bliss for me. I imagined myself as a picture-perfect mom, doing chores with Clover strapped to my chest, making everything from scratch. But the reality is exhausting. And I shouldn't be surprised. I never deserved an easy go of motherhood.

"Honestly, not really. It's a lot harder than I thought it would be," I admit, blinking back the emotions creeping to the surface.

Tabitha's face softens. "Oh, sweetie, I'm sorry. And here I am talking about how much I love it."

Before I can respond, Clover begins to fuss. I knew this peace wouldn't last. I start rocking her stroller, but the fear that I am a bad mother gnaws at me. I unbuckle her, pulling her into my arms as she begins to wail. I bounce her, feeling like I'm failing at this too.

"See?" I say, wiping the tears away that prick my eyes. "I'm not good at this. You're a natural, Tabitha. I'm just holding on by a thread."

"Maybe you're being too hard on yourself," she says, reaching for Clover. "Here, let me take her."

Relieved, I hand her my daughter. Instantly, Clover calms in Tabitha's arms. It should make me feel better, but instead, it only deepens the ache. I'm not cut out for this. The perfection I'm trying to create is crumbling around me.

Tabitha, ever gentle, rocks Clover effortlessly. "You always try to put on this appearance of perfection, Amelia. It's okay if things aren't perfect."

She doesn't understand. I *have* to be perfect. If I'm not, Timothy will see it, and when he does, it'll be over. He'll decide I'm not worth it. I've already messed up so much. I've ruined things before.

"What's on your mind?" Tabitha asks, concern in her eyes.

"I'm just... I'm lucky to have a friend like you," I say, dodging the question. But inside, I'm spinning out of control.

The letter, the nanny service, Timothy's family—everything is falling to pieces. It's only a matter of time before my perfect life shatters.

Back home later that afternoon, I try to shake the feeling of unease, but it's there, simmering under the surface. I finally find my laptop buried in a basket of clean laundry. I check my email, and my heart drops when I see another message from the nanny service. It takes only a glance for my panic to spiral.

"Hello, Amelia. There seems to be a discrepancy in the background information provided..."

I slam the laptop shut, my hands trembling. They're already onto me. How long before Timothy is too?

Someone knows the truth. They've known all along.

And now they're waiting for me to make a mistake.

TEN
AMELIA

Later that night, Timothy and I are in the bedroom getting ready to go to dinner at his parents' house.

Clover is lying on the center of our bed, kicking her feet happily. Why is she always so happy when other people are around? There is a pang in my chest, like a reminder I am the bad mother I know I really am.

"I just don't understand," he says. "I thought hiring a nanny was what we agreed on, to help you out?"

"I know. It just didn't feel right," I say truthfully. Though he doesn't have a clue what felt wrong. "I felt weird about it."

"Weird how?" he asks.

Explaining to Timothy why I don't want the nanny service feels impossible. After their inquisitive email requesting my background information, I felt like they were going to get too close. And having a nanny in the house meant a stranger could be watching me more closely. And I don't want any more eyes on me right now.

"I don't know it just... didn't." I reply, lamely.

Timothy's wearing his boxers and a white T- shirt as he

enters the walk-in closet, looking for a clean suit to change into before we go to dinner.

I don't want to go, but he is insisting we make a family appearance. His sister will be there, and I've avoided family dinners for the last two weeks. Earlier, I tried to make up an excuse—a headache, feeling exhausted from the baby—but Timothy's eyes turned to steel.

"We *need* to go, Amelia," he had said, his voice soft but with that firmness underneath, a tone I only hear when he's pushed too far. He's kind and thoughtful, but when I resist... there's this coldness that makes me falter.

"I'm just tired, Timothy," I'd murmured.

"I know you are," he had responded, his tone icy. "But this is *important*."

There was no arguing with him, not when he had that look in his eyes.

"I know it isn't your favorite thing to have dinner over there, but my parents love seeing Clover," he says now. "And it will be relaxing for you. She never seems to fuss when I'm around."

I roll my eyes as I turn away, not wanting my husband to see my frustration. The last thing I want is for Timothy to think I'm anything but a good mother and wife. He doesn't understand what it is like caring for a newborn because he's gone for ten hours a day. He barely sees Clover. And when he does, she's usually rested and fed because I spent the day trying to meet her needs. He swoops in and gets to pick her up, cooing over her perfection. Meanwhile, I'm the one doing the dirty work.

"Are you going to change?" he asks. He is making a Windsor knot on the tie around his neck, standing in front of the full-length mirror.

"You don't like this?" I look down at myself. I'm wearing a black wool dress that hits my calves. It's loose, but I thought it was pretty.

"No, it's fine," he says quickly. "You look wonderful. I didn't mean that. I just thought... I'm sorry. I'm not trying to upset you." He steps toward me, resting his arms on my shoulders. "Amelia, are you okay?"

I blink back tears. "Why wouldn't I be?" I ask, trying to keep my voice from faltering. "I'm perfectly fine."

"You're just not acting like yourself. You're always worked up about Clover. You seem so tired, and yet you won't accept any help. I feel stuck, like I don't know how to make any of this easier on you. I thought you *wanted* to be a mom."

"I did. I *do*. Of course I want to be a mom," I say to him, pushing down my deepest feelings of inadequacy. Feelings that took root decades ago. "It's just a big adjustment."

"I know, love." He pulls me into a warm embrace. "We've had a big year."

He is right about that. After we met and I spent the night at his house, we fell into a quick rhythm of him picking me up after work, sweeping me away to some high-end restaurant in the city, or treating me to long weekends away. One time he took me to the coast, another was a weekend in the mountains. The first time he asked if I would like to take a business trip with him to France, I pressed a hand to my chest, shocked. But then I shook my head.

"Flying terrifies me," I had lied. The truth was I didn't have a passport let alone a valid ID. I wasn't sure how I could procure one without revealing my real identity.

"No, it's fine. Of course, it was a last-minute idea," he said, smiling at me. "But let's plan a trip soon," he said. "Somewhere special."

"I've never been to the San Juan Islands," I told him quickly. "I'd love to take a ferry there and do some whale watching.

He grinned. "I know when we could go there," he says.

"When?" I asked.

There was a sparkle in his eye. "For a honeymoon."

I remember patting him on the shoulder playfully. "Don't say those sorts of things to a girl unless you mean it."

He changed the subject, but somehow we wound up there four months later, reclining on a sailboat on Orcas Island, a ring on my finger, a baby in my belly.

I know he only proposed so quickly because I was pregnant with his child, but I knew he loved me. I *know* he loves me.

We didn't mean to get pregnant, of course. I never intended to ever become pregnant. We'd only been dating a few months when I missed my period. My breasts felt tender. Then I started throwing up.

I remember the morning I walked out of the bathroom in his high-rise condo, sunlight streaming through the big open windows. My face was ashen. I felt depleted. He looked up from where he was reading in bed.

"What is it?" he asked.

"I got sick again," I told him.

"Do you think maybe..." he said at the very same time I voiced out loud, "Do you think I could be pregnant?"

He ran down to the pharmacy on the corner and bought several tests. I took them one after another. By the third test with two pink lines, he was laughing incredulously.

"I can't believe it," I said, forcing a smile. "Pregnant? I never imagined I..."

But he didn't know the whole truth. I never imagined this moment would come, not for me. As the reality set in, I felt the pressure of yet another secret building. Tears filled my eyes, and he asked if I was okay.

I lied and said, "Yes, of course I am. I'm so happy. I'm... Can we do this?" I asked, my words a flurry.

He took me by the hands and he kissed my fingers. And then he kissed my lips and he looked into my eyes and he said, "I love you, Amelia. I love you with all my heart. I want to have this baby with you. I want to have a life with you. Marry me."

I laughed. I was in a nightgown, my hair a mess. He was in his boxers. He rushed to his dresser, pulling out a small box. Dropping to one knee, he said, "Marry me. Be my wife, the mother of our child, my forever."

"It's all so fast," I said, overwhelmed by the whirlwind of the morning.

"Lucky us," he laughed, holding out the ring. The fact he had bought the ring and had already planned on proposing, even before knowing I was pregnant, made my answer easier.

He slid the sparkling diamond onto my finger, and through teary eyes, I said, "Yes."

I always wondered how long he'd had that ring. Had he planned to propose before I told him the news? It didn't matter, I told myself. We were happy, and that's what counted, right?

He didn't understand then how foreign this whole unfolding was. I'd spent so many years living under a rock, dating only one other person in my life, not wanting to be seen —but Timothy wouldn't let me disappear.

He said he loved my naivety, my willingness to say yes to a new experience and how I marveled at simple pleasures in life.

Part of me felt, and still feels now, like I am novel to him, as if the reason he loves me is that I'm so different from all the other girls. Different than all the Celestes he knew before.

After I saw her at the market, I Googled her again, of course. Beautiful brunette hair, shiny and luminous, a bright white smile, eyes with nothing to hide. An interior design consultant.

I don't know if that means she's out of work and living at her mom's house or if she's just here for a break from city life, but I knew the instant I saw her photo online that I wasn't anything like her.

She'd attended an Ivy League school, just like Timothy, and previously worked at a boutique design agency in Los Angeles before coming back to Cutter's Island. Celeste's Instagram revealed brunches with friends and trips to Europe, beautiful clothing in every image. And her laughing, head tossed back, sophisticated. The opposite of me in every way.

I shake the thought of Celeste from my head. Timothy had explained the situation, and I knew I was obsessing over his ex for no reason. I needed to let it go. My world was small, and I kept it that way on purpose. Tabitha was my only real friend—my old boss Cal from the bakery didn't count. I hadn't seen him since Clover was born. And I had no family to fall back on, no mother to turn to when things got rough.

Timothy thought I grew up in foster care and that I never knew my parents. He was proud of me for pulling up my bootstraps and making things work, but I know I'm not the kind of girl his family imagined for him, not the kind of wife or daughter-in-law they would've picked for themselves.

It's not that I never had bigger ambitions, it's just my life got small so quickly and I was too scared to let it expand.

Nothing's changed now as I stand in the bedroom with my husband and my daughter, knowing I need to change my clothes so I look more presentable for my husband.

"What should I wear?" I ask, forcing a playful tone, trying to get the evening—and my mood—back on track.

"Something that will show off your curves," Timothy says with a smile, squeezing my ass. Then he takes my hand and leads me into our walk-in closet. It's full of beautiful clothes and shoes and handbags. If I wanted, I could play the part of an elegant wife, because it just feels like costumes to me.

But now, he's picking out a dress for me. I own only designer clothes because of the shopping spree his mother and sister dragged me on right after Clover was born. My body didn't feel like my own—everything had changed, and I knew it would continue to fluctuate. But they insisted.

"Now that you're not pregnant," Isabelle had said, "you need a new wardrobe."

I had smiled, trying to go along with their game, but later told Timothy none of it felt like me.

"You don't have to wear them," he'd told me. "Take my credit card and buy anything you want that feels more you. But I like you just as you are. In fact, I fell in love with the girl wearing clogs and a flour-covered apron. I'm not looking for you to be anything but yourself."

He'd kissed me then, deeply, the same as he kisses me now in the walk-in closet. Clover is happy in the center of our king-size bed, so when Timothy pulls me toward him, kissing me more deeply, I give in.

We undress quickly, my black woolen dress on the floor, my panties on a pile next to his boxers, and he takes me quickly, completely. I'm breathless when we finish. His kisses feel warm on my neck.

"You're beautiful, Amelia, just as you are. And all of this will get easier," he promises.

When I look back up at my husband, I feel a love, a longing, a knowing. He may not know everything about me, but he accepts me just as I am.

I wish I could tell him everything, the whole truth and nothing but the truth.

"So," I say, after we've composed ourselves, "you said you wanted something that shows off my curves?"

He growls, "Yes, please."

"And my cleavage? Should that be revealed?" I tease.

He chuckles. "Always."

Not long after, we're dressed and walking over to his parents' house, Clover in the stroller. When we reach the estate, I unbuckle her and lift her into my arms protectively. Timothy reaches for the diaper bag, and as a family, we walk into his parents' house.

Of course, I thought it was just a family dinner.

So when I see the beautiful woman in Louis Vuitton heels

and a cream-colored suit in the corner drinking a cocktail with Isabelle and Lydia, I'm caught off guard.

"Why is she here?" I ask Timothy as we enter the living room, the same room where we had our photos taken for the magazine.

"Oh." His voice falls. "That's Celeste. Didn't I mention she was joining us for dinner?"

ELEVEN
AMELIA

I'm holding Clover as I stand in the living room, taking it all in. My husband's ex-girlfriend is here with his family, fitting in so effortlessly it's as if she was born for this life—*born* to be Timothy's wife.

Timothy wraps an arm around my waist, his mouth on my ear. "I'm so sorry. I should have said something, but that is Celeste, my ex." He squeezes my hip. "My mom and her have stayed in touch. It's not personal."

I look at him out of the corner of my eye, trusting him and resolving to be brave no matter how this night goes. He's never been a liar—at least, I don't *think* he's ever been a liar.

"It's okay," I say with genuine confidence. I am not going to be usurped by my husband's ex. "I'm a big girl."

He kisses me on the cheek, and then, with the sort of care I've always wanted, he says, "I'll have a word with my father."

He walks away, joining Alexander in the corner of the room where he's pouring bourbon.

I walk toward the women, Clover in my arms. "Good evening," I say.

"Amelia!" Isabelle says, her voice high. "I'm so glad you

could make it. I didn't think you were coming." There's a glimmer in her eye, something almost mean lurking beneath her polished smile.

"Sorry, I haven't been able to get it together the last few times you've had dinner together," I say. "Still adjusting to the new routine."

"That's all right," Isabelle says. "So long as Timothy makes it, I won't complain too much."

"Right," I say, recognizing her words for what they are. I'm irrelevant. Her son is her golden boy and I'm just the unwanted wife.

Lydia reaches out and gives me a quick hug. "Hey," she says, "you look good tonight." Her words are kind, but they sound, though, as if I usually don't.

Brushing her comment aside, I bounce Clover, shifting my body so they can look at the baby. "Clover's looking well tonight as well," I say.

"Isn't she always?" Lydia says, leaning down and kissing Clover's forehead.

Looking straight at Celeste, I smile brightly. "I don't think we've met. I'm Amelia Sterling," I say, emphasizing my new last name.

"Of course," she says, her pearly teeth shining as she smiles at me. "I'm Celeste Salsberg. I'm your neighbor."

"So I've heard. My husband told me all about it."

Lydia's eyes narrow as she meets mine, but she doesn't reveal that she told me this tidbit of information.

"I was hoping to meet you sooner," Celeste continues. "But you never appeared at the last few family dinners I've attended."

"Sure," I say, storing that information for later. "Right now, my priority is ensuring Clover has what she needs."

It feels odd that Timothy would've omitted the details of his time with his parents. What if he did mention it, and I've been so sleep-deprived I didn't even notice? Still, that detail seems hard to miss.

Isabelle smiles at me, but it's cold, barely touching her eyes. "I need to speak with the cook and make sure there's another setting at the table for Amelia." The way she says it, the place setting feels more like an inconvenience than a welcome.

I feel a pang of jealousy—they have a table setting for Celeste but not for me.

Lydia places a hand on my elbow and asks if I'd like a glass of wine.

"Wine sounds lovely," I say too brightly. Timothy walks over with his bourbon and asks if he can hold Clover for me.

"Thank you," I say with a smile.

Timothy puts his glass on a side table and effortlessly takes our daughter from me. She doesn't fuss or cry in his arms, but a wave of dread washes over me. Whenever she's away from me, I get this knot in my stomach, like something might happen to her. Like there's always the chance of an accident lurking just out of sight, waiting to strike when I'm not there to stop it.

But Timothy is perfectly capable of caring for his child, even though he doesn't do many hands-on daily duties. No slight to him; he's working, and I'm at home. So her routine has become my responsibility.

I turn back to the women. Lydia hands me a glass of red wine, and I sip. It's delicious, rich and full-bodied.

"Dinner is ready," Isabelle announces. She glances my way, a sharp smile tugging at her lips. "Now that *everyone's* finally arrived, it might be a squeeze, but we'll make it work."

Before we exit the living room, I reach for Timothy's bourbon and carry it to the table for him. Once inside the dining room, we take our seats, and I place his glass beside mine.

"Oh, I've arranged seating for tonight," Isabelle announces, her voice firm. "Amelia, you're there." She points to the seat next to her husband at the head of the table. "And Timothy, you're down here, next to me. And of course, Celeste," she adds with a purr, as if it's the most natural thing in the world.

I look across the table, feeling the distance between Timothy and me like a chasm. Celeste effortlessly fits in, her polished smile never wavering. They look so natural together, like they were meant to be side by side. Even Clover, who's content in her father's arms, seems to adore her. Celeste looks at Clover with an almost maternal gaze—adoring, soft, like she belongs. They're the perfect picture of a family, a life that's not mine.

Celeste slides in next to my husband, who's now diagonally across from me. The table leaves have been removed, so there's just enough seating for six. It's intimate, and I appreciate that, though I wouldn't say I like sitting across from my husband's ex-girlfriend all night.

Timothy is still holding Clover, who's resting happily in his arms. "She's such a good baby," Celeste says softly.

And just then, Clover giggles at her—her little face lighting up in delight. It's not rational, but it feels like the ultimate betrayal.

"She truly is," Timothy says. "She hardly cries at all."

I look at Timothy, wondering how he manages to sleep through Clover's middle-of-the-night screams. Instead of venting my frustration, I turn my attention to Celeste.

"So, Celeste, do you often come to dinner when you're in town?" I ask, keeping my tone deliberately light.

"Oh, well, she's practically *family*," Isabelle jumps in before Celeste can answer. "Now that she's back, it's so lovely to have her around again, just like old times."

"Right," I say slowly, as the cook begins serving the roast chicken. I take my portion and reach for the green beans. The whole dynamic feels... off. Like I'm the one intruding, not her.

"It's interesting," I say, trying to keep my voice steady, "I didn't realize you all had stayed so close with Timothy's ex."

As I pick up my knife and fork, my engagement ring glitters on my finger, a reminder of my husband's promise. I feel a stab of panic. *Was the ring really for me? Was it always meant to be mine?* The thought is ridiculous, yet there it is, clinging to me like a shadow now that his ex-girlfriend is near.

Alexander clears his throat as if willing the meal to steer away from confrontation, but I don't care. The intimacy of this dinner, just six of us at the table, feels far too personal to ignore the elephant in the room.

Timothy glances at me, his expression unreadable. "Celeste is helping with the properties. We've been in touch more recently since she joined the team. It's why she returned to Cutter's Island."

My stomach drops. This isn't just about dinner. He *hired* her. He wants her here. The betrayal lurches through me. Has he been lying about working late every night too?

What else has he been keeping from me?

"In which capacity are you helping with my husband's condos?" I ask, trying to maintain my composure.

Celeste beams, as if unaware of the tension, her white smile almost blinding. "I'm handling all the interior design—selecting the hardwood, tile, fixtures. All the fun stuff."

"And might I add," Isabelle chimes in, "her choices have been absolutely impeccable."

"Well, thank you." Celeste sits with her back straight, all confidence as she begins cutting a piece of chicken. She turns to me, her voice syrupy. "And what kind of work do you do, Amelia?"

I force a smile. "I was a baker before I met Timothy. Then, of course, we had Clover."

"Oh, that's so charming," Celeste coos, her tone patronizing. "Did you go to school for that?"

"No, I never went to college." I press my lips together,

trying not to take the bait. "I didn't grow up with the privileges of Cutter's Island."

Lydia, sitting next to me, lets out a nervous laugh. "Oh my gosh, is this *awkward?*"

"*Unexpected* might be the better word," I mutter, trying to maintain my calm.

I wonder if Timothy was so intent on me wearing a revealing dress this evening because he wanted me to look different than I usually do. If I am here, I'm playing a part.

Regardless, I am ready for the topic to change. I don't want attention on me and what I used to do before the baby was born.

"Where did you train?" Celeste asks. "Were you a pastry chef?"

"No." I glance at Clover, who's awake now and sucking on her fingers in her father's arms. I feel a twinge in my chest. I know it's time for her to eat. "Self-taught mostly. I got a job in a bakery, and they showed me the ropes."

"That's so... industrious of you." Celeste smiles tightly.

I take another bite of my chicken before Clover starts fussing. I want to say something like, *See, she's not a perfect baby. She gets upset sometimes.* However, Timothy stands from the table, bouncing Clover gently, his hand on her back. "Just finish eating, babe," he directs me. "She's fine." He's so relaxed, so easy with her.

My entire body tenses when I am trying to keep her settled. It's strange to feel jealous of my husband now, but I do.

I take one more bite before pushing away from the table. "It's fine," I decide. "I'm going to take her and feed her in the living room," I explain.

"The diaper bag's already in there," Timothy informs me.

I stand and reach for my daughter. When I pull her to my chest, she begins to wail. Isabelle clucks her tongue as if I've done something wrong, but I know I haven't.

I leave the dining room defeated, feeling like I don't belong.

I hear Alexander clear his throat as I go to the living room. "It is so nice to have you at the table again, Celeste."

My blood feels like it's going to boil. Why did they even want me in the family portrait if they are intent on destroying my marriage? As I unfastened the button on the front of my dress to offer milk to my daughter in the living room corner, I try not to take it all so personally.

But the truth is, it *is* personal. The Sterlings are actively showing me that they don't want me here. But what does Timothy think? What have I ever done to any of them? Don't they love Clover? Tears fill my eyes, and I try to stop them from falling.

Lydia walks into the living room, her steps cautious. "There you are," she speaks softly, sitting beside me on the couch.

"It's really fine," I falter, my voice shaky. "We don't need to talk about it."

She hesitates. "I should've told you about Celeste coming tonight. I didn't want to make things worse."

"Why is she here, Lydia? It feels like I'm being replaced."

"That's not true," Lydia quickly reassures. "Mom's just always had a thing for Celeste, you know that. And Timothy... well, he didn't want to upset you by telling you she had joined his project. You are already going through so much with the new baby."

"Timothy is equally a new parent, you know?"

"I do know, but... well, I think..."

"You think what?" I ask, but Lydia licks her lips nervously, looking away.

Quietly, Lydia adds, "I think you should be... careful."

My blood runs cold. "Careful of what?"

My mind races. Do they know? Have they found out who I really am? Is this their way of replacing me—bringing Celeste back, the one who belongs, while they quietly push me out? I can feel it, the way they look at me. I'm the misfit here, the one who doesn't belong in this perfect picture. And Celeste... she's waiting for the moment they finally get rid of me.

"I don't know what Celeste is planning, but she's the girl who's always gotten what she wants," Lydia whispers quickly. "Everything with you and Timothy happened so fast. Meeting and getting pregnant and getting married was a whole whirlwind, right? Celeste didn't know how serious things were before it was too late." She looks genuinely worried. "But now that the baby's here and things have calmed down, she's swooping in for a reason, like she wants what she always hoped to have. They'd stopped dating for only a month before Timothy met you."

My heart pounds. "I didn't know that," I disclose. "I didn't realize I was a... rebound." I shake my head. "We promised each other that what was in the past was the past and that we were just going to live in the present. We never discussed past relationships."

"Interesting," Lydia ponders, raising an eyebrow. "Most women wouldn't want to do that."

I shrug, trying to sound indifferent. "Maybe I'm not most women."

Her eyes narrow. "Or maybe you just don't want Timothy asking *you* the same questions."

I swallow, suddenly on edge. "What are you getting at, Lydia?"

She shrugs casually, but there's a glint in her eyes. "I don't know. Maybe you've got some skeletons in your closet? Something you don't want Timothy to know about."

I feel the tension in my chest tighten. "It's really nothing, Lydia. You should go back to dinner."

Lydia rolls her eyes. "They're all so boring, anyway. Talking about Timothy's development, the security systems my dad wants to add to his condo project. It's just another Sterling Enterprise thing."

I nod absently, but her words swirl around me. Why is she pushing this? Why is she implying I'm hiding something?

She gives me a look, her voice dropping. "Just be careful, Amelia."

The warning hangs in the air like a threat. "Careful of what?"

Lydia stands, her gaze lingering on me for a moment before she walks away. "You'll figure it out," she says over her shoulder, and then she's gone.

I sit there, Clover in my arms, my thoughts spinning wildly. *Be careful.* What does she mean? Does she know about my past? Does the whole family know? Have they been setting me up from the start—Isabelle, Celeste, Lydia? Was this their plan all along?

The notes. My stomach twists in horror. Could one of *them* have sent those notes? Isabelle, so cold and distant. Celeste, who slid back into Timothy's life as if she never left. Lydia, with her veiled warnings.

My breath comes in short bursts. They know. They must know.

And now they're closing in.

TWELVE

Then

Have you ever been to a baby's funeral? The casket's so small, it looks like a toy.

We're standing graveside, my sister gripping my hand, crying. Mom's wailing, practically hysterical. The pastor drones on about eternal rest, but I've never felt more awake. I can't cry. What's the point?

Vera's gone.

My other sister is shaking beside me. I grip her hand tighter, keeping her anchored, but inside I feel nothing. There's nothing to feel. The people from the complex scraped together enough money for this burial, and now it's over.

Life goes on.

Back at the apartment, my sister collapses on the bed, her eyes glued to the empty crib in the corner.

"She's never coming back," she whispers, voice breaking. "I can't stand it. I can't stand it one bit."

I shrug. "We should take it down tomorrow. It's just going to upset Mom more."

My sister stares at me, tears streaming down her face. "Why are you so cold? She was our *sister*."

Her sobbing intensifies. "If I had been more careful, if I hadn't—"

I grab her shoulders, forcing her to look at me. "You *weren't* careful. That's why she's *dead*. And you'll spend your whole life making up for it unless you promise me something."

"What?" she stammers.

"A sister pact," I say, matter-of-factly. "We both make a promise to never have a child."

Her face crumples. "It was an accident. I didn't mean—"

"You'll never have a baby. Ever. You can't be trusted. You killed Vera, and you'll kill another if you're not careful. Make this promise and I'll keep your secret. I'll make sure no one knows what really happened."

She looks at me, broken. "I promise."

"Good," I say, stepping back, satisfied. "And if you ever break that promise, I'll tell everyone the truth."

But as I watch my sobbing sister, I know I can never do that.

Because the truth of what really happened that day would destroy us both.

THIRTEEN

AMELIA

I squeeze my eyes shut, feeling lightheaded from lack of sleep, hunger and stress. My life is pressing in on me, from the letters that have been haunting my mind since they arrived to Clover's constant fussing.

Outside, the sky is a gray sheet, covering the sun, typical for February in the Pacific Northwest. Cutter's Island sits under its usual damp blanket, the Sound's mist curling around the pines like fingers. The cold air seeps through the cracks of our immaculate home, despite the double-paned windows.

I can't stop pacing the kitchen, the smooth hardwood under my feet. Clover is in her swing, her cries grating against my last nerve. I've tried everything, but nothing seems to calm her today.

All I can think about is that last letter and the chilling feeling that someone knows too much.

The wind rattles the windows. My thoughts spiral as I work to clean the kitchen. I wipe down the counters and the state-of-the-art appliances. But it doesn't feel like my home, it feels like a cage, and my in-laws next door have the key. Something about this life I have chosen feels wrong—like it's all a facade.

The doorbell rings, cutting through the eerie quiet. I freeze. Another ring—insistent.

I force myself to walk to the door, my heart pounding. The wind tugs at the hem of my sweater as I pull it open, the briny, wet smell of the salt water rushing in.

Mrs. Salsberg, Celeste's mother, stands on the front steps, clutching a plate of homemade cookies. She wears a green wool coat with a cheerful plaid scarf and sensible shoes. The opposite of her sophisticated daughter, Mrs. Salsberg looks grandmotherly.

"Hello, dear," she says, her voice smooth as honey. "I thought I'd bring you some shortbread. I made it this morning."

I hesitate, gripping the door tightly. "I'm sorry, what do you want?"

She tilts her head, her smile not faltering. "I just thought we could have a little... chat. Maybe I could pop in for some coffee?"

"I don't need cookies," I say, sharper than I intend. "And I don't need a chat."

Her expression tightens, but she doesn't back down. "I was being neighborly, Amelia. I know how hard life can be with a newborn."

"You think you know me?" The paranoia creeps back in. "Why are you really here?"

She takes a step back, but there's something too knowing in her eyes, like she's keeping secrets of her own. "I just wanted to help. But if you don't need it, I won't keep you."

I slam the door shut quickly, my hands trembling. What is she playing at, especially after the scene she must know I caused at dinner last night? Does she know something? I turn back to the kitchen, feeling off balance. Why is everyone acting like they know more about my life than I do?

I pick up Clover, needing her warmth against me. Her cries soften as I hold her close, her small body fitting against mine. "I won't let anyone hurt you," I whisper, my voice thick with emotion. "I promise. I'll protect you."

My phone buzzes on the counter, interrupting the moment. It's a text from Tabitha.

Up for a walk?

I look out the window at the dreary drizzle coating the trees and the narrow roads. It's not just the weather—everything about Cutter's Island feels stifling today, like the whole place is watching me. I quickly reply to her text.

Feeling tired today. Hope you understand. XOXO.

A moment later, guilt gets the better of me, so I send another message.

Did you end up talking to Keith about extending maternity leave? Did you make a plan?

Her reply is instant.

That's what I wanted to talk about. It didn't go so well. :(

I bite my lip. Despite my exhaustion, I know she needs to talk.

Come over. We can talk.

Her reply pings in quickly.

Give me ten!

I set down my phone and glance out the window, where the

rain has started up again, lightly tapping on the glass. The sky is dense, the island blanketed in a mist that seems to cling to the trees and roads, leaving a sense of isolation.

The knock at the door comes quickly, and I check it's Tabitha through the peephole before opening it. She looks as tired as I feel, her messy bun and red eyes a mirror of my own struggles. Johnny is nestled in his baby carrier against her chest, his tiny fists curled up.

"Hey," she says softly, her voice apologetic. "Sorry to impose..."

"Don't apologize," I say, waving her inside. "Do you want some coffee? I just made a pot."

"That sounds great," she says, settling into the warmth of the kitchen, where the smell of fresh coffee at least offers some comfort.

She glances at Clover, who's finally sleeping in her swing. "You getting any rest?"

I shake my head, pointing to the coffeepot. "Not enough. Hence the caffeine."

Tabitha gives me a sad smile. "I'm sorry I'm here. You should probably be sleeping while you can."

"It's fine. Adult company is nice." I reach into the fridge for half-and-half, pouring it into her cup the way she likes. The quiet hum of the refrigerator fills the space, making the kitchen feel too perfect, too curated for the chaos in my life.

"I thought you would have had enough adult conversation last night at the family dinner?" she teases, wrapping her hands around the mug.

"Yeah," I sigh, leaning against the counter. "But it was a whole mess. Celeste was there."

Tabitha's eyes widen. "Wait, Timothy's ex-girlfriend? What was she doing there?"

"I guess she's been going to the dinners I've missed." I groan before taking a sip of my coffee. "Apparently, she's helping him with his condo project. I didn't know until last night. It's like... like they're already *replacing* me."

Tabitha shakes her head. "Oh, stop. You just got married. You're madly in love."

"Am I? Or is he already hiding things from me?"

She gives me a sympathetic look. "You're overthinking it."

I let out a bitter laugh. "Maybe, but everything feels off lately. Like Timothy has all these secrets, and I'm the only one not in on them."

Tabitha takes a long sip of her coffee before answering. "Well, I'm in no position to judge. Things with Keith are rough. I told him I didn't want to go back to work, and he freaked out. If I don't work, we might not be able to stay here. He wanted the whole 'Cutter's Island dream,' but now we're drowning in bills."

"I get that." I exhale, glancing around my kitchen. "Before I married Timothy, I worked under the table, baking. I never imagined I'd end up here, in this glamorous life."

Tabitha nods, her eyes dancing around the room. "Your house is beautiful though. It's like something out of a television show."

"It doesn't feel real," I admit. "Not when Timothy's ex is sitting across the table at dinner, acting like she's part of the family. I'd trade all of this for normal."

"*Normal?*" Tabitha muses with a laugh. "I don't think normal exists. We're all just faking it."

We sit in silence for a moment, the rain drumming softly on the roof. The air is thick with the smell of coffee and the underlying tension we both feel.

"I told Keith I don't care about keeping up appearances, but he wants the fancy life," Tabitha admits. "Now we're stuck, and I don't know what to do. I don't want to be a working mom, but if I don't go back, he's going to resent me. I feel trapped."

Listening to her, I realize I'm not the only one on this island with a perfect facade that's crumbling. Not everyone in this luxury community has their life together, no matter how it looks from the outside.

Tabitha sighs. "I feel like I'm in a no-win situation. You're lucky, you know, to have Timothy."

"Lucky?" I mumble, staring into my coffee. "It doesn't feel that way. It feels like everything is falling apart. Ever since that article came out, I've felt paranoid, like it's all going to come crashing down."

Tabitha frowns. "Paranoid?"

"I don't know," I falter, shrugging. I so desperately want to tell her everything, but I know I can't. "Like this life Timothy gave me is about to disintegrate."

She gives me a wry smile. "Well, if you two split, you'll walk away with a lot of money."

I shake my head. "I signed a prenup."

Tabitha groans. "Oh no..."

"It's not about the money," I quickly promise. "But what if he leaves me for Celeste? What will I do? I have to take care of Clover somehow."

"Don't think that way." Tabitha dismisses my fear, waving a hand. "Deal with the facts in front of you. Right now, Clover's asleep, and you should take a nap too. I'm going to head out and figure out what to do with Keith. You should figure out your own plan with Timothy." She lifts her eyebrows. "Maybe make a nice dinner. When he comes home, wear something cute. Reignite the flame that may have gotten lost in pregnancy and childbirth. And *then* ask him what he's doing with his ex-girlfriend."

I grimace. "I feel like that's all so weird, seducing him to get information. Do you think it's a good idea?"

She twists her lips. "Look, we're both sleep-deprived new moms. I'm not saying my idea is good," she laughs. "But I am saying Timothy has the information you want. You might as well try to get it out of him without a fight."

As Tabitha leaves, I walk to the front window, staring out at the gloomy drizzle. Everything feels ominous, like the island is pressing down on me, choking me with its perfection and its secrets. Unable to stop myself, I slip on my shoes and head to the mailbox, the damp air clinging to my skin.

Inside is another envelope.

My heart stutters in my chest as I pull it out and tear it open. The paper trembles in my hand.

You can't hide forever. I know what you did.

The words send a shiver through me.
They know.

FOURTEEN
AMELIA

I can't solve the mystery of who is writing the letters right this moment. But I can try and salvage my marriage.

So while Clover takes an unexpected afternoon nap, I take Tabitha's advice. After jumping in the shower, I exfoliate with a grapefruit body scrub and deep-condition my hair before running a razor over my legs. Drying off, I rub lotion on my skin, appreciating how soft and smooth it is. It's been ages since I did that.

Wrapped in a thick white bathrobe, I walk down the hall to check on Clover. She's still sleeping soundly in her crib. Relieved, I exhale, choosing to dry my hair and run the curling iron through it afterward. After that, I apply moisturizer and foundation to my face, swipe mascara on my lashes and use a brow pencil to curve the arch perfectly. I rarely wear makeup, so it feels special.

Knowing Clover is bound to wake up soon, I walk into the closet and choose a tight black turtleneck and my favorite pair of high-waisted Levi's. I remember that they were Timothy's favorites too while we were dating before I got pregnant.

He'd slide his hands in my back pockets and tug me close.

I'd stand on my tiptoes, leaning in for a kiss. I'm trying to focus on those good memories instead of the new ones trying to disrupt my vision of a happy life on Cutter's Island.

When Clover wakes up, I pull milk from the refrigerator where it is thawing and prepare her a bottle in the milk warmer. I bounce her happily, cooing, remembering that I can do this. I can be a good mom to my daughter.

I push the threatening letters far from my mind as I offer her the bottle and she takes it happily. I sit on the couch with her—my phone in one hand, she in the other—and I think about how much I've let the past control my present.

Maybe I've made a massive mistake telling Timothy all of these lies. He doesn't know where I spent my teenage years or what happened because of the secrets.

Not sure how to fix the situation, I continue to focus on what I can control. I open my phone and place an order with our favorite Italian restaurant downtown. I order him filet mignon and a Caesar salad. I order myself a caprese and their Bolognese pasta. I request a delivery time of 7 p.m.

I'm doing something good for a change, for Timothy and me. When was the last time I put any effort into our relationship? Maybe I've been the problem the whole time.

Clover finishes the bottle and begins fussing again. I pick her up, placing a burp cloth on my shoulder before gently patting her back.

"There you go, baby," I whisper as I carry the bottle to the sink. The house is clean, for the most part, and I set Clover into her swing while I load the dishwasher.

Once that's finished, I light a candle on the kitchen counter and then walk to the wine cabinet, choosing a bottle that I know Timothy loves. I pick a bottle from the vineyard where our wedding took place. It wasn't far from here, at Caraway Estate. It was a small wedding, just Timothy's family and friends. I didn't have anyone to invite except for my boss from the bakery, Cal.

I remember how surprised he was at the expense thrown for our wedding. He pulled me aside at the reception and laughed, "I had no idea you were marrying up. I've always been paying you under the table without any questions because I'm sure you have your reasons. So this is a surprise."

I lowered my eyes. "I'm pregnant," I confessed quietly.

Not many people knew. Once we found out about the pregnancy, we married within a few months, before I even began to show.

"Oh." He paused. "Well, are you happy? Is this what you want?"

I remember laughing back at him, shrugging at my boss, who was a round-faced man with a thick mustache. "I think it's too late. If I wanted to be a runaway bride, I should have done that before the ceremony."

"I mean it though. Are you happy?" Cal pressed, concern creasing his brow. He'd always looked out for me.

I met his eyes. "Yes," I stated. "I'm in love. Timothy is wonderful and the baby..."

"You want it?" he pressed.

Not having family or friends, no one else had asked me that simple question. Timothy certainly hadn't. He assumed that having a child was a part of my dream. He didn't know about my deepest fears. I hadn't told him that about myself, the heartbreak of losing my sister all those years ago.

Cal didn't know either, but there was something in the pause, the way his eyes met mine, the way he wanted to be sure I was all right.

"It'll be good," I promised, trying to convince myself as much as him. "I've been floating all these years, and maybe it'll be nice to settle down."

Cal frowned. "Not exactly the words of a happy bride."

My eyes darted around the reception. There was a big dining room at the vineyard where we were having a five-course sit-down dinner, a first dance and a cake cutting. It was a simple affair but lovely nonetheless. I wore a big white gown, and all the guests wore suits and long dresses.

It was beautiful, but standing there with Cal, I distinctly knew how different my life was from Timothy's.

"You don't have any family here," he reflected.

"You know I don't *have* family," I lied.

"That's what you've always said, but sometimes, on someone's wedding day, family members come out of the woodwork, you know?"

"Not mine," I told him firmly. "I promise you, I'm okay."

"If you're ever not okay, you can call me. I mean it. Even though you're out on Cutter's Island and I'm in Seattle, I'm always just a boat ride away. I want you to know that, Amelia."

"I do, Cal, and thank you. Without the job at the bakery, I don't know what I would've done."

"Well, you would've figured it out. You're a smart girl, and truly one hell of a baker. If you ever want a job again, no one makes as good a scored sourdough loaf as you."

I smiled then, grateful he was at the wedding but wondering what everyone else must have thought. *Poor Amelia, without any family to speak of.*

Now, I carry the bottle of wine to the dining room table. I set out wineglasses, plates, silverware and cloth napkins.

I look at the clock. It's just after 6 p.m. I pick up Clover as she begins to fuss again. "There you are, baby girl," I say. "Mama's here."

I carry her upstairs and bathe her, changing her into cute pink pajamas. I ensure she's nice and cozy before turning down the lights in her room and nursing her one last time before I attempt to put her to bed.

Luckily, she goes down without a hitch. I smile as I creep

out of the nursery. She lies there with her eyes closed as if she always goes down this easily.

As I tiptoe downstairs, there's a soft knock at the door—the food delivery.

"Thank you," I say, signing the check. The young man delivering the food gives me a nod before walking away.

I carry the bag into the kitchen and begin plating the meal. It's still hot from being prepared, and I'm grateful to Tabitha for giving me this idea. Inspired, I reach for my phone and take a photo, sending it to her.

At-home date night. Thank you. :)

Just then, another text comes through from Timothy. Quickly, I open it.

Running late.

I text back.

How late?

Not long. Probably home by 8:30.

I frown in frustration. I'm tempted to send him the photo I just sent Tabitha. But instead, I walk to the front window and look out at the street.

Across the drive, I see Celeste exiting her mother's house. She looks fantastic in a long wool coat. She gets in her sports car and drives off. Of course, there's an unsettled feeling in my stomach. Is she leaving to meet my husband for dinner?

Feeling slightly embarrassed that I'm here alone, I uncork the bottle and pour myself a glass of wine. Clover is asleep, after all, and there's no reason to waste this food.

The Bolognese is delicious. I eat every bite, savoring my second glass of wine.

I scroll through photos of Clover on my phone as I enjoy my caprese salad, trying to block out my worst nightmare coming true.

Well, many nightmares colliding all at once.

Someone is sending me threatening letters that could destroy everything I've worked so hard to keep hidden. At the same time, my husband may be having an affair—not so secretly —with his ex-girlfriend, who happens to live across the street. And my in-laws? They seem to be in on it, watching from next door as everything begins to cave in around me, as if they are willing it to happen.

I want to sob. I want to fall apart, but then I hear Clover crying upstairs, waking, probably hungry again. I take a bottle from the fridge that I prepared earlier and warm it.

I had a vision that Timothy would lead me up the stairs, and maybe we would fall into bed together, laughing after our delicious dinner, his hands roaming over my now soft and smooth skin.

But he's not with me as I move up the steps. I'm utterly alone. I gently pick up Clover from the crib, not wanting to stimulate her. I offer her the bottle, swaying with her in my arms as she suckles.

I look outside through her nursery window at the street below.

I watch as Celeste's car returns to her driveway, just as Timothy's pulls into our driveway right behind her.

My stomach falls, fears realized.

Clover sleeps through my worry. I lay her back in her crib, going downstairs just as Timothy walks in the front door.

I don't have anger or rage that is ready to be unleashed. The feeling inside of me is a lot more tender. Even though Timothy and I were swept up in an unexpected romance, I still believe he loves me and chose me.

He had that ring all picked out *before* I told him I was pregnant. I've always held on to that. It made everything feel... right. But now, alone in this house, the thought gnaws at me, darker, sharper.

I swallow hard, the silence pressing in, the echoing distress in my mind. What if the ring really wasn't for me at all? Maybe he had that ring picked out for *her*. My stomach turns as Celeste's face flashes in my mind. It would make sense, wouldn't it? The perfect timing, the way she fits so easily into his life. Into *this* life.

Was I just a rebound that got out of hand when I fell pregnant?

The house feels suddenly cold, and I wrap my arms around myself. If he loved me, *really* loved me, why does this feel like a question I've been too scared to ask?

Perhaps he had bought the engagement ring for Celeste and had never returned it, and it was just in his dresser drawer. What if when I told him I was pregnant, it was the perfect chance to save the day and be a hero?

I reach the bottom step as he's hanging up his coat, setting down his leather briefcase. "Hey," he greets me, "you look nice."

I run a hand over my curled hair, feeling foolish for putting on makeup and his favorite pair of blue jeans. I shrug. "There's dinner..."

"Oh, great I'm starving," he groans.

"You are?" I ask, as he walks into the kitchen.

"Oh, wow, Amelia, look at what you did."

I press my lips together. "I was trying to do something nice for us. I got takeout from Campelli's and..."

He grins when he walks to the table and sees the bottle of wine. "Our wedding wine."

I nod. "Yeah. Sorry, I already drank half of it."

He chuckles, turning to face me. He runs his hands over my arms, taking me in. "You look beautiful."

"Thank you," I whisper, softly, as he steps toward me, kissing me. When he pulls back, I resist the urge to smell him, inhale deeply and try to decipher if he's been with someone else.

But I hear his stomach growl, so if he's saying he's hungry, he's not lying.

"Of all the nights to be late. I'm so sorry. I've been in back-to-back meetings all day," he apologizes. "I'm so hungry."

"I can just microwave that for you real quick," I offer him. "I'm not sure if filet mignon is great heated up, but..."

"No, no, it's perfect," he affirms. He pours us both a glass of wine and then sits down as I carry the plate to the microwave.

He runs a hand through his thick blonde hair, loosening his tie at the neck.

"Is everything going okay with the project?" I ask him.

"I suppose," he says, "It's just... I think I might be in a little bit over my head."

"Do you need any help?" I ask, as the microwave beeps. I open the door, lift out the hot plate and carry it to the table, then I go into the refrigerator for the boxes of tiramisu that I ordered for dessert.

I pluck a fork from the silverware drawer and carry the cake to the table, sitting across from my husband. "It's nothing I want to worry you with. I know you have a lot on your plate with Clover. How was she today?"

"She's fine," I tell him honestly, "but I have other things on my mind right now..." I begin, trailing off.

"Like what?" he asks.

"We haven't spoken about dinner at your parents' house last night."

He groans. "About Celeste?"

"Yeah," I push, "I don't know why you're lying to me."

"I'm not *lying*. I just knew it would be a whole thing."

"You're avoiding the truth to... what? Protect yourself, or protect me?"

"Both of us," he declares. He sighs as his phone buzzes. "Just a sec," he says, answering it. "Hello, Mother. Yeah. No, I just got home. I'm having dinner right now. Oh, okay. I'll let her know. I'm not sure she's going to want to." He looks at me. "Okay. I'll let you know what she says. Love you too."

"What was that about?" I ask.

He exhales, setting his phone on the table with the screen down. "There's a reporter who wants to do a piece."

"A local reporter?"

"*The Seattle Tribune.*"

At the mention of the newspaper, my heart picks up pace.

"A piece about what?"

"Our family. A follow-up to the article."

"Is that typical?" I lower my eyes. More publicity is the opposite of what I want.

"I think so. *American Journal* is a national magazine, and it makes sense that *The Seattle Tribune* would want to do a follow-up article on us. Anyways, the journalist, Jack Canfield, he's—"

"Jack *who*?" My shoulders tense, the fork in my hand, filled with espresso-dripped mascarpone, shakes.

"Jack Canfield," Timothy repeats calmly, not noticing my distress. "He's a reporter for the *Tribune.*"

I know exactly who Jack is.

Jack is my ex-boyfriend.

Timothy continues, oblivious to the sudden alarm that must be written on my face. "He's coming out to Cutter's Island tomorrow morning to do a short interview with my parents. He met with Lydia today. He wanted to know if he could talk with us too. I have appointments in Seattle most of the day, so I'll meet up with him there later, but I told my parents he could stop by here, if that's all right?"

My heart skips a beat. "Your parents?"

Timothy nods, completely casual. "Yeah, Mother specifically requested him. She liked his last piece apparently."

My stomach twists. Isabelle picked Jack. Isabelle chose him *specifically*. Does she know? Could she have found out about Jack and me? Is this her way of making me panic? The thought makes me feel sick, paranoia creeping in like a wave of nausea.

I swallow hard. "Right. Of course, that's fine." My voice sounds thin and distant, but Timothy doesn't seem to notice. He gives me a quick smile, completely at ease, while my mind races, desperately trying to piece together why this is happening.

Had Isabelle discovered the connection between us, or was this just a cruel coincidence? Either way, it feels like the walls are closing in.

"I mean, after all, do I have a choice in this?" I ask Timothy, pretending to laugh.

He grins. "I know you don't want to do this, but it would mean a lot to Mom."

It would mean a lot to his family if Celeste were to replace me.

I hesitate for a moment, unsure of how to respond. His grin fades, and his eyes narrow just slightly—harder, colder. "Let's not do this again, Amelia," he says, his tone firm. "It's not a request." The sudden shift in his demeanor sends a wave of unease over me.

But all I can think about is why Isabelle has asked Jack Canfield to come to my house.

FIFTEEN

Then

When I returned to middle school at the end of that summer, Vera's death gave me something I'd never had before: attention.

Tommy was the first person to notice me. It wasn't all pity—Tommy liked that I was different. There was a depth to me that made me seem older, and in middle school, being different meant I stood out. I wasn't just the quiet girl anymore; I was the girl who had been through something tragic. Tommy liked that about me. He saw someone strong, someone who wasn't afraid to handle the hard stuff. He liked my edge.

His parents, though, never really saw it that way.

They tolerated me, sure, because Tommy wanted me around. But I wasn't the type of girl they pictured for him—their golden boy. He was easygoing, good-natured and had a bright future ahead of him playing football. I was a little too much for them—too tough, too controlling, too *damaged*. I could feel the way they stiffened whenever I was around, their disapproval thinly veiled behind polite smiles.

I didn't care.

I had Tommy, and that was all that mattered.

By the time we were in high school, Tommy wasn't just my best friend—he was my boyfriend. With Tommy's approval, I became popular. *Wanted*.

Tonight, on our high school graduation night, I'm getting ready in the cramped bedroom I share with Meadow. Vera's crib is long gone, and in its place are two twin beds and a dresser each. It's still small, but I've outgrown the space in more ways than one. I've got a future now, and it's bigger than this town.

Meadow stands next to me, running her hands over her sundress, a pale blue thing with embroidered daisies that I lent her. "You look amazing." Her voice is soft, admiring.

I catch my reflection in the mirror and smile. My black dress hugs my newfound curves, and my strappy heels give me height, making my legs look endless. I swipe on some lip gloss, the kind that makes my lips shimmer, and toss my hair over my shoulder.

"Thanks," I reply, casually. I'm aiming for effortless and sexy, like I saw in *Cosmopolitan* magazine. I read it's the perfect blend that boys can't resist.

Meadow, in her simplicity, looks beautiful. She glows in that natural way she doesn't even realize, and for a moment, I almost feel bad for being hard on her. For lying to her for all these years.

"Do you know where Mom is?" I ask, trying to keep my tone neutral.

"She went to an AA meeting after graduation." Meadow frowns briefly, then tries to lighten her tone. "Did you have fun at Tommy's house?"

"Yeah, it was amazing," I lie quickly.

In reality, Tommy's parents barely spoke to me. His mom handed me a graduation card like it was an obligation, not a celebration. She didn't even make eye contact when she gave it to me, and when I opened it, there was no cash, just a generic note. His dad, on the other hand, avoided me altogether, spending the evening in the garage talking with Tommy's older brother about some home improvement project.

I don't tell Meadow any of this. She wouldn't understand, and besides, my life with Tommy is mine, not hers.

As we're getting ready to leave the bedroom, Mom walks in, her arms full of books and notepads.

"Hey," she brightens, smiling. "I just want to say again how proud I am of you, Hazel."

I roll my eyes. "Like you care," I mutter.

"I *do* care," she insists. "And Meadow told me you got accepted to WSU. You didn't even tell me."

I shrug. "Why would you want to know?"

"Because I love you, Hazel. Because I'm your *mom*."

I stiffen, not wanting her approval. "Why do you have all those notebooks?"

Mom's smile widens. "I've been journaling. It's cathartic, you know? My sponsor at AA suggested it. "Day 63," she adds. "I'm proud of myself."

Meadow beams at her. "I'm so proud of you, Mom."

I roll my eyes again. I can't bear it when they're like this. "Great, I'm glad everyone's happy. But tonight isn't about you, Mom. It's my graduation night."

Mom nods, her smile faltering. "Right. Be safe, okay?"

Mom gives us her car keys, making us promise not to drink and drive. It's pathetic how she thinks some motherly advice can make up for years of bad parenting.

At the party, I feel Tommy's eyes on me the moment I walk in. The crowd parts, and there he is, like a king among his friends. He grins at me, and I know exactly why he loves me. I'm different. I've been through things other girls haven't. I'm tougher, harder, and I wear it like armor. Tommy likes that I don't break, that I'm not like those easy, soft girls his parents would rather see him with.

Later in the night, Tommy pulls me close, sneaking us off to a bedroom. As we lie there afterward, he asks if I'm okay, and I almost tell him the truth. Almost tell him my plan for our future. But before I can, there's a knock on the door.

"Dude, Tommy! You gotta see this."

He grins at me. "It's grad night. I can't miss it."

I laugh, shaking my head as he pulls his jeans back on and kisses me on the cheek. "I love you," he says.

"I love you too," I reply, watching him rush out the door.

The future I've set differs significantly from the one everyone thinks I have planned. But that doesn't matter, not right now. I'll play the part of Hazel Carlisle a little bit longer. Soon enough, I'll be more than just Tommy's girlfriend.

Finally, at the night's end, Meadow finds me.

"Can we go home?" she yawns. "I'm so tired. It's almost two."

"Sure," I agree. "Looks like everything's ending here anyway."

I find Tommy and kiss him. "I'm just leaving too," he says. "I'll call you tomorrow."

We walk outside to our cars, and Meadow and I pull onto the main road.

We realize the car is out of gas and we turn around to stop at a station. Meadow fills the tank.

When we get back on the road, Meadow brings up Mom. "I just don't know why you're so rude to her," she says softly.

"Can we not? It's two in the morning. Do we need to talk about Mom right now? I want to go home and sleep."

"I'm not trying to bring up anything, except ever since Vera died, Mom's been having a hard time—"

I hate hearing Vera's name. If I say it, it's okay—because I'm telling the story I want to tell. But Meadow knows things that no one else does, and I don't want her subconscious to ever remember the truth about that day.

That *I* left the door open.

That it was *my* fault. That *I* killed my sister.

The argument distracts us—our car is going faster and faster, over a wet and dark road. Too fast to even see the other car. Not until it is too late.

We scream, horrified as our car careens into the other. There is no way to stop the hunk of metal from spinning into the oncoming vehicle.

The crash is head-on.

If Mom's car weren't so old, maybe the airbags would've gone off. But they don't, and instead of me getting knocked out like Meadow, I see everything. Crystal clear.

The worst part isn't the crash.

It's that when I look up, I see the driver of the other car.

It's Tommy.

SIXTEEN
AMELIA

The morning after my failed at-home dinner date, I text Tabitha a recap. I know it's dangerous to share too much, but I can't hold the tension in any longer. I need to talk to someone, and I know there's only one person in the world I can trust right now.

> Tabitha: *Wait, you're saying your ex-boyfriend from Seattle is coming to your house later today to do an interview!!??*
>
> Amelia: *Yeah. Wild, right? I feel like the universe is playing some sort of creepy trick on me.*
>
> Tabitha: *Want to come over for coffee and hash it out?*
>
> Amelia: *Sure. Give me a few minutes to get Clover ready.*

Now Clover is lying in the middle of my bed while I root around my dresser for some clean clothes. I pull on a pair of vintage-washed barrel-legged jeans and a cream-colored thermal shirt. Then I add a chunky knit red cardigan and a pair of thick Fair Isle wool socks.

Maybe not the look glamorous in-laws would choose for my interview with my ex-boyfriend, but nobody said I needed to look any particular way for today. If Isabelle and Alexander have some interview tips they want me to follow, that's fine, but I'm not going to invent them on my own.

When Timothy left this morning for work, I was still in bed, Clover nestled in my arms. After her 5 a.m. waking, I had brought her to bed with me—a small comfort for both of us during these sleepless stretches. Timothy never complains about it, and for that, I'm grateful. He just accepts it, without a word, which is one of the things that makes me feel like we're still a team.

The early-morning light filtered through the curtains, casting the room in soft shadows. The house felt calm, the muted sounds of the island outside blending with the gentle rise and fall of Clover's breathing. But my heart was already thumping uncomfortably in my chest, knowing what I had to do today.

Timothy leaned down to kiss my cheek and then placed a gentle kiss on Clover's head, his touch warm and lingering. For a moment, everything felt right, as if we were a picture-perfect family. But recently there's always a faint shadow behind his eyes, something I can't quite place.

"I'm heading to Seattle for the day," he tells me, pulling back.

I nod, remembering he told me that last night, trying to shake off the creeping unease that stirs each time he leaves.

"Let me know how the interview goes," he adds, his tone casual, but something beneath it feels off, like an unspoken expectation.

"All right," I say, groggily. "What time is that again?"

"I'll text you to confirm, but I'm pretty sure he said 1 p.m."

His voice is still light, but when I ask, "And when will you be home?" something flickers in his expression—just for a moment. His jaw tightens and pulses.

"Not till late. I'm going to meet with the reporter after he sees you and after my five o'clock appointment, which I think will put me on a ferry home around eight."

The air feels colder, his words just a little clipped, as if my question has annoyed him.

"That's a long day," I murmur, trying to smooth over the moment. "I'll miss you. We both will."

For a moment, the softness returns around his eyes. "I'll miss you guys too. I'll see you ladies tonight, all right?"

But then, just as he turns to leave, his eyes harden again, his voice losing the warmth it had just a few seconds ago. "Let's not make today complicated, Amelia. I don't have the energy for it."

His words hit me like a cold splash of water, and I swallow hard. The room suddenly feels smaller, the warmth of Clover in my arms no longer enough to chase away the chill in his tone.

"All right," I whisper, watching as he walks out the door.

He left and I was able to fall into a fitful sleep for a little while. Clover seems to do her best rest in these early-morning hours.

Now, after getting dressed, I'm fighting a yawn, looking for a hair tie to pull my red locks into a messy bun. While Clover lies there dreamily, I walk into the en suite bathroom, rinsing my face with soap and water, adding moisturizer to my skin. The winter weather has left it feeling dry. In fact, my whole body is parched, as if life is being sucked out of me.

Once I'm ready and have sneakers on, I lift Clover from bed. "You ready for a little adventure?" I ask her softly.

I buckle her into the stroller, and then we head out the back door. I quickly lock everything up, unsure of who may be watching me. At the end of the drive, I pluck open the mailbox, wondering if there will be a not-so-subtle reminder of my past.

And sure enough, nestled between bills, there's a familiar envelope.

I want to open it before I walk down the end of the lane where Tabitha lives. Above me, it's a cloudy dreary sky, but thankfully it's not raining. The chill in the air though makes me wish I had put on a down jacket, not just this cardigan.

I double-check on Clover, but she's cozy in a blanket, happily sucking on her fingers. Not wanting to read this letter in front of my friend, I need to open it here.

My eyes flicker up, darting across the street, wondering if Mrs. Salsberg is watching from behind her curtains. If she is, so be it. It's not like she hasn't made it clear she's always keeping an eye on things. And maybe she has something to do with this, or maybe her daughter does. Or maybe it's all in my head—just another layer of secrets I'm not ready to untangle.

But it doesn't feel like just Mrs. Salsberg. It feels like the whole island is watching me. Like every set of eyes behind the manicured hedges, the pristine windows, are on me. Waiting. Judging. As if they already know everything I'm so desperately trying to hide.

Regardless, my eyes run over the page. Terror lacing the vessels of my heart as I take in the words.

Do you ever miss being locked up behind bars?

How do you sleep at night knowing what you did to your sister?

My heart pounds, my hands shake. I shove the envelope into the pocket of my jeans, wiping away the tears that have filled my eyes so quickly. The past is so close. It is as if I am caving in after trying to carry it for so long. It threatens everything I've built. Everything I have to live for.

I press my fingers to my temple, remembering to breathe in

and out, in and out. But then suddenly, anger wells up, sharper than fear. How *dare* someone dredge this up now?

But the memories claw at me, pulling me back to *that* night. I hear the sirens, the chaos, the cold air against my face. I see the headlights, the car twisted in on itself. The smell of gasoline lingers in my mind, acrid and sour.

I don't let myself remember too much. Just glimpses. Flashes of what happened. My heart races as I push the stroller faster toward Tabitha's house, my head down against watchful eyes.

I still see the flashing lights. I still hear my sister's low voice, calm in the middle of it all, telling me to keep quiet. My own voice, terrified, caught in my throat. And that overwhelming sense that nothing would ever be the same again.

Maybe I should have told the truth. Maybe I should have let the blame fall where it belonged, but I didn't. I stayed quiet. And now... now it feels like it's all about to disintegrate. This life feels so close to becoming nothing but a memory.

I glance around, feeling eyes on me from every direction. Maybe it's the neighbor. Maybe it's Timothy's family. Maybe it's all in my head. But I can't shake the sensation that someone is watching, waiting for me to stumble.

Pushing the stroller, I pause, hovering at the end of Tabitha's driveway. My fingers linger over my phone, heart pounding as I glance down the street. The air is cold and biting, and every sound—the wind rustling the leaves, the distant hum of a leaf blower—seems amplified, too close. I can't do this. I can't pretend everything's normal, not right now.

I grab my phone and quickly tap out a message:

Amelia: *Hey, I'm so sorry, but Clover's fussy today. I need to stay close to home. Can we catch up later?*

Tabitha: *Of course, sweetie! Let me know if you need anything. XOXO.*

I slip the phone into my pocket and turn the stroller around, pushing it faster toward my house. My hands grip the stroller bar, my body tense as if I might buckle from the pressure any moment. As I walk, the events of the past few days swirl in my mind. The letters, Timothy's secrets and now this latest note eating away in my pocket.

Once inside, I lock the door behind me and rush to the living room, collapsing onto the couch. The envelope feels heavier than paper should, and with trembling hands, I pull it out of my pocket to reread it.

I unfold the note again, and the words sear into my mind like poison:

Do you ever miss being locked up behind bars?

How do you sleep at night knowing what you did to your sister?

My chest tightens, and I can hardly breathe as flashes of the past break through the surface—fragments of a night I've tried so hard to forget.

The flashing lights.

The screech of tires.

The sickening thud.

Tommy.

I squeeze my eyes shut, pressing my hands against my temples, trying to push the memories back down, but they won't stop. I see the car again, its front crushed like paper, and the unmistakable eyes of Tommy, wide in shock, just before it all went black.

I gasp, forcing myself to breathe. *In and out. In and out.*

The worst part wasn't the crash, it was the aftermath. The

lies. The manipulation. The way the truth was buried deep inside me, just like I had been kept behind bars. I remember the sound of the cell door closing, that metallic finality. I never thought I'd be free again, not really.

I glance at Clover in her stroller, her tiny chest rising and falling so peacefully as she sleeps. My beautiful accident, my miracle. How can anyone make me feel guilty for having her? After everything I've been through—everything I've sacrificed— I *deserve* this happiness.

Don't I?

But the guilt lingers, clawing at the edges of my mind. I broke the pact. I broke the promise I made, one I thought would keep me safe. Now, it's all crashing down around me. The past is catching up, and I'm terrified of what's coming next.

I glance at the note again, the lines blurring as tears fill my eyes.

Do you ever miss being locked up behind bars?

As I choke back a sob, I wonder if maybe I was never really free...

The doorbell rings, startling me, and I cry out. Quickly, I shove the letter back into my pocket. The air feels too thick to breathe as I stand up, heart pounding, head swimming. My hands shake as I approach the front door, my mind spinning with dread.

I press my forehead against the cool wood of the door for a moment, gathering myself before opening it. Whoever is out there, and whatever is coming next, I know it's too late to run from it.

But first, I need to face what I left behind.

SEVENTEEN

AMELIA

I stand frozen in the hallway, still staring at the door as the bell rings again. My heart pounds, and my body feels cold. I long for sunlight to stream through the window. But there are nothing but dark clouds in the sky.

I reach for the door handle, trying to steady my breathing. The past is crawling back too quickly, trapping me. But when I open it, it isn't Jack.

It's Isabelle.

My mother-in-law stands there, impeccable as ever, a faint smile playing on her lips. She's dressed in a cream blouse and tailored slacks, the perfection of her appearance making me feel instantly disheveled in my worn jeans and loose sweater.

"*Darling*," she says, stepping inside without waiting for an invitation. She doesn't ask to sit, and I don't offer. Instead, we stand awkwardly in the foyer, the tension between us thick. Her gaze sweeps over me, lingering just long enough to make me feel judged.

I close the door behind her, my body stiff. "I wasn't expecting you," I say, trying to keep my voice steady.

"I thought it best we talk in person," Isabelle explains

lightly, though her sharp gaze flicks to Clover in her stroller. "Jack will be here soon, and I wanted to go over a few things before the interview."

I swallow hard, my fingers tightening around the stroller handle. "What do we need to talk about?"

Isabelle steps closer, her heels clicking softly on the polished floor. "I just want to ensure you're clear on the points we want to highlight—motherhood, Timothy's new development and, of course, how much you *love* living on Cutter's Island." Her words are smooth, but there's an underlying sharpness that makes my skin crawl.

I bite the inside of my cheek, resisting the urge to step back, away from her. "Why is Jack coming here to speak with me? Can't he just meet with Timothy in Seattle?"

Her eyebrow arches slightly. "Do you have a *problem* with being interviewed?" There's something in her tone, something subtle, that makes my stomach twist. Could she possibly know about my history with Jack?

"Well, not really, I am just busy is all, with Clover," I reply, my voice tighter than I intended. I glance down at my daughter, who is beginning to stir. Remembering Timothy's directive before he left for work, I add, "But I'll do my best with the interview."

Isabelle's smile is polite, but her eyes are cold. "I'm sure you will, darling. But it's important to focus on the family. This interview is about Timothy's success, and you'll want to support him."

I bristle at her words, my fingers gripping Clover's stroller a little harder. "And by support, I assume you mean not bringing up his ex-girlfriend coming to family dinners?"

Her smile falters for just a second, and Isabelle's eyes narrow. "Timothy doesn't mind Celeste being there. In fact, it was *his* idea."

Her words hit me like a punch to the gut, but I refuse to give her the satisfaction of seeing how deeply it affects me. "Regardless, I think it's inappropriate. If you want me at those dinners, she shouldn't be there. It's uncomfortable."

Isabelle steps closer, her eyes locking onto mine. "I didn't realize you were the jealous type, Amelia."

"I'm not jealous," I snap, unable to keep the edge out of my voice. "I just don't think it's appropriate to keep bringing his past into our present."

Her gaze sharpens, the tension between us crackles like static. We're standing too close now, her presence stifling. "Oh, *darling*," she says softly, her voice dripping with condescension. "You and I both know you're not comfortable because you've never really allowed yourself to be part of this family."

I feel my jaw clench, the anger rising in my chest. "You don't know me," I say, my voice barely above a whisper. "We've known each other for a few *months*, not years. And frankly, I don't appreciate you trying to control how I handle my relationship with Timothy."

Isabelle's eyes flicker with something—satisfaction, maybe—as if she's enjoying this little dance of power. "Perhaps not," she says, her voice still light. "But I do know that today isn't about you. It's about Timothy. The Sterling family always comes first, Amelia. I suggest you keep that in mind when you speak with... *Jack*."

Her words send a shiver down my spine, and I feel a cold sweat breaking out on the back of my neck. Does she know? Does she know about Jack, about my past, about everything I've been trying so hard to keep hidden?

She steps back, her hand resting lightly on the doorknob as if she's already preparing to leave. "And one more thing," she says, her tone dropping to something more menacing. "Make sure you don't let your... *personal* issues cloud the interview. We all have our roles to play."

I stand frozen, watching as she opens the door and steps

outside, her smile never once wavering. "We'll see you at the next family dinner," she calls over her shoulder, before the door clicks shut behind her.

I'm left standing in the foyer, Clover still cradled in my arms, my heart pounding in my chest. The heft of Isabelle's words settles on me like a threat. She knows more than she's letting on, I'm sure of it. The walls are closing in, and I can feel the cracks beginning to form.

I look down at Clover, her tiny hand gripping the edge of my sweater, and my breath catches in my throat. This isn't just about me anymore. It's about her. It's about protecting the life I've built for us, the life I fought so hard to create.

But Isabelle's words echo in my mind.

The Sterling family comes first.

I stand there for a long moment after Isabelle leaves, trying to shake off the lingering discomfort of our interaction. Her presence clings to the air, mingled with the overpowering scent of her perfume, threatening to choke me.

I exhale, reminding myself that I have to keep it together.

For Clover.

EIGHTEEN

AMELIA

With the front door closed on Isabelle, I take a long shaky breath, determined to calm myself, refusing to collapse to the floor and cry. I cannot let my mother-in-law turn me into someone I'm not. I'm strong.

At least I want to be.

I turn and head up the stairs toward the nursery, my legs shaking after my confrontation with Isabelle. I will the familiar creak of the floorboards beneath my feet to ground me as I walk. This is *my* home, *my* life. I am safe here. Aren't I?

Inside Clover's bedroom, soft light filters through the curtains, casting a warm glow over the space. It's a room that's become my sanctuary, a place where I can focus on being a mother, on the things I can control.

Gently, I lay Clover on the changing table, her small face scrunching as I change her diaper and soothe her back into comfort. The mundane task gives me a moment to collect myself, to push aside the unease that's been building all morning.

Once I've finished, I pick her up and settle into the rocking chair, draping a blanket over my shoulder as I bring her to my breast. As she nurses, I close my eyes, focusing on the rhythm of her breath, the quiet sounds of her feeding. For a moment, the world outside feels distant, and it's just the two of us.

Just as I'm about to shift her, the doorbell rings.

Jack.

I stand slowly. Clover, now sleeping, is resting against my chest. The familiar scent of her soft skin is comforting, but my pulse drums in my ears as I walk down the stairs toward the front door.

When I pull it open, there he is. Jack, standing on my perfect, polished front porch, looking like a ghost from a life I thought I'd left behind.

He is as handsome as ever with his scruffy beard and shaggy brown hair. His hazel eyes are warm and invite me in. He has a leather satchel and a dark denim barn coat. Like he might have been lifted from the pages of a rugged outdoor clothing store.

He looks at me as if he's slightly embarrassed. Ashamed even and, I realize with rising anger, he should be.

"What are you doing here?" I hiss in a hushed voice.

"Is that question on the record or off?"

"Isn't the person getting interviewed the one who should ask that?"

"*Touché.*" He clucks his tongue. "May I come inside?"

I roll my eyes. "Yes, but be quiet. My baby just fell asleep."

"The princess and heir to the Sterling fortune, right?"

"Is that what this is about?" I ask him. "You want to somehow cash in on the fact that you used to date me, someone connected to the Sterlings?"

"You're not just connected," Jack pushes back, leaning casually against the doorframe, an amused glint now in his eyes. "You're a Sterling, at least as far as the marriage records show—which I looked up. Part of me wondered if the whole thing was some elaborate setup. You know, if you were just some girl they dressed up for the glossy spread."

His words feel like a punch to the gut, but before I can react, he adds, "Actually, it was Isabelle who reached out first, you know, to give me the family rundown. She was pretty adamant I get everything right."

The room tilts slightly, and I hold Clover closer to my chest, my heart hammering. So Isabelle *did* reach out directly to Jack.

"And how was that? Speaking with Isabelle?" I ask, trying to keep my voice steady.

Jack smirks slightly. "She's thorough, I'll give her that. Wanted to make sure I had all the... *details* before I spoke to anyone else. Kind of like she's managing the family PR on her own terms."

His tone is light, but his words press down, forcing a load on me I can't bear to carry. Isabelle didn't just suggest Jack interview the family—she *orchestrated* it. And now, he's here, not because he randomly got assigned the piece, but because she wanted him here.

A surge of panic flares inside me. Is this a coincidence? Or is Isabelle playing a deeper game, knowing exactly what she's doing bringing Jack back into my life?

Jack doesn't seem to notice my unease as he continues, "I guess she's just making sure the local follow-up aligns with the national piece. You know how these families are—they like their image to stay squeaky clean."

I nod, my throat dry, trying to swallow the rising tide of dread. This wasn't a coincidence. Isabelle knew exactly what she was doing when she called him. My past, my secrets—everything I've tried to bury—is suddenly dangerously close to being unearthed.

I walk into the kitchen. Instead of giving any sort of theatrics, I grab myself a cup for water and fill it from the refrigerator door. I don't offer him any.

As if he thinks I'm making a point, he laughs. "No worries. I wasn't thirsty anyways."

I walk to the armchair with my glass, Clover in my arm. He follows and sits on the couch opposite me.

"It's nice in here," he observes. "It reminds me of your old studio apartment."

"Oh yeah? I think this might have been just about $5 million more."

He chuckles. "I know the place wasn't glamorous like this, but it was cozy. I remember that quilt you had on the bed, some old wrought iron bed you found at the thrift store?"

I nod, a lump in my throat. "I loved that bed."

"And I remember in your kitchen you had all these old vintage plates that you said you got at an estate sale." He snaps his fingers. "And cloth napkins. Right? Do you still avoid paper products?"

"Wow," I admit. "It seems like you kept quite the inventory of Amelia."

"Yeah. Well, you were the girl who got away."

There's an uncomfortable beat of silence.

"Is that how it happened?" I roll my eyes, trying to lighten the mood. "I remember you breaking up with me."

"Only because you refused to come home and meet my parents. Yet here you are, close as a bug in a rug with the Sterlings. Are you secretly a money-hungry gold digger?"

I laugh softly. "Yep, that's me all right."

"How did it happen?" Jack asks.

I shake my head. "No, no you don't get to start asking me questions like that. I'm asking *you* a few first."

"Fine," Jack agrees, leaning back against the sofa.

I reposition Clover in my arms, my shoulders falling as I breathe in her sweet baby smell. For the first time in my entire experience being a mom, I feel at ease. Like this is something *familiar*. Like I'm capable of doing it, caring for her. She's happy. She burps and I see her eyes shut as she falls back asleep. I pat her back gently, breathing her in.

"Why are you really here, Jack?"

"Look, I knew there was a story. A story I was intrigued by in the first place after I saw it in *American Journal* because of you. Your photo."

My body tightens. If he saw me and knew who I was, who else might have?

"I didn't realize you had gotten married, let alone had a baby. We'd only broken up, what, eighteen months ago?" Jack's tone is casual, but the impact of his words hits harder than I expected.

I nod slowly, feeling the floor tilt beneath me. *Eighteen months*. Not even two years since we ended things, and here I am—married, with a child I never imagined having. His words sink deep, unsettling everything I've built since.

Jack keeps talking, oblivious to the storm he's just stirred up inside me. "You always told me you were never going to have kids."

The truth stings and I have to look away. I had told him that. His words pull me back to promises I broke, mistakes I made. My heart pounds, the guilt creeping in before I can suppress it.

"I suppose fate had other ideas," I manage, my voice tight. Clover resting in my lap keeps me grounded, reminding me of what's real now. But the past is tugging at me, refusing to let go.

"So," I continue, forcing myself to breathe, "you saw the article, and then what?"

"Well, actually, my editor came to me," he reveals, leaning forward, his expression curious. "Apparently, your mother-in-law, Isabelle, reached out to the paper directly. She wanted *me* to do a follow-up piece—local coverage to complement the national story. My editor agreed that I'd be a good fit, so here I am."

My stomach tightens. None of this was random. And now

I'm sitting across from my ex-boyfriend I ran away from, trapped in some twisted plan I didn't even see coming.

"Did you tell your editor that we used to date?" I ask quietly, my voice shaky despite my best efforts.

"No." Jack shakes his head. "I thought about it, but I didn't want to complicate things. Conflicting interests, you know? If they'd known, they might've passed the piece to someone else."

I nod, trying to keep my face neutral, but my mind is spinning. Isabelle didn't just invite Jack here for the interview. She wanted *him*. She knew. Whether she understands our history or not, she's orchestrated this meeting with a precision that leaves me feeling exposed. What else does she know?

"I could let your editor know the truth, or the entire Sterling family for that matter," I tell him. "And I don't think my husband would like the idea of my ex-boyfriend being in my home alone."

"Do you care about that?" Jack questions, raising an eyebrow. "What your husband might think? I hear he is working on his new development project with someone from *his* past."

I frown. "What do you know about that?"

"I know that Celeste Salsberg is his designer for his massive real estate venture that should net the family $40 million."

"I didn't realize it was that lucrative," I admit.

"Well, yeah. They're building on Cutter's Island."

"Right." I close my eyes, realizing I somehow missed that fact. I knew the project was big, but sometimes I forget the scale with which the Sterlings influence things.

"Anyway," he continues, "I heard about Celeste from Lydia, Timothy's younger sister. We spoke yesterday."

"You've been on Cutter's Island longer than just this morning?"

"Yeah, I've got lots of facts to check. But enough about that. Tell me about *you*."

"What about me? I am..." I press my lips together trying to

remember what Isabelle asked me to discuss. "I am loving motherhood," I tell him with a smile. "Clover is a beautiful baby and I'm enjoying getting to spend my time with her." I pause.

Jack looks unconvinced. He doesn't fill in the silence.

"Oh," I add, "also, I *love* living on Cutter's Island. What an idyllic community and I am so pleased to be able to raise my child in such a beautiful place. My highlight of the week, of course, is going to the Sterling estate for a family dinner. It's always a joy to watch Clover's grandparents admire her so warmly."

Jack laughs, jotting things down on a notepad in his lap. "Sounds pretty... canned."

"Which part?" I ask, not wanting to show an interest in his critique, but unable to refuse asking nonetheless.

"Your whole response. It's pretty fake, Amelia."

"It's the truth." My words are flat.

"Okay," he pivots, "then tell me this, because honestly, this is what I'm most interested in knowing. As I was doing my fact-checking and background digging, trying to get an angle for the story, I figured something out, Amelia. Something I always wondered when we were together."

His voice is calm, but his words hit me like a punch to the gut. My heart skips, my breath catching in my throat. *This is it.* I force a smile, but it's weak.

"And what is that?" I ask, though dread is already pooling in my stomach.

Jack leans in slightly, as if to close the distance between us. "You were always so quiet about your upbringing."

"That's not true," I quickly deny, defensive. My pulse is racing, hands clammy. "I told you, I grew up in foster care."

His eyes narrow, studying me. "You told me that, but when I looked into it—there's no record of you with the Department of Child and Family Services in the state of Washington."

I freeze. A chill washes over me. "You—*what?*" My voice falters, disbelief mixing with fear. "Isn't that *illegal?*"

He shrugs, a smile tugging at the corners of his mouth, but there's no malice. "I've got a contact. And it wasn't just foster care. I checked school records, private and public, and... *nothing*. It's like you didn't exist until a few years ago." He pauses, watching me closely. "You've never even filed taxes. Your entire life, in ten years out of high school, is a blank. It's like you've been hiding in plain sight."

I feel sick. My chest tightens, and I can barely focus. "I worked cash in hand," I manage, my voice thin. "For Cal."

"Convenient, huh?" he states softly, but his eyes gleam with something deeper—curiosity maybe. Or concern.

"What are you getting at, Jack?" My voice wavers, dread bubbling under the surface. I feel the past creeping up, threatening to drown me now.

He leans back, arms crossed. "I'm just surprised, Amelia. The Sterlings are smart people. How did they not dig this up before they let you marry into their family?"

I can feel the panic rising in my throat, my vision narrowing. "Timothy and I got married quickly," I blurt out, the words tumbling out too fast. "We became pregnant unexpectedly, and then we decided to make a go of it. It happened fast. Then Clover was born, and we're just coming up on a year. We've only been married six months."

His eyes search mine, as if trying to see beyond my words. "Interesting," he says. "But what happens this tax season, Amelia?"

"What do you mean?" My voice is barely a whisper now, the room spinning around me.

"Well, surely you can't keep using a Social Security number you're hiding." His voice is calm, almost gentle, but it cuts through me like a knife.

I can barely breathe. I feel the walls closing in, my past

crashing against the fragile life I've built. "Why are you doing this?" My voice trembles, barely above a whisper. "Why now?"

"I'm a reporter," he states, but his tone softens, his expression almost regretful. "This is what I do, Amelia. I *dig*."

I shake my head, tears welling in my eyes. "But you used to love me," I whisper, the words slipping out before I can stop them.

He hesitates, the mask of professionalism faltering for a moment. His gaze softens, and for a brief second, the Jack I knew is there—the one who used to hold me close, the one I trusted with my heart. "I did," he admits quietly. "I still—" He stops himself, clearing his throat. "Look, I'm not trying to hurt you. I didn't come here to destroy your new life."

"Then why are you here?" I whisper, my heart pounding so hard it hurts.

His expression tightens, conflicted. "I was curious. And part of me still cares about you. You know that." He reaches out as if to touch me, but then stops himself.

I pull back slightly, my emotions warring inside me. Anger, fear and something deeper—something that feels dangerously close to hope. "Well, I'm hoping your curiosity has been satisfied," I manage to say, but my voice cracks, betraying me.

Jack looks away, running a hand through his thick hair, clearly torn. "It was... but now, being here, seeing you like this..." His voice trails off, and when he meets my gaze again, there's a flicker of something—regret? Longing? "It was fun to go to the Sterling estate and meet the billionaires themselves, but I think the real story is *you*, Amelia."

His words are a punch to the gut, and the panic surges. My head spins. "No," I choke out, tears blurring my vision. "It's not. Please, Jack, don't do this." I'm begging now, and I don't care. "Just let me have my life. Please, go and let me keep what I've built."

He watches me for a long moment, the truth of our past

hanging between us. His face relaxes, but I can see the struggle in his eyes—the tug of duty against something more personal. "Amelia," he says tenderly, "I don't want to ruin anything for you. I promise. For what it's worth," he adds, "I believe you."

"Believe me?"

"I believe you have something you have to protect. Something terrifying or heartbreaking, something that could ruin everything for you."

My heart pounds and I try to steady my breath. The last thing I want to do is startle Clover now and have her begin to cry. I want Jack out of my house before that happens.

"The thing is," he observes, "secrets always have a way of coming to the surface if you let them stay still long enough. You ever heard that analogy? Eventually muddy water settles and the truth becomes clear."

"I don't want the truth to come out," I tell him, my voice raspy, steely, scared.

"So you *do* have a secret."

"Stop it, Jack," I beg, but there's no denying it from him. "You know I do. You wouldn't be here if you thought I didn't. Just tell me what you want," I gulp. "Tell me what you want, and I'll make it happen."

"I just want you to be happy, Amelia." He exhales. "If that's even your real name."

NINETEEN

Then

I hear police sirens approaching. An ambulance, fire trucks, emergency vehicles surround us. And soon an officer is at the car, ripping open our doors. The noise seems to have jostled Meadow awake. I look at her, stunned. Blinking, I try to process what is happening. What has been done.

A scream of terror builds in my chest as I look through the window, registering Tommy's car across from us.

I look at Meadow, blood running down her forehead, her hands on the steering wheel.

"Are you okay?" His words are gruff, but caring. "Are you both here, alert? Anyone else in your car?"

"It's just us." Meadow's hands grip the steering wheel tightly, her knuckles white. She blinks, looking around, as if jolted awake, confusion flashing across her face.

I watch her, the confusion on her face clear. She went unconscious at impact—she doesn't realize what has happened. That Tommy is in the other car.

Is the only boy I have ever loved dead?

I feel sick, horrified at the truth of what is happening. This cannot be happening.

"Ma'am, I need you to listen to me carefully. You're going to be removed from the vehicle and taken to the hospital. Do you think you can stand?"

"Yeah." Meadow nods. "I can stand."

I began to speak. "My sister hasn't been driving long. She just got her license a few months ago. It was dark and she was driving fast and..."

"Is the other driver okay?" I ask. "Please tell me she didn't kill him."

Meadow's head turns toward mine slowly, as though whiplash has affected her movements.

"*I killed someone?*" She shakes her head, her voice trembling. "Oh God. No." Her eyes fill with tears. She shakes her head. "Please say it isn't true."

I can't stand to look at her one more moment—I need to know. I need to see for myself.

Tommy has to be okay. He has to be.

I jerk open the passenger door, the cool night air rushing over me, sharp against my skin. The dampness from the nearby woods mingles with the acrid stench of gasoline and burnt rubber. Meadow's confusion stings, but I can't face her questions right now—not with Tommy's car crumpled in front of us.

I stumble out onto the dark road, gravel crunching under my shoes, and head straight for the wreckage. Tommy's car is still smoking, the metallic scent of destruction filling my lungs. An officer steps in my path, his flashlight catching the reflection of twisted metal.

"Ma'am, we're trying to extinguish the fire."

"No!" I cry, my voice raw. "That's my boyfriend's car..."

The officer pauses, lowering his flashlight. "Your boyfriend?"

I nod, heart pounding. "Tommy Donahue. He was driving. We just left a grad party."

His eyes widen. "And your sister hit him?"

"Yeah," I say, swallowing hard as the reality looms over me, pressing in from all sides. "Oh my God. My sister killed my boyfriend." My legs buckle, and I fall to the wet pavement. It's an act—I have to play it perfectly. I can't afford to slip up now.

The night sky is wide open above me, but it feels like the air's been sucked out. I watch as Tommy's body is pulled from the wreckage, limp, his face unrecognizable. It's like the world has caved in. His family's hope, my future—all gone in an instant.

Meadow's sobs carry over from where the medics are trying to coax her into an ambulance. She's shaking, repeating my name, but I can't go to her—not now. "I can't be with her," I tell the officer, forcing my voice to break, feeling the tears sting my eyes. "Not if she killed Tommy."

Two officers glance at each other, silent communication passing between them. One picks up his radio. "We'll get you another ambulance," he says.

I nod, cradling my head in my hands as Tommy's lifeless body is loaded into the ambulance next to the one with Meadow. The night is eerily still, save for the hum of the engines and the hiss of extinguishers on the wrecked car. The pine trees stand tall around us, shadows against the midnight-blue sky, but nothing feels solid anymore—nothing but the cold pavement under my hands.

Meadow's voice rises again in the darkness, desperate. "Where's Hazel? I need my sister..."

But the ambulance doors close, muffling her cries, and it speeds away, leaving me behind. Another ambulance pulls up, and I'm ushered inside.

The medics strap me in and begin taking my blood pressure. "Oh, Tommy..." The tears fall freely now, mixing with the salt of the sweat on my face. My body is trembling. "This can't be happening," I whisper, but it's like the words are lost in the cold still air.

As the doors close, shutting out the scene of twisted metal, flashing lights and smeared blood, a horrifying realization dawns on me: Tommy is gone. My way out—the future I'd banked on—is gone. The summer night feels suddenly oppressive, the smell of rain lingering in the air, but there's no relief. Only dread.

I press my hands harder against my chest, trying to steady my breathing.

I look out at the pine trees through the ambulance windows, the night closing in around me, and my breath hitches. I can't think about what comes next. I just know that Tommy's future died tonight, and maybe mine did too.

Meadow will go to jail, surely. Tommy's family will make sure someone pays.

I close my eyes, sinking into the seat as the ambulance races toward the hospital, the flashing red lights painting streaks across the wet pavement, my hands clenched tight across my growing belly.

The life I thought I would have has been taken from me.

And it is Meadow's fault.

TWENTY

AMELIA

Jack stands to leave, his presence like a cloud of old memories I've been trying to forget. I follow him to the door, my heartbeat uneven, Clover resting against my chest. My mind races, thinking about what his digging into the past could mean for my life now.

"This life that I have," I tell him, my voice shaking, "it means something to me. Clover is my whole world. Do you understand the damage you could do by looking for cracks in my story? In my life?"

He gives me a crooked half smile, that same mysterious grin that melted me when we first met. Back then, he was like a breath of fresh air in my complicated life. But now, that grin unsettles me. The memories it stirs are anchors tied to my ankles, threatening to pull me under.

"I'm not trying to hurt you, Amelia," he says softly, stepping back. "You know that, right?"

I nod, though deep down, I'm not sure. Jack has always been kind, but he's a reporter now. He's looking into things better left buried. He doesn't realize the damage his curiosity could cause.

"You've changed," he continues, studying me with those

dark, thoughtful eyes. "You were so different back then. We used to talk about living a simple life, remember? You didn't care about money. You were content."

I flinch at his words. He doesn't understand. He never did. *Content* was never enough for me. I needed security. I needed to escape my past.

"People change, Jack," I express gently. "I'm a mother now. Life's different."

He shakes his head, his expression soft, but sad. "I know. But even now, it feels like there's still something missing. Like you're hiding behind walls."

"I'm not hiding." I deny his accusation, but the words feel like a lie on my lips. *I've been hiding my entire life.*

He watches me for a moment longer before finally nodding. "All right. You know, I'm here, same number, in case you ever need someone to talk to. You don't have to do this alone."

"Thanks," I murmur, opening the door wider. "I appreciate it."

As Jack walks down the driveway toward his beat-up Volvo, I lean against the doorframe, my heart pounding. I watch him get into his car, and for a moment, I'm transported back to when things were simpler—when the biggest secret I was keeping was a past I could hide. But now, there's Clover. And Timothy. And the life I've built here.

I lock the door behind him, feeling the burden of the past pressing down on me, choking me with each breath. *How much longer can I keep it hidden? How much longer before everything unravels?*

I carry Clover upstairs, trying to shake off the lingering dread. The nursery is quiet, the soft hum of the white-noise machine filling the air. I change her diaper, feeling her tiny heartbeat under my hand. I hold her close, pressing a kiss to her head.

"I love you, baby girl," I whisper, my voice cracking. "I hope one day I can tell you the truth. On my terms, not because someone else forces it out of me."

I lie down with Clover in my arms, exhaustion pulling me under. Her little body is warm and comforting, her steady breaths lulling me into a half sleep.

When I wake, the room is still and quiet. Clover is asleep, her hair damp with sweat, cheeks flushed. I watch her, my heart aching. *Will it always be like this?* A barrier between me and the people I love, built by secrets I can never share?

Tears fill my eyes as I think about the lies I've told—about the parts of myself I've buried so deeply that even Timothy doesn't know them.

It's one thing to lie to the man I married. But to lie to my own daughter?

I close my eyes, willing the tears away. *She deserves better.*

I hear the front door open suddenly, a sound that jolts me upright. My heart races, panic flooding my veins. Who would be here in the middle of the day?

I hold Clover tighter, my mind spinning. I don't want to call out. What if it's someone here for me? What if the past has finally caught up?

But then I hear Timothy's voice, muffled but familiar. "Amelia? Darling, I'm home."

I exhale, my whole body sagging in relief. He enters the bedroom moments later, looking pale and disheveled.

"You're home?" I ask, trying to keep my voice steady.

"I sent you a text," he says, pressing a hand to his stomach. "But your phone's on 'do not disturb.'"

"I'm sorry," I say, blinking away the remnants of fear. "I was trying to take a nap. I thought you had an appointment later with the journalist?"

"I did, but I think I came down with something." He grimaces, clutching his stomach. "I feel awful."

"Oh, no," I say, reaching for him. He steps back, shaking his head.

"Don't get too close, in case it's contagious. I'm going to take a shower and crash in the guest room, try to sleep it off."

"There's medicine in the cabinet," I say, but he waves me off.

"I think it's just food poisoning. I'll be fine."

He disappears into the bathroom, and I sit there for a moment, holding Clover, feeling the burden of my own thoughts pressing down on me. How many more lies can I juggle before it all collapses?

I need to get outside. I need to breathe.

The cold wind cuts through my coat, stinging my cheeks as I step outside on my porch, desperate for some fresh air. Clover is pressed tightly against my chest, her tiny body warm under the thick blanket, and I hold her close, as if she's the only thing keeping me grounded.

The wind bites again, and I turn slightly, adjusting Clover's blanket as her small fingers curl into my shirt. I look out across the property, only to see Lydia—impeccable Lydia—standing by the entrance to the estate, her blonde hair perfectly slicked back despite the wind, her tailored coat cinched at the waist. Even here, on this damp isolated island in the middle of February, she looks flawless.

She sees me, and with that effortless grace of hers, she makes her way over. Her heels click softly on the wet pavement, each step calculated, each movement controlled. As if nothing ever rattles her.

"Amelia!" she calls, her voice smooth despite the wind whipping around us. "Is everything okay?"

I force a nod, though my chest tightens at the sound of her voice. I don't want to talk to her right now—not when I'm feeling like this, not with Timothy upstairs, and certainly not with what's been weighing on my mind since Jack's interview.

Lydia stops in front of me, her eyes sweeping over Clover nestled in my arms, then back to my face. "I heard Timothy isn't feeling well." She says it lightly, but there's something probing in her tone.

"Yeah," I manage, adjusting Clover in my arms. "He's not feeling great. I just needed some fresh air."

Lydia studies me for a moment longer, then her expression shifts—just a fraction, enough for me to notice the gleam in her eyes. "So," she begins, her voice dipping into something softer, almost conspiratorial, "I hear Jack interviewed you earlier. What did you think of him?"

My heart skips. She had her own interview with him the day before. But why is she asking? Is she testing me, waiting to see if I'll slip, if I'll admit the truth?

I force a smile, feeling the damp chill sink deeper into my bones. "It was fine. He's thorough."

Lydia's lips curl into a slight smile, and I can feel it—that subtle pressure she's applying, like she knows more than she's letting on. "He certainly is. He asked all the right questions when we talked. *Very* insightful." She pauses, her gaze drifting over me, a hint of amusement in her eyes. "He's quite charming too, don't you think?"

My stomach tightens. *Charming*. Lydia's testing me—I can feel it.

"I suppose," I say, my voice shaky. I pull Clover closer, her soft breath warm against my chest.

Lydia's smile widens, and there's something sharp behind it. "I was thinking," she continues, her tone as light as the wind, "maybe I'll ask him out."

The words hit me like a punch, and I grip Clover's blanket tighter, my knuckles white. *Ask him out?* My heart pounds in my chest, and the wind feels colder, harsher, whipping at my face. Is she serious? Or is this another one of her games? Is she trying to see if I'll admit it—admit that Jack wasn't just some random reporter? That he was *my* past?

"I don't know if that's a good idea," I manage to get out, my voice barely above a whisper.

Lydia raises an eyebrow, the wind catching her hair but not a strand out of place. "Why not?"

I can feel her eyes on me, waiting, watching for a crack in my facade. She's pushing me, trying to get me to slip up, to expose the truth. But I can't. Not now. Not after all this time.

"He's just... writing an article about the family," I say, my voice tightening. "We wouldn't want it... biased."

Lydia tilts her head, studying me with a mix of amusement and curiosity. My throat constricts, and the words stick. I feel Clover shift slightly in my arms, her tiny fingers gripping my shirt, anchoring me to the moment. Lydia is pushing, probing, waiting for me to confess something I can't.

"It's just a thought." I force the words out, trying to sound casual, but I know Lydia can hear the strain in my voice.

She lets out a soft, almost musical laugh, and it makes my skin crawl. "Interesting," she chimes. "Jack and I had quite the conversation the other day. He didn't seem too concerned about biases to me."

Her words hang in the air, heavy and biting. My heart races, and I feel a cold sweat break out along my spine. Lydia's eyes gleam with something darker now, something almost triumphant. Is this a game to her?

Lydia's phone buzzes in her pocket, and she pulls it out, glancing at the screen. Her smile never falters. "Well, I'll leave you to it," she says, slipping the phone back. "But let me know if you hear anything interesting about him. I think I'll ask him to dinner next time I see him."

The words twist like a knife, and I force a nod, my voice gone.

Lydia gives me one last smile, a smile that feels more like a warning, before turning and walking back toward the estate. I watch her go, my heart pounding in my chest, my mind spinning with everything left unsaid.

I look down at Clover, her tiny face calm and peaceful, and the truth of our situation crashes down on me. It's as if the Sterling family is waiting for me to break, to slip. And the worst part is, I'm not sure how much longer I can hold it all together.

Having had more than my fill of fresh air, I take Clover back inside, and we walk up the stairs to the nursery. Once there, I focus on changing her diaper and offering her milk. She settles against me, warm and content. I rock her gently, staring out the window as rain begins to pound the quiet street below. Lydia is back at the Sterling estate, but there's someone else out there.

A figure standing by my mailbox. A woman, hooded, her back to me. My heart stops.

No. It *can't* be.

I squint, pressing my nose against the window, my breath fogging up the glass. With the water droplets running down it thick and fast, I can barely see.

But the way the figure stands, the slope of her shoulders— it's too *familiar*.

I freeze, my pulse thundering in my ears.

Could it really be her?

I press my hand against the glass, feeling it cold against my palm. The woman turns slightly, but I can't make out her face in the darkness. The rain is lashing down, harder than before. *I can't see...*

My stomach twists, a sickening knot of disbelief. *Is it her?*

I stumble back from the window, my legs trembling as everything falls into place.

It has to be.

But the figure is moving away, disappearing into the night.

But it can't be.

I clutch Clover to me, feeling her heartbeat quicken against mine as I watch the hooded figure grow smaller. I close my eyes, a tear slipping down my cheek. The past never stays buried, does it?

And maybe... just maybe, she has come back.

My sister.

TWENTY-ONE
AMELIA

I'm standing at the nursery window, clutching Clover to my chest, trying to steady my breathing. The rain is still coming down in relentless sheets, but it doesn't blur the figure that I am sure was just there.

Hazel.

In the moment, I would have sworn it was her. I'm not losing my mind. I *saw* her.

Didn't I?

With trembling hands, I place Clover gently in her crib and run down the stairs to the front door, pulling it wide open. The rain hits me like a slap in the face, cold and sharp, but I don't care. I step barefoot into the storm, calling out.

"Hazel?" My voice cracks as I shriek. "Hazel, I see you!"

But there's no answer and no one is there. The street is empty. But I'm sure she was here. I saw her just a second ago. My heart is pounding, the world spinning as I sprint out into the driveway. The rain makes it hard to see, turning the night into a blur of shadows and streetlights. My feet slip on the slick pavement as I run toward where I saw her figure disappear.

I call her name again, my voice swallowed by the downpour. My chest heaves as I stop at the end of the driveway, squinting through the rain. The street is deserted. No car, no person, nothing.

She's gone.

I crumple to my knees, sobbing, the cold rain mixing with my hot tears. Everything is slipping through my fingers—my past is creeping up on me, threatening to ruin everything. *Hazel has found me, and I don't know what she wants.*

I hear the distant rumble of thunder as I force myself to stand, drenched to the bone, shivering as the terror grips me. My legs wobble as I stumble back toward my driveway. The mailbox catches my eye, and dread coils in my stomach.

Slowly, I pull open the door and reach inside. The envelope is soaked through, the ink smeared.

My heart stops. I clutch the letter with shaking hands. My nightmare is realized.

I barely make it back inside, my hands trembling so violently I can hardly even tear the letter open. The envelope falls to the floor as I collapse against the wall, gasping for air. She's going to ruin everything. It's what she does.

I read the letter, a single line meant for only one thing: to terrify me:

You'll pay for what you've done. Murderer.

I force myself to stand, stumbling upstairs and toward the bathroom off my bedroom. I need to pull it together. I need to be strong. For Clover. For this life I've built. My hands fumble with the shower knob as I strip off my wet clothes, my body trembling as I step into the scalding water.

But no amount of heat can thaw the ice-cold dread that's spreading through my veins.

As the water beats down on me, my mind races. The letter.

The life I've tried so hard to leave behind. It's all crashing down around me.

My breath comes in shallow gasps, panic clawing at my chest. I grip the tile wall, my knees nearly buckling beneath me. I blink hard. Already my mind is playing tricks on me. I thought it was Hazel, I could have sworn it, but how can it be, after all this time?

As the shower room fills with steam, I try to remember what I saw. In Clover's bedroom I could have sworn I saw my sister, but now I'm not so sure. I really saw only a flash of dark hair, the way she moved...

But whoever she is, she's not just here to torment me. The letter proves that. She's here to destroy everything.

And if it was my sister, and I wasn't imagining it, what does she want?

The thought of Timothy upstairs, completely unaware of what's happening, makes me feel even more alone. My dark past was literally on the front lawn, and my husband doesn't have a clue.

I turn off the water and wrap myself in a towel, my mind still spinning. I can't let her do this to me. I have to figure out if it was her and what she's planning. But the more I think about it, the more I realize I can't be sure that was my sister—did I just imagine her? Either way, I'm not ready for the truth.

As I pull on jeans and a sweater, I hear Clover start to cry from the nursery. I rush to her, scooping her up, not wanting her cries to wake Timothy in the guest room. I have to be the perfect wife. The perfect mother. I can't lose it all.

I press her tiny body against mine, trying to calm both of us. My hands still tremble as I cradle her in my arms, kissing the top of her head.

I think back to what I saw. I can't let whoever it was take this all away from me. This life. This family.

As I head downstairs, Clover snuggled against me, I force

myself into autopilot. After putting Clover in her swing, I start dinner, but everything feels wrong. My hands fumble with the rice, spilling grains everywhere. I manage to get the pot onto the stove, trying to focus, but my mind is stuck on the letter. The rice burns almost instantly, filling the kitchen with smoke. I curse under my breath, waving the smoke away as Clover fusses in her swing.

I'm barely keeping it together.

Just as I'm pulling the charred rice off the stove, there's a knock at the door. My heart lurches into my throat.

For a split second, I think it must be whoever left that note, back to finish what they started, but as I walk to the front door, I can see through the window—it's Eleanor Salsburg, holding an umbrella against the downpour.

Not now.

I open the door, forcing a smile, but my face feels tight. "Eleanor," I say, trying to sound calm. "It's not a good time."

She steps in without hesitation, shaking off her umbrella. "I saw you outside earlier," she says, her voice soft, but her eyes are sharp. "You were crying. In the rain."

I freeze. *She saw me.* I try to brush it off. "It was nothing," I lie, but my voice cracks. "Just... overwhelmed."

Eleanor's eyes narrow, scanning my face. "Are you sure? You looked... *frightened.*"

Her words hit me like a punch to the gut. "I'm fine," I assure her, but my hands are still trembling. I can feel the letter in my back pocket, itching to be dealt with. *Does she know?*

Eleanor's gaze shifts to the kitchen, where the burnt rice sits smoking on the stovetop. "Dinner's not going well, I see."

I nod, too numb to care. "I got distracted."

Just then, there's a cry from the kitchen. I exhale. "Sorry. I have to go. My daughter's just woken up."

"Oh, can I meet her?"

"Um, sure," I concede, annoyed at this woman's invasion of

my privacy. I walk into the kitchen and unbuckle Clover from the swing's seat, pulling her into my arms. "This is our daughter, Clover."

"What a... *unique* name."

"Yes," I soften. "She's my good luck charm."

Eleanor smiles. "How lovely. It's somehow reminiscent of a meadow, is it not?"

The way she says it, the way she pauses. Instantly, it puts me on edge and I can barely breathe.

Meadow.

"Why do you say that?" I look at her in the eyes, wondering if maybe she knows more than she's letting on. Maybe she knows everything. The way she looks at me makes my skin prickle with fear.

I was certain it was Hazel leaving these letters. And I just saw her, didn't I? But what if something else is going on? What if Eleanor is connected in ways I don't understand?

"I went to Ireland once when I was much younger, before I had Celeste, and I remember the green *meadows* there, just beautiful and completely covered in *clover*." She relaxes in her memory. She steps closer, her voice dropping as she raises an eyebrow. "Amelia, is something going on? You were outside earlier, crying in the rain."

"I-I'm just tired," I stammer.

She nods slowly, but there's something unsettling about her smile. "Well, I just wanted to check on you. I know Timothy has been busy. And with Celeste always around..."

My stomach clenches at the mention of Celeste. "What about Celeste?" I ask, trying to keep my voice steady.

Eleanor gives me a knowing look. "She's very ambitious, my daughter. Always has been. But I worry about her sometimes. The way she attaches herself to certain people... certain men."

My heart races. *Is she talking about Timothy?*

Eleanor steps even closer, lowering her voice to a whisper.

"You must feel so exposed, living in this neighborhood. Everyone watching. Always talking."

I stiffen, my blood runs cold. *Exposed.* That's exactly how I feel. Like everyone is holding their breath, waiting for me to make a mistake.

Does she know who I am?

I swallow hard, trying to regain my composure. "I appreciate your concern," I say, my voice tight. "But I'm really fine."

Eleanor smiles, but it doesn't reach her eyes. "Of course, dear. But just remember—some things are better left buried."

Her words send a shiver down my spine. She knows. Or at least, she suspects something.

As she turns to leave, she glances back at me. "Take care of yourself, Amelia. And remember, I'm always just across the street if you need anything."

I watch as she steps out into the rain, her umbrella snapping open. She walks back to her house, disappearing into the blur of the storm.

I stand there for a long moment, shaking. *She knows.*

Maybe it wasn't Hazel I just saw at my mailbox. Maybe it was Eleanor. Or even Celeste.

The words in the letters burn in my mind, a constant reminder of the threat lurking in the shadows. My stomach twists as I glance at the clock. Timothy is just upstairs, completely unaware of the storm brewing inside me and what's happening in his own house.

I feel like I'm crumbling beneath the load. *Hazel could be here. Eleanor is watching. Celeste is too close.*

I don't know how much longer I can keep this up.

I close the door behind Eleanor and check all the locks, still rattled by her unexpected visit, her words sticking to me like burrs. My breath comes in shallow gasps as I lean against the doorframe, trying to regain control. The rain is coming down harder now, as if the sky itself knows what's lurking just beneath the surface of my life. My life that's about to implode, all because of *her*.

The person I saw. The figure that fled. *Hazel?* Or someone else?

I take a shaky step toward the kitchen, but then I hear them—deliberate footsteps above me. Timothy's. A pulse of panic surges through me. He's coming downstairs, and I'm standing here, chest heaving, shaking like a live wire. *He can't see me like this.* Not now.

I quickly smooth back my wet hair, desperate to appear calm. But I can't get the image out of my head—the figure running away, the way the rain is blurring everything except the raw, unmistakable *truth*. Someone is here. Someone is watching me.

When he appears at the top of the stairs, I can't help but notice how casual my husband looks—too casual. His sweats and T-shirt hang loosely on him, and it's unnerving, like he's trying to fit into something that doesn't suit him. Timothy is always so... composed. Polished. But today, he's undone. It makes me feel exposed, like I'm teetering on the edge of something I can't control.

"How are my girls?" he asks, descending the stairs, his voice steady. Too steady.

I clutch Clover tighter, my arms stiff, and force a smile. "I was just making dinner."

His eyes flick to the kitchen, where the smell of burnt rice still lingers in the air. "Dinner?" His voice is laced with a subtle, unspoken question. As if he knows something's off but can't quite place it. *Or maybe he can...*

"Who was here just now?" he asks, his tone casual, but there's an edge to it. "I heard voices. Were you on the phone?"

"No." My voice is too quick, too tight. I clear my throat, trying to appear unfazed. "It was Eleanor Salsberg, Celeste's mother."

Timothy frowns, his casual stance stiffening ever so slightly. "Why was she here?"

My breath sharpens in my throat and I fight to swallow. "She said she wanted to make sure we felt welcome in the neighborhood."

His frown deepens, his eyes narrowing. "Does that happen often?"

The question is loaded, and I feel it settle in the room. He's always asking things like that. Always looking for cracks in the foundation, as if he's waiting for me to slip, waiting for me to reveal something. Something I've been so careful to keep hidden.

"No, not often." I shake my head. "I guess she's just... trying to be friendly."

"Friendly." He repeats the word slowly, like he's testing it, and it sends a shiver down my spine. He knows. He has to know. But his face gives nothing away, only the faintest flicker of something dark and unreadable in his eyes.

I need to get a grip.

"Is there a reason we wouldn't feel... welcome?" His tone is deceptively light, but I hear the bite beneath it. The suspicion.

I laugh, but it sounds hollow, even to my own ears. "Well, after dinner at your parents' house the other night, things felt a little... tense."

"Tense." He repeats it like he's considering the word for the first time. "What *exactly* do you mean by that?"

I hesitate, unsure of how to respond. My throat tightens, and I can't tell if it's the lie or the truth that makes me feel buried alive. "You know... with Celeste. It was just... uncomfortable."

His eyes darken, but his voice remains eerily calm. "I told you, there's nothing to worry about. Celeste is just a coworker."

Coworker. The word grates on me, and I laugh again, this

time with less control. "A coworker? I thought she was more like a contracted employee."

His jaw tightens, but he doesn't respond immediately. Instead, he moves toward the kitchen, dismissing the tension with a wave of his hand. "What smells so good?" he asks, changing the subject with a deliberate nonchalance that only makes me more uneasy.

"I was making chicken and rice," I mutter. "But the rice is ruined."

"Doesn't matter," he says, too easily. "I'm starving."

I watch as he takes Clover from my arms, cradling her with practiced ease, but my stomach twists into knots. I can't shake the feeling that he knows more than he's letting on. *That everyone knows more about me than they're letting on.* Eleanor. Celeste. Timothy.

As Timothy settles onto the sofa with Clover, my nerves are frayed, raw. He stretches out, too comfortable, as if everything in our world is still perfectly intact. As if it hasn't been crumbling from the inside out since the moment I saw *her* face.

"Did we get any mail today?" Timothy asks, the question harmless on the surface, but it cuts through me like a blade.

My hand instinctively moves to the pocket where the letter is hidden, and I feel the edges of the paper, damp but still sharp and accusing.

"No," I say, my voice strained. "Nothing that mattered."

He nods, seemingly satisfied, but I can't shake the gnawing dread in the pit of my stomach. My whole body aches with the knowledge of the letters I've been receiving, the secrets they hold. *The threats.* And now Timothy is sitting there, seemingly blissfully unaware, while my past is clawing its way out of the shadows, ready to tear everything apart.

I go through the motions of preparing dinner, but my hands are shaking so badly I almost drop the pan. Timothy watches me from the sofa, his gaze steady, unnerving. He doesn't say anything, but I can feel his eyes on me, burning the back of my neck, like he's waiting for me to slip.

I carry the food to the table, my heart pounding in my chest. I can't focus. I can't think straight. I can't stop thinking about Hazel—what she wants, what she's here to do. Is it revenge? Or something worse? And am I sure that was really her?

When dinner is ready Timothy takes a bite of chicken, chewing slowly. I watch him, wondering if he can taste my fear in the food. If he can sense how close we are to disaster.

"How's everything with you?" His voice is laced with something I can't quite place.

"Everything's fine," I lie, my stomach in knots.

He doesn't say anything else.

But as I sit there, my mind spinning, I know it's only a matter of time before everything is destroyed.

TWENTY-TWO

Then

I stare at my reflection in the bathroom mirror, trying to recognize the person looking back at me. My skin is pale, my eyes hollow, and my lips are pressed thin like I'm holding my breath—like I've been doing for weeks. I press my hands against the cool porcelain sink, trying to ground myself. Tommy is dead. Meadow is locked up for it. But me? I'm still free.

I don't deserve to be.

A fresh wave of nausea rolls through me. I barely make it to the toilet before I throw up again. Everything is slipping away, and I don't know how much longer I can pretend that it's not.

But I can't lose control. If I do, everything will fall apart. From the living room, I hear Mom crying again. She's been stuck on the couch for days now, clutching her mug of "tea"—except it's not tea. It's vodka. She doesn't even bother to hide it anymore. The smell wafts through the small apartment like it's part of the air now.

"Meadow's such a good girl," she sobs on repeat, her voice cracked and broken. "She didn't deserve this."

I bite down on the anger bubbling up. *What about me?* Tommy was supposed to be *my* future, and now he's gone. But all Mom can do is cry for Meadow.

"She'll be fine," I say coldly, stepping into the kitchen. "It's not like she'll be in there forever."

Mom looks up at me, her face swollen and blotchy from days of crying. "She'll never be the same," she whispers, her voice trembling. "This will haunt her for the rest of her *life*."

The guilt cuts deep, but I can't let her see that. "She'll get out in two years." I dismiss her fears, trying to sound indifferent. "It's not a life sentence."

"She's just a *kid*, Hazel," Mom whispers, her hands shaking around the mug.

I swallow hard, forcing myself to stay composed. The memory of that night claws at me—Tommy's body slumped over the wheel, blood on his face, the panic flooding my veins...

Now she's locked away, and I can't even bring myself to visit her.

"What about Tommy's funeral?" Mom asks, her voice breaking through the silence. "Why didn't you go?"

The question cuts through me like a blade. "They didn't want me there," I say, my voice quieter than I intended. "His family... they told me to stay away."

Her face crumples, and she rubs at her eyes. "You were his girlfriend."

"They don't care about me, Mom," I snap, turning to face her. "They only care about their son. And Meadow killed him. They don't want anything to do with any of us."

Mom shakes her head, wiping her tears. "It's not right. None of this is right."

I know it's not right. But what choice do I have? If anyone finds out what really happened, my life will be over. Tommy's family will destroy me.

"What about college?" Mom asks suddenly, her voice still thick with emotion. "Are you still going?"

College. The word hits me like a punch to the gut. I think about the lie I've been carrying for months. "No, I'm not going," I mutter, keeping my back to her.

"What?" Her voice is sharp now. "What do you mean you're not going? You've been planning this for years, Hazel. You got the scholarship—"

"I said I'm not going!" I snap, spinning to face her. The truth hangs on the tip of my tongue, but I can't say it. I can't tell her that I never got in. That everything I've told her was a lie. "I'm not going to college, okay? Just drop it."

She stares at me, her face a mix of confusion and disappointment. "What happened?" she asks, softer now. "What changed?"

"*I* changed," I say, my voice trembling with anger. "Everything changed."

She doesn't understand. She never will.

Mom sighs, rubbing her temples. "Is this about Tommy? Is that why you're throwing everything away?"

I flinch at the mention of his name, the guilt wrapping tighter around my throat. Tommy was supposed to be my future. My escape. But he's gone now, and with him, any hope of a way out.

I turn away, shaking my head. "Just let it go."

Mom's quiet for a long moment, and I can feel her disappointment, her sadness. But then she sighs again, this time deeper, more resigned. "Maybe we need a fresh start," she suggests.

I laugh bitterly, turning back to her. "A fresh start? Where are we going to go, Mom? We can barely afford this place."

"I got a job," she tells me quietly.

I blink, caught off guard. "A job?"

She nods. "On Cutter's Island. My sponsor helped me get it. Housecleaning. We'd live in a guest house on the property."

"Cutter's Island?" The words feel strange in my mouth. Cutter's Island—the place where all the rich people live, far from the mess we've made of our lives.

"It's a chance to start over," she says, her voice soft but hopeful. "Away from Bellport. Away from all of this."

I stare at her, the idea swirling around in my head. *Cutter's Island*. A place where no one knows us. A place to hide.

"And you think running away will fix everything?" I ask, my voice thick with doubt.

"It's not about fixing everything." She pauses, her eyes dark. "It's about... surviving."

My chest tightens. *Surviving*. It's all we're doing. But maybe she's right. Maybe it's all we can do now.

"What about Meadow?" I ask quietly. "We're just going to leave her behind?"

Mom's face falls, and she looks away, her voice barely a whisper. "We can't help her right now, Hazel. There's nothing we can do for her."

I feel the bile rising in my throat again, but I force it down. I can't think about Meadow. I can't think about her. If I do, I'll fall apart.

"I can't face her," I admit, my voice shaking. "Not after everything."

Mom doesn't say anything for a long time, just stares at her hands, her silence soft. "We've all made mistakes, Hazel," she murmurs.

I bite my lip, the guilt clawing at me. *Not like this. Not like what I've done.* She doesn't know. She'll never know how deep my lies go. She'll never know the lengths I'll go to protect myself.

"I'll go with you," I say finally, my voice tight.

Mom looks at me, her eyes filled with relief, but I can't feel it. Cutter's Island might be her fresh start, but for me, it's just another way to run. Another way to hide.

"I'll pack tonight," I mutter, turning away. As I walk to my room, the guilt feels heavier than ever. I glance at Meadow's empty bed, her things still untouched. It's like she's just gone on a trip, like she'll be back any moment.

But she's not coming back. Not anytime soon.

And I can never look her in the eye again.

I sit down on my bed, staring at the wall, the past pressing down on me. Cutter's Island won't save me.

But for now, I'll run.

For now, I'll survive.

TWENTY-THREE

AMELIA

Timothy has been acting strangely all day, but I've learned not to be surprised by his behavior, just suspicious. After he finishes his chicken and rice, he tells me he's going out, and it feels like a final blow to an already overwhelming day.

The letter arrived this morning. Then Isabelle stopped by to corner me. Jack's interview rattled me, then Timothy came home early with some excuse about a stomach bug. Lydia tried to claim my past, and Eleanor started intruding on my privacy. And worst of all, seeing *her*.

Now, Timothy is suddenly recovered enough to leave the house. Just like that.

"Where are you going?" I probe, trying to keep my voice steady, though inside I'm coming apart.

"I'm going to my parents' house," he replies, pulling on his raincoat. "I want to check in with them about how their interviews went. I need to be prepared for mine. It's been rescheduled with Jack in a few days' time."

The lie stings.

I force a tight smile, but suspicion coils in my chest. "Clover and I could come too?" I suggest, desperate not to be alone. The idea of staying here—after everything that's happened today—feels unbearable. I think of who I saw, or who I *think* I saw, earlier near the mailbox. My nerves are raw, shredded.

Timothy's expression tightens, that familiar flash of darkness in his eyes again, and I brace myself for his rejection. "No, that's fine," he says too quickly. "Clover's probably going to bed any minute. I don't want to bother you."

Bother me? I swallow hard, holding Clover a little tighter, using her perfect presence to ground me. "It's not a bother," I insist, my voice trembling. "I've been in the house all day. I'm feeling a little stir-crazy, actually—"

"Like I said," Timothy's tone hardens, his patience thinning, "I think it's best if I just head out by *myself*."

My heart pounds in my chest. He's hiding something—Celeste, maybe? Or something worse? I hate that I'm even thinking this way, but I can't stop the spiral. Not anymore.

I follow him to the front door, Clover cradled in my arms like a shield against whatever's about to break between us. "Aren't you going to kiss Clover goodbye?" I ask, my voice shaky.

He turns and smiles at her, but it's brief, detached "I love you, sweetheart." He kisses her cheek. Then he looks at me. "And I love you too." He gives me a quick kiss, barely brushing my lips, and opens the door.

As soon as he's gone, the house feels cavernous and cold. The walls press in on me, and my legs feel weak. I pull the curtain aside, watching him walk across our lawn toward his parents' home, his shadow disappearing into the rain.

My gaze flickers across the street, searching for Celeste exiting her mother's home. I know I'm being irrational, but I can't shake the fear that she's going to follow him, that there's something more going on. *What if it's not just an affair?*

I close the curtain and press my back against the wall, clutching Clover as if she's the only thing holding me together.

My breath is shallow, ragged. My head is spinning, the strain of it feeling unbearable. I can't let go of the feeling that someone is coming for me. *What if it wasn't Hazel I saw earlier? What if it was someone else?* I don't know which terrifies me more.

Clover squirms in my arms, her tiny fists clenching as she starts to cry again. The sound pierces through me, rattling my already frayed nerves. I try to nurse her, but she pushes away, wailing louder. "It's okay, baby," I whisper, my voice cracking. "It's all right."

But it's not all right. Nothing is.

Her cries echo through the house, amplifying my panic. I feel like I'm going to shatter. I grab my phone with shaking hands and text Tabitha.

Amelia: *Clover is so fussy. I don't know what to do. I'm losing it.*

She replies almost immediately.

Tabitha: *Johnny just went down and Keith is here to watch him. Want me to bring over a bottle of wine?*

Amelia: *Please. I can't do this alone.*

Tabitha: *Be there in ten. Hang tight.*

I bite my lip, blinking back tears as I try to calm Clover, but her screams just keep getting louder. My chest feels tight, and my breath hitches in my throat. I carry her downstairs, trying the baby swing again, setting it to the highest speed. The swing whirs to life, and Clover's cries begin to subside, though my pulse doesn't slow with them.

I lie down on the floor in front of the swing, watching my daughter slowly drift to sleep. My hands are shaking so badly I can barely hold my phone, but I clutch it like a lifeline. The silence feels fragile, like it could shatter at any moment.

There's a knock at the door. I jump, my heart slamming against my ribs. I rush to open it, almost desperate for the relief of Tabitha's company.

She steps inside, dripping from the rain, holding a bottle of wine like a trophy. "I drove," she says, glancing back at the storm outside. "You doing okay?"

I'm not, but I nod anyway, too tired to explain. "It's been a long day," I mumble, my voice barely above a whisper.

Tabitha slips off her jacket, and I lead her to the kitchen, grabbing two glasses. "Clover's finally asleep," I say, though my voice is hollow, like I'm trying to convince myself that everything is fine.

Tabitha watches me closely as I pour the wine. "You seem... on edge," she says gently. "What's going on?"

I let out a shaky breath, my hands still trembling as I hand her a glass. "Timothy left. *Again*. He's been acting strange all day, and now he's just... gone."

Tabitha frowns, concern clouding her face. "What do you think's going on with him? Is it to do with Celeste?"

My shoulders fall, feeling crushed by it all. "Of course I think something is going on. He's distant, and I'm just... I'm afraid."

"Afraid of what?"

"Of everything ending." The words tumble out before I can stop them. "I think he's lying to me. I don't know what's happening between him and her, but I have this sinking feeling that everything's about to fall apart."

Tabitha's eyes soften. "You're not alone, Amelia. You don't have to deal with this by yourself."

I blink back tears, my chest tight as it holds in secrets I can't ever release. "I haven't told him everything," I admit, my voice barely above a whisper. "There's so much he doesn't know about me."

Tabitha sets her glass down and leans in closer. "What haven't you told him?"

I hesitate, ashamed with the need to unburden myself. "My past... it's not what he thinks. There are things I've done, things I've kept hidden."

"Are they secrets that could get you in trouble?"

I bite my bottom lip, "I'm not sure exactly, but they're the kind of secrets that could *change* things."

"For the better?"

I blink back tears. "If it were for the better, I would be honest, but it would be for the worse. And I have Clover to think about now."

"I know you guys got married quickly. You hardly knew each other and didn't plan on the pregnancy," Tabitha says. "So surely there are things that you don't know about Timothy and he doesn't know about you? You haven't even been together a year yet."

"I'm scared," I finally admit, "that our life is about to crash and burn, and this thing with his ex-girlfriend just makes it worse"

"And *your* ex-boyfriend," Tabitha adds.

"Right," I sigh, remembering Jack sitting where Tabitha is now.

"How did it go today?" she asks, sipping her wine.

"It felt familiar, but also unsettling," I say, being as honest as I can. "I don't think he's out to ruin things for me, and I think he's genuinely trying to understand my new life. Because just like you said, I'm cryptic with everyone, and that's how he felt about our relationship, I always keep things wrapped up tight."

She eyes me critically.

"Things have happened in my past," I finally tell her, the words tumbling out. "That I regret. And unless people knew the whole story, not just *my* version of events, they would see me in... a not very good light."

"But friends forgive, and love conquers all," Tabitha says with a hopeful smile. "Surely Timothy will appreciate you even more if you're honest with him."

"I don't know, his family image means a lot... the Sterlings and the whole business. I don't want to jeopardize anything for him."

"They say no press is bad press," Tabitha says with a smirk.

"But I don't want to be labeled something I'm not," I tell her. "So I'd rather just..."

"Lie?" Tabitha asks, filling in the silence.

I nod. "Yeah."

"Aren't you tired of it?" she asks me. "Of not being... real?"

"I've lost a lot because of it, maybe too much," I confess. "But I was young when things happened, and you can't exactly go back in time. But I just have a feeling that everything's catching up to me. The past that I've tried to keep hidden is not as escapable as I once thought."

"That's why you didn't want to be in the magazine?" she deduces.

I nod, unable to stop the tears that fall down my cheek. "I don't want my face anywhere. I don't want to be remembered by anyone..."

Tabitha rests a hand on my arm. "But Amelia, the cost of that choice means you've been forgotten."

There's a pause where I feel more exposed than ever. Tabitha's eyes are filled with sympathy, but there's nothing she can say to fix this. Nothing anyone can say.

Just as the silence settles between us, the front door rattles. My heart leaps into my throat, and for a second, I think it's someone else—Hazel, or worse, the person I thought was Hazel, someone who knows the truth.

But it's Timothy.

He steps into the kitchen, rain dripping from his coat, his expression unreadable. He looks at me, then at Tabitha, and something dark flickers in his eyes.

"Everything okay?" Tabitha asks, her voice cutting through the tension.

Timothy's eyes meet mine, and for a split second, I see something in his gaze that sends a chill down my spine.

"Yes," he says unsmilingly. "Everything's fine."

But it doesn't feel fine. Not at all.

He knows.

TWENTY-FOUR
AMELIA

Once Timothy is home, Tabitha makes a quick exit. I watch as she pours the remainder of the wine from her glass down the kitchen sink drain. It is as if she can't get out of our home fast enough.

I don't blame her.

Timothy's presence feels threatening. The opposite of a supportive spouse coming home after a long day.

In bed, I toss and turn wishing I had feigned my own stomach bug and chose to sleep in the guest bedroom. Instead, I feel myself stewing over the possible ways my husband is out to get me. Is everyone?

After Clover wakes for a midnight feeding, I fall asleep in the armchair a few feet from Clover's crib. Her presence is the only sure thing I have.

Once morning comes, I focus on taking care of myself and my little girl. After slowly getting ready for the day, we make our way to the kitchen. I make myself a bowl of oatmeal and am just sitting down to eat it when my phone buzzes.

I'm surprised to see his name on my phone. Jack Donovan.

After everything that's happened in the last few days—

Timothy's strange behavior, Eleanor's unsettling visit, the letters—I feel a momentary flicker of relief. *Jack*. He feels like a small anchor to my past when things were simpler. Before my life became entangled in the Sterling family and its secrets.

My thumb hovers over the screen. I could ignore him. But I don't.

"Jack?" I hold the phone between my ear and shoulder as I rock Clover's swing gently.

"Amelia," he says. "Hey, you doing okay?"

The way he asks—the softness in his voice—it throws me off. *Am I okay?* I'm not sure anymore. I swallow down the lump in my throat, knowing I can't answer his question. "What's up?" I ask instead, trying to keep it casual.

"Well, I'm back on Cutter's Island. I wanted to follow up, get a few more interviews from the locals about the Sterling family."

"Uh-huh..." I'm already feeling a twist in my stomach.

"I wasn't sure whether to tell you this or not," Jack continues, "but I just saw Timothy at the coffee shop. He's there with... well, with Celeste."

I freeze, every muscle tightening. "They're working together," I manage, trying to sound indifferent.

"I figured. But they looked... I don't know, Amelia. It didn't look like *just* work."

"Jack, are you saying my husband having coffee with his ex-girlfriend is inappropriate?" I try to inject some humor, but my voice cracks.

"I'm not trying to stir things up," he says gently, "but I thought you might want to know. They seem... very close. You okay with that?"

My heart is racing, my pulse thudding in my ears. How close is too close? I can't even think straight. My brain feels like it's on fire.

"Which coffee shop?" I ask quickly, the words tumbling out before I can stop myself.

"Cutter's Island Roasting House. You know it?"

"I'll be right there."

I hang up before Jack can respond. *What am I doing?* But my body is already in motion. I grab Clover, bundling her up in the stroller, my mind spinning out of control. Why didn't Timothy tell me he was meeting Celeste this morning? He said he was going straight to the office. I feel like my life is slipping away from me.

The walk to Main Street is a blur. I look over at Eleanor's house, but I don't even have the energy to care if she watches me rushing out of the house. My chest tightens, panic clawing at my throat. I pause at the mailbox, barely able to breathe. What if there's another letter?

My fingers tremble as I open it, and there it is—another letter in the same, slanted handwriting.

You took things from me and never looked back.

You will pay.

I shove the letter deep into my coat pocket, bile rising in my throat. *Hazel.* It has to be her. Doesn't it? But why now, after all these years?

I glance back at Eleanor's house again, and I'm sure I see a curtain twitch as a dark figure moves away from the window. Hazel... or Celeste? It's the first time I realize how similar they look, especially at night. Did I mistake my sister for my husband's ex-girlfriend? I took something from her, after all, as everyone on this damned island never stops reminding me. And I took something from Eleanor by doing so, I ruined her daughter's chance to marry into one of the wealthiest families in America.

Pushing the stroller faster, my breath comes in ragged bursts as I zip past my in-laws' estate. I think about Isabelle's cold smile as I move past the iron gates. I took something from her as well, although I never meant to. I took away the daughter-in-law she wanted—no, that she *expected*—for her son. I shiver at the thought.

By the time I reach Cutter's Island Roasting House, I feel like I'm going to collapse. The cold drizzle pricks my skin, but it does nothing to cool the heat inside me.

Jack's waiting on the corner, his hands stuffed in his coat pockets. For a brief moment, seeing him there—his familiar face, his genuine concern—it calms me.

"Hey," he says gently, his voice laced with worry. "You okay?"

I shake my head, forcing a smile. "No. But I'm here."

Jack looks across the street, nodding toward the café window. "They're in there. Still... *together*."

I glance over, my heart sinking as I see them—Timothy and Celeste, sitting side by side. *Too* close. Celeste is laughing, her hand resting lightly on Timothy's forearm. She looks perfect, with her sleek blonde hair and flawless skin, while I feel frayed at the edges, like I don't belong in this town.

"She looks..." I trail off, unable to finish. *Like she fits beside him. Like I don't.*

Jack watches me closely. "You don't have to do this," he assures me. "We can leave. Go for a walk—"

But I can't. I need to know. "No. I have to see this for myself."

I push Clover's stroller across the street and walk into the café, the warm scent of coffee washing over me. But it doesn't comfort me today. All I see is Timothy. And her.

"Amelia," Timothy says, clearly startled, standing up. "This is a surprise."

I try to smile, but it feels forced. "Just out for a walk with

Clover." I glance pointedly at Celeste, who is watching me with the same tight smile she had at dinner.

Timothy pulls out a chair for me, but the tension between us feels crushing. "Can I get you something? Coffee? Tea?"

I nod. "A latte would be great." My voice sounds too high, too cheerful.

As Timothy walks to the counter, Celeste leans back, her eyes flicking to me with something close to amusement. "I didn't expect to see you here this morning," she says, her voice smooth.

"Same," I reply, my heart pounding in my chest.

She crosses her long legs, her manicured hand resting on her lap, every movement elegant, controlled. "Timothy and I were just finalizing some project details," she says, gesturing to the sketches and samples on the table.

I try not to flinch. They look like they're planning their future. And I'm not in it.

"That's great." My voice is hollow. "I didn't realize things were moving so quickly."

Celeste's smile widens. "Timothy's a hard worker. He really puts his heart into *everything*."

I feel my stomach churn. He used to put his heart into *us*.

At that moment Timothy returns, placing the latte in front of me. When I look down, I see it's a takeaway cup. It's clear he wants me to leave. I can't bring myself to take a sip. The heat between us is stifling now.

"I think we need to talk." I stand, my voice shaking.

Timothy frowns, his smile slipping. "Right now?"

"Yes. Please."

He glances at Celeste, and I see the flash of irritation on her face before she covers it with another tight smile. Timothy sighs and stands. "Okay. Let's go outside."

As soon as we step out into the cold, the tension between us snaps.

"What is going on with you?" Timothy asks, his voice low but firm. He grabs my arm, hard, pulling me around the corner of the building where we can't be seen. "You're acting... strange."

"*Strange?*" I echo, my voice rising. "You've been spending all this time with *her*, and you didn't think it was important enough to mention it to me?"

His face hardens. "I told you before, Amelia, it's just work."

"But *is it?*" My voice cracks and tears burn as I blink them furiously away. He doesn't even seem to notice my distress. "Because I feel like I'm losing you, Timothy. Like you're slipping away, and I don't know why."

He stares at me, his jaw clenched. "You're being ridiculous, Amelia. Nothing's happening between me and Celeste, as I've already told you."

I wipe at my eyes, trying to pull myself together, but I'm falling apart. "Then why didn't you tell me she was in town, working for you? That she was living across the street from us? Why all the secrecy?"

"Because you've been acting paranoid, like you're waiting for something to go wrong," he snaps. "You're not making any sense." He steps back, shaking his head in disbelief. "You need help, Amelia. You're breaking down."

And maybe I am. Maybe everything is already broken.

He catches something in the corner of his eye, focusing on someone across the street.

"Is that Jack, the reporter from the *Tribune?*"

I turn around to look. I hesitate. "Yes," I say. "Which is something else I wanted to talk to you about."

He frowns. "What is it?" He waves Jack toward us. I have a sinking feeling. This isn't going to go how I hoped.

"Jack is the one who called me and told me you and Celeste were having coffee. Said I might want to come check it out."

Timothy frowns. "I didn't realize you and the journalist had such a... camaraderie."

"That's the thing, Timothy. Jack Canfield isn't just some random reporter. He is my ex-boyfriend."

TWENTY-FIVE
AMELIA

There's a beat of silence.

"I can't believe you honestly think I don't already know that," Timothy says slowly, his voice low and dangerous.

I freeze, my heart stopping in my chest. *What?* The air thick between us, and I suddenly realize I've underestimated my husband.

"You... you *knew*?" My voice is barely audible.

Timothy steps closer, his eyes cold. "Of course I *knew*. Jack's been lurking around for weeks, sniffing for something. Do you seriously think I wouldn't look into him?"

I feel the ground shift beneath me. "Why didn't you say anything?"

"Because I wanted to see how long you'd *lie*," he snaps. "How much you'd hide from me."

I shake my head, trying to catch up. "I wasn't hiding anything. It's not like that," I whisper, my voice trembling. "Jack's here for work. That's it."

Jack crosses the street. "Hey," he says, joining us. "Am I coming in at a bad time?"

Timothy shakes his head and runs a hand through his thick

blonde hair. "My wife was just illuminating me on the fact that you and she were lovers."

"My God, Timothy," I breathe.

I look at Clover, who's beginning to fuss, as if she can recognize the tension. I unbuckle her from the stroller and bring her to my shoulder, trying to calm her before she begins screaming. Jack runs a hand over his jaw, clearly unnerved.

Timothy chuckles. "She was just telling me that you used to date. Though, of course, I already knew that."

"Well, I'm sorry," Jack says. "I'm not trying to stir things up."

"*Aren't* you though?" Timothy says, looking at him more closely, a frown creasing his brow. "It seems like you might have some sort of alternative reason why you wanted to interview the Sterlings in the first place. Clearly, you knew Amelia was my wife, if you saw our article."

"I did," he said. "And I was curious. I hadn't heard from her since our relationship ended, and I wanted to see how she was doing. But also, it's a good story and it's a good job. I wanted to write the piece."

"What kind of angle were you going to lead with that you weren't disclosing?" Timothy demands.

"Can we not?" I plead. Clover is beginning to fuss more loudly and I jostle her on my shoulder. "I think I should take her home," I say firmly. "I want to go to the house and feed her and put her down for a nap."

"Convenient," Timothy scoffs.

"You can come with me," I tell my husband firmly.

He looks at Jack, eyeing him suspiciously. "Is there anything else I should know?"

"Of course not," I say to Timothy. Though it isn't the truth. Not one bit. There is so much he should know. But confessing could cost me this entire life we've built.

"I guess this is my cue to leave," Jack mutters. "Sorry, I

wasn't trying to start anything," he says to me. There's a look in his eye I can't quite place. "I mean it."

"I know," I tell him. "It's fine."

Timothy smugly watches Jack cross the street. Then he turns to me, his tone icy once more. "You have some explaining to do, Amelia."

I roll my eyes as I buckle Clover, who's now wailing at full volume, back into the stroller. "Yeah, I suppose you do too."

Timothy mimes at Celeste through the window that we're leaving, and I realize she's been watching our entire argument—me, Timothy and Jack, fighting in the middle of the street. The look on her face is unreadable, but if I had to guess, it looks close to smug. I quickly look away. I can't do this now.

We leave Main Street, and Timothy begins pushing the stroller for me. I'm holding my latte and wondering where this is going exactly. Timothy and I have never had a fight, not a real proper throwdown. I've done everything I can to go out of my way to be perfectly amiable, as generous and easygoing as possible.

I have only once gotten unreasonably upset, and it was that one time I was so hungry when I was eight months pregnant and all I wanted was a dill pickle and a lemon Popsicle. Timothy was able to find them both for me, and once in hand, I stopped my hysteria.

This feels different though. This isn't about pregnancy cravings. This is about secrets. This is about lies.

This is the kind of fight you might not recover from if you don't tread carefully. And God, I want to be careful. This is not the time to undo things. Not before I get to the bottom of why I am being sent these letters.

My stomach is a knot as we walk at a very brisk pace back to our home. "Where's your car?" I ask him.

"Downtown."

"We could have got in it and—"

"No, it's fine," he says. "I need to be outside right now. I need space to think."

"Are you mad with me?"

He sneers, shaking his head. "Am I mad? God, Amelia, what do you think? You were here in our home, alone with your ex-boyfriend, doing an interview, and you didn't think to mention it to me, your husband?"

I swallow, his words hitting hard. "I didn't think it mattered. It was just for the article—"

His voice is sharp, cutting through my explanation. "You think I didn't already know about Jack? You think I haven't known all along? The fact that you hid it from me, *that's* the issue, not that he was here."

My heart pounds, and I'm suddenly at a loss for words.

"You could have told me. You *should* have told me," he adds, his tone growing darker. "But you didn't."

"I didn't mean to hide anything." My voice shakes. "It's in the past. Jack doesn't mean anything to me now—"

Timothy's eyes grow cold. "Clearly. And yet, you still didn't trust me enough to mention him. And you trusted him enough to come running to the coffee shop today. That says a lot, doesn't it?"

The heaviness of it all is overwhelming. All my secrets are pressing down. "I didn't mean for it to be like this."

"You never do, do you?" His words hang in the air, harsh. "Always keeping things to yourself, Amelia. Always holding something back from me."

"But you didn't say anything about working with your ex-girlfriend," I point out. "That seems much more treasonous. She came to family dinners without me present, and you didn't tell me about them. I don't feel like I should have to defend myself to you."

"Is that what our marriage is going to be?" he asks as we round the corner to our home.

I can't help but dart my eyes side to side, wondering if there's an unfamiliar car nearby, a person getting out from it who could be dropping off one more letter as we speak. I don't see anyone though. I glance at the houses either side of us, but the curtains are still. I swallow. "I don't want a relationship that's tit-for-tat or full of secrets," I tell him honestly.

He laughs. "Fine, that's how you're going to play it?"

"I'm not playing anything." I feel defeated as we round our driveway.

We walk around the back of our beautiful home to the side door at the kitchen. He unlocks it before pushing the stroller inside. Clover has fallen asleep from the fast pace of the walk and the cool air, and the house seems eerily quiet. Timothy walks to the kitchen sink and pours himself a glass of water. I drop my empty paper cup from the coffee shop into the garbage can and pull out a barstool sitting at the island, looking on as he drinks the entire glass of water.

"I love you," I tell him, my voice trembling. "When I heard Jack was doing the interview, it had been a long day. You'd come home late. You sprung it on me. I didn't want to get into another fight. I was so tired. I'm always so tired."

"I know." Timothy's voice is steady but somehow distant. "That's why I said you should hire a nanny. We've talked about this. We don't have to be working ourselves to death, Amelia. You can relax, take a break every once in a while."

"I don't want a nanny," I mutter, feeling defensive. "I want to figure this out on my own. I don't want strangers in my house."

"Fine." His voice is tight. "I'm not going to argue with you about Jack and whatever your relationship was. But I think it's suspicious that you kept it from me. I should've known."

A flicker of guilt runs through me, but my irritation flares. "And I think it's suspicious you and Celeste were cozying up in the coffee shop this morning," I push back, my voice sharper than I intended.

His jaw tightens, and for a moment, I think he's going to snap at me. But instead, he sighs. "I don't know how to explain the Celeste thing to you." His voice is strangely soft now, as if he is changing his tactic. "You didn't grow up on Cutter's Island. You don't understand how things work with my family. They've always had their own way of doing things."

"I'm getting a pretty good idea." Bitterness that I can't fight creeps into my tone.

Timothy's eyes flicker, a hint of something dark behind them. "Look, my mother may be putting on a show, pretending to accept our marriage, but if she had it her way, Celeste would be in this house, not you. You know that. It's not a secret she's trying to hide."

The words sting more than I want to admit. "Great. Thanks for reminding me." I feel my stomach churn with a mix of anger and insecurity.

"I'm not trying to hurt you." He steps closer. "I love you, Amelia. I love everything about you. The way you tie your hair up when you're baking, the way you get so lost in your recipes that you forget the time."

His words sound sweet, but all I can think is: *Is he only saying this because I caught him with her today?*

I stare at him, trying to gauge whether this is genuine or just an attempt to smooth things over. The tenderness in his tone, the way he's suddenly being vulnerable—it feels too convenient. Too perfect.

"I loved that night we met at the bakery," he continues, his voice low. "You were so perfectly yourself. No pretense, no games. You didn't care about my family's name or money. You were just... *you*."

My chest tightens. *Why is he bringing this up now?* My mind races. Is this a way to distract me from what I saw at the coffee shop? From Celeste? My thoughts swirl, paranoia creeping in.

"I didn't tell you about Celeste because I didn't want you to think I couldn't handle my own life. I didn't want you to know how much my parents still control everything I do. I didn't want you to see me as... weak."

Weak. The word hangs in the air between us, and for a second, I wonder if this is another layer of manipulation. Is he playing on my emotions, trying to make me feel guilty for suspecting him?

"You're not weak," I whisper, even though a part of me wonders if I really believe that.

"Maybe you don't really know the real me," he says, his voice dropping to a near whisper. "Not all of me."

A chill runs down my spine. "Don't say that." I blink back tears.

His vulnerability feels real, but it also feels calculated. Like he's pulling me in, getting me to drop my guard, right when I should be questioning him the most. I can't shake the nagging feeling that something's off—something bigger than just Celeste.

I reach for his hand, my fingers trembling. "I love you, Timothy." My voice cracks. It's all too much. The money, the house, everything. *Was all of this a mistake?*

He pulls me closer, his arms wrapping around me as if trying to shield me from my own doubts. "I love you too." He runs a hand over my hair. "I love you more than anything."

His words should soothe me, but instead, they heighten the tension coiling in my chest. *Is this love—or is it control?*

I lean into his embrace, trying to ignore the growing sense of dread. "I just don't want to lose what we have," I confess, the tears slipping free.

"You won't," he promises, gripping me tighter. "As long as we're totally honest with each other, everything will be fine."

But those words only make my heart pound harder. *Honest?* How can I be honest when I'm hiding so much from him? And how honest is he really being with me?

He wipes away my tears, his touch tender, but there's something in his eyes—a flicker of something I can't place.

I pull back slightly, trying to smile, but the thought gnaws at me, insidious and dark. I've been receiving those threatening letters for weeks. I've been living in fear, terrified of who might be sending them.

But now, standing here in Timothy's arms, a horrifying possibility creeps into my mind.

What if it's him?

What if Timothy has been sending me these letters all along?

TWENTY-SIX
AMELIA

That night it feels nearly impossible to fall asleep with Timothy beside me. I keep checking the baby monitor on my bedside table, constantly thinking I hear Clover waking, needing something from me. I jump out of bed several times, and rush into the nursery feeling a sense of panic I've never felt before.

I find myself pacing in her bedroom in the middle of the night, cradling her in my arms, ruminating over all the letters I've received.

I'm coming for you. I'm coming for you. I'm going to make you pay.

I press my lips to Clover's head, kissing her soft skin.

"I love you, sweet girl," I whisper into the night.

I don't know what time it is when Timothy appears in the doorway of the nursery, his figure casting a shadow over the dimly lit room. Clover's soft breathing is the only sound, but my body stiffens at the sight of his silhouette.

"Amelia, are you okay?" His voice is low, but something about the way he says it sends a jolt to my heart.

I startle, instinctively pulling Clover a little closer to me as if protecting her from some unseen threat. I blink, trying to focus, but my thoughts spiral.

Is Timothy here to comfort me—or is he here for something else?

My mind races, flickering between the tenderness he showed me earlier and the growing doubts that have been gnawing at me. His words had seemed sincere in the kitchen, but now, in the quiet darkness of the night, everything feels different. His presence is suddenly too much, too close, as if he knows something I don't.

I swallow hard, my voice barely above a whisper. "I... I'm fine."

He steps closer, his eyes unreadable. "You've been in here for a while."

The way he says it makes my stomach tighten. Is he watching me? Has he been keeping tabs on my every move?

"I was just—Clover was fussing." I force my voice to sound steady, even though I can't shake the feeling of unease creeping up my spine.

Timothy takes another step forward, and for a moment I wonder if he's going to reach for Clover—or for me. But he stops just short, his gaze fixed on mine, searching, as if trying to read my thoughts in the dim light.

The air between us is charged with something I can't name. I can't tell if Timothy is my protector, or if he's the one I need protection from.

My hands tremble as I adjust Clover's blanket. My mind whispers questions I don't want to ask: *Does he know about the letters? Is he the one sending them?*

"I'm here for you, Amelia." His words feel like they carry a double meaning, something more than what he's saying. "You don't have to worry."

But I do. I can't stop worrying. Because I no longer know if the man standing in front of me is my husband—or my enemy.

"Come back to bed. You've been singing lullabies for hours, and Clover's not crying. She's out cold, babe." He walks toward me, pressing a hand on the small of my back.

"I just want to hold her." I kiss her head.

Timothy walks toward me and takes my daughter from my hands, placing her in the crib. I am so fatigued I don't fight him. "Let her sleep." He takes my hand in his, pulling me back.

He's right. She's sleeping. Nearly three months old and such a good baby. *Our baby.*

"It's our one-year anniversary next week," he tells me softly.

"I remember," I say as he guides me to the bedroom.

"Maybe we should do something special? Ask my sister if she can babysit and go out to a nice dinner?"

"I don't think I want to leave Clover—"

"I know you say that," he interrupts gently, "but it might be good for us. We haven't had a night out, just the two of us, since she was born."

"She could come with us to dinner," I say as we crawl into bed, already panicking at the idea of leaving Clover with any member of the Sterling family.

"Not sure that's exactly what I was thinking when I imagined a romantic night out with my wife," Timothy murmurs sleepily, and there's a smile in his voice.

"I'll think about it," I whisper into the darkness.

But I already know the answer. There's no way I'm leaving Clover right now. Not after the letter I received today. I'm already anxious leaving her anywhere without me. Even being ten feet away in the nursery terrifies me. What if someone came and got her while I was in my bed? What if something happened and it was all my fault? I couldn't live with myself. But I can't tell this to Timothy. Not until... Well, not ever, I realize.

I crawl under the covers, the baby monitor on the nightstand next to me. Timothy tries to draw me close, but I pull back, wanting my ear closer to the potential cry of my daughter.

I know it's insane how scared I am, but I remember Hazel, the way she looked at me when we were growing up, how convincing she could be, how ruthless, how she was perfectly fine with me taking the fall and spending two years of my life behind bars, how perfectly fine she was with me being labeled a murderer when in fact she pinned her mistake on me.

I squeeze my eyes shut, trying to push her face from my mind.

I fall into a fitful sleep, praying for a miracle.

In the morning, after Timothy leaves for work, the house feels claustrophobic. Like a cage, a home meant to keep me trapped inside. The soft hum of the heater and the occasional creak of the floorboards are the only sounds to keep me company. The gray February sky hangs low, casting a dull lifeless light through the windows.

I sit at the kitchen table, hands wrapped around my coffee mug, staring blankly ahead. My chest feels tight, my heart racing for no specific reason I can name. I haven't slept well in weeks. Every muscle in my body aches from exhaustion, and the quiet only amplifies the unease simmering beneath my skin.

The noise of my phone vibrating on the table snaps me back to reality. It's Tabitha.

Tabitha: *Coffee today?*

For a moment, I consider ignoring her. The thought of having company, even someone as familiar as Tabitha, triggers my unease. But then again, maybe I need it. Maybe seeing her will pull me out of this fog.

Amelia: *Come over. I just made a pot.*

Not long after, there's a soft knock at the door. I open it to find Tabitha standing there, Johnny strapped to her chest in his baby carrier. She gives me a warm smile, but the concern is clear in her eyes as she looks at me.

"You doing okay?" she asks gently, her eyes taking in my rumpled hair, my stained clothes, the bags under my eyes.

I force a laugh, rubbing my eyes. "I look that bad?"

She steps past me into the kitchen, heading straight for the coffeepot. "You don't usually text back so fast," she says, pouring herself a cup and grabbing the creamer from the fridge like she's lived here her whole life. Her ease, her familiarity—it should make me feel safe, but instead, it only highlights how untethered I've become.

I follow her, bouncing in my arms Clover, who's fussy again, refusing the pacifier no matter how many times I try. "I've just been... tired." My voice shakes, the understatement of the century.

We settle in the living room, Johnny on the floor with his rattle while Tabitha takes Clover from me, cradling her in her arms like it's second nature. The moment she's nestled in Tabitha's arms, Clover quiets. Although I'm happy she's calm, it feels like a betrayal. As I watch her, I feel like a bad mother. I sit across from her, every nerve in my body screaming at me to stay alert. Every creak of the house, every shadow through the window—it feels like something's creeping closer. Something I can't escape.

"You seem more than just tired." Tabitha's voice is gentle but probing. "Did you get any sleep at all last night?"

I groan, sinking back into the chair, unable to hold it in any longer. "I confronted Timothy yesterday," I admit. "And Celeste. God, I don't even know what I was thinking."

Tabitha's eyes widen. "You did *what*?"

"I know, it sounds insane. Jack—remember him, the reporter? He told me he saw them together at Cutter's Island Roasting House, so I went down there."

Her mouth opens in surprise. "So you and Jack—your ex-boyfriend—went to spy on your husband and *his* ex-girlfriend? Are you living in a soap opera, Amelia?"

I laugh bitterly. "Yeah, apparently."

She shakes her head, grinning, but there's concern in her eyes. "Okay, but what happened? Did Timothy say anything about him and Celeste?"

I fill her in on the whole awkward confrontation, my stomach twisting tighter with each word. "Everything's fine on the surface, but underneath... I don't know. I can't shake this *feeling*."

Tabitha leans forward, her voice quieter. "You think he's lying?"

"I don't know. I *want* to believe him."

Tabitha sets Clover in the swing, her face serious now. "Amelia, you've been through a lot. I don't want to overstep, but have you thought about... *talking* to someone? A doctor, maybe?"

"A doctor?" I scoff. "You think I'm that crazy?"

"No!" She quickly reaches for my hand. "I'm not saying you're crazy. But you've been on edge ever since Clover was born. I can see it—hell, anyone can see it. You're not sleeping, you're anxious all the time, you're biting your nails down to nothing... I just... I think it might help you."

I blink, fighting back the tears stinging my eyes. Looking at my fingernails that have been bitten to tatters, I know my friend is right. Tabitha doesn't even know the half of it. She doesn't know about the letters, the threats, the constant worry gnawing at my insides.

"I appreciate it," I say, "but I'm fine. I just need to figure this out."

She gives me a sad, knowing smile, but doesn't push. "Just think about it, okay?"

Before I can answer, there's a sharp knock at the door, and my heart leaps into my throat. Tabitha looks over, confused at my reaction. I stand, my palms suddenly damp with sweat. I tell myself it's just someone dropping by, but my mind is racing—what if it's something worse?

I open the door to find my mother-in-law. Isabelle Sterling stands with her posture stiff, her expression as cold as ever. My heart sinks.

"Amelia," she says, stepping inside without waiting for an invitation. "I hope I'm not interrupting anything." She looks me up and down and the distaste on her face is clear.

I swallow hard, forcing a smile. "My friend Tabitha is over."

Isabelle's eyes flicker to Tabitha and the babies, before resting back on me. The tension in the air thickens instantly, and a sense of alarm rushes through me. Her presence is a reminder that I'm never truly free. She's always just next door. Always watching, always judging.

"I just heard the article with *The Seattle Tribune* was canceled," she says, her voice sharp, every word deliberate. "Needless to say, the family is not pleased."

My mind races. *Canceled?* Why would Jack cancel the article? Did something happen? Did he uncover something... about me?

"I-I didn't know," I stammer, the words sticking in my throat. "No one told me."

Isabelle's eyes narrow slightly, her lips curving into a thin, disapproving smile. "Interesting. Considering you were the last person he interviewed, I would have thought you'd be the first to know."

The blood drains from my face. She's not just disappointed—she's accusing me of something. My mind scrambles for an explanation, but I can't think straight.

"I... I don't know why he didn't write it," I whisper, barely able to get the words out. "Maybe Jack... I mean, Mr. Donovan just decided not to run it."

Her smile doesn't reach her eyes. "I find that hard to believe. But then again, the Sterling name is a powerful one, and any association with scandal must be avoided at all costs."

Tabitha, sensing the tension, steps forward. "Isabelle, Amelia's been under a lot of stress. She's a new mom, and—"

Isabelle holds up a hand, cutting her off without even looking at her. "Thank you, Tabitha, but this is family business." Her gaze is icy. "I trust you'll get to the bottom of it, Amelia. And remember, the Sterling family doesn't tolerate... surprises."

As she turns to leave, my chest tightens. I feel like I'm about to break. The walls are closing in, and the air feels too thick to breathe. The moment the door shuts behind Isabelle, I collapse into an armchair, my hands trembling uncontrollably.

"Amelia," Tabitha says delicately, sitting beside me and taking my hand in hers. "You don't seem okay."

I can't answer. My throat feels tight, and all I can do is shake my head. Why did Jack cancel the article? Why didn't he tell me? Paranoia churns in my gut. Personally, I'm thrilled it was canceled, but as far as how this might further deteriorate things with my in-laws I'm terrified.

Tabitha's voice is gentle but firm. "I think you really need to see a doctor, Amelia. This is too much for anyone to handle alone."

I nod, but my mind is elsewhere. I can't shake the feeling that Isabelle's words carried a deeper threat. That somehow, she knows more than she's letting on. And if Isabelle knows about my relationship with Jack... what else might she have uncovered?

I stand, looking out the window at the gray sky, feeling eyes on me from every shadow, every corner. The paranoia gnaws at my insides, and for a moment, I wonder if I'm losing my grip on reality.

Then, with a sinking dread, a new thought creeps into my mind.

What if Jack didn't cancel the article because of me?

What if someone else got to him first?

TWENTY-SEVEN
AMELIA

Once Tabitha leaves, the house feels too quiet. The silence presses in on me, soul-crushingly. I get that familiar creeping feeling, a knot tightening in my stomach. The letters have been in my head for days now, clawing at me, but what if there's another one waiting?

The thought won't leave me alone.

I push open the front door, the February chill biting at my skin as I step out onto the porch. The wind rustles the trees, and for a moment, I just stare at the mailbox. Is there another letter in there?

Before I can check, movement catches my eye.

There's someone here.

I freeze, my breath catching in my throat as I spot a figure behind the apple trees at the far side of the yard.

"*Hey!*" My voice trembles. "Who's there?"

The figure steps out slightly, and the wind catches their hoodie, pulling it back just enough for me to see long dark hair.

Celeste? My stomach flips. *Hazel?*

"Hazel?" I call out, my voice breaking. "*Celeste?*"

The figure doesn't answer, but they turn their head ever so

slightly, and I see her profile—just enough for me to know. My heart races as panic mixes with desperation.

It's her. It's Hazel.

But it can't be.

"*Hazel!*" I shout, louder this time, my legs shaking, adrenaline rushing through me. I want to run to her, to demand why she's here.

But she turns and starts moving away, quicker now, her speed surprising me as her dark hair whips out behind her.

"No, wait!" I yell, stumbling forward, but by the time I reach the bottom step, she's already gone, vanishing into the street. I stand there, trembling.

That was her. It must be her, right?

But at the same time, I know I must be imagining it. That was the Hazel I remember from all those years ago, not Hazel as she would be now.

Clover lets out a little sigh, still asleep in her stroller, completely oblivious to the storm raging inside me. My knees feel weak as I glance around, searching for any trace of my sister, but the street is empty now.

Shakily, I push Clover back into the house, my mind spinning. No, I tell myself, it *was* her. Hazel was here. She was here just a few moments ago. But why? What does she want?

Once inside, I pull off my jacket and shoes, but the panic won't leave me. It's gnawing at my insides, twisting tighter with every breath I take. I glance at Clover—still sleeping, unaware of the chaos that's brewing around her—and grab my laptop from the side table. My fingers are numb, fumbling to open it as I sit down on the couch, my heart still racing.

I haven't used this computer since I canceled the nanny service. But now, I need it. I need answers. My fingers hover over the keyboard before I type the name that's haunted me for years: Hazel Carlisle, Bellport, WA.

The first thing that pops up is an old photo from high school —Hazel, smiling with Tommy beside her.

My throat tightens when I see her face, and I quickly scroll past it, refusing to let myself get lost in the memories. *Focus*. But then, I find it—her social media account, barely active. The profile is sparse, just a handful of photos. I click on them, my pulse pounding. I gasp as I see familiar spots around Cutter's Island.

There's a photo of the ferry, another of the park. The lookout point where Timothy and I have walked together. I pause, my eyes scanning the pictures. None of them have her face, just images of the island.

I look over at Clover, still sleeping in her stroller. Tears fill my eyes. Why is my sister tormenting me? Why does she want to hurt me? Everything tied to my biological family has always led to pain. I don't want any of it anymore. I don't want it at all.

I bury my face in my hands and sob. My shoulders shake as the strain of my past presses down on me. I wonder how I'm ever supposed to fix this. How am I supposed to come clean to Timothy, to anyone, about who I really am?

I'm not Amelia Sterling. I'm Meadow Carlisle.

And my past has finally caught up to me.

The lies, the secrets—they're fraying faster than I can keep up. And when the truth comes out, I'll lose everything.

I killed a boy. I sound like a monster, even to myself. I killed Tommy on graduation night. And Hazel lost the love of her life because of *me*. His family lost their son because of *me*. Tommy lost his bright future, all because of *me*. And before that, our baby sister, Vera, lost her life on my watch because of *me*.

I was never meant to be a mother. I was never meant to have this life. I made a promise to my sister.

Clover stirs, her tiny body shifting as if she can feel the pain radiating from me. And when I cry, she cries too. I scoop her into my arms, holding her tight as I rock her back and forth, tears rolling down my face, wishing I could be a better mom. A good mom. But I'm not. I'm a bad mother.

"I'm sorry," I whisper to her through my tears. "I'm so sorry I'm not better for you." I wish I had my own mom here. I wish *she* could help me now, the way she tried so hard to help herself after Vera died. I remember her face when she came to visit me in juvie, the way her eyes looked when I knew she'd started drinking again. It broke me then, and the memory is breaking me now.

I keep looking at the photos on Hazel's photo account, and when I reach the last one, my breath catches in my throat as I read the comments below.

So pretty, Mom.

I stare at the words, and the tiny image of the face that wrote them, my heart hammering in my chest.

Mom.

My sister has a daughter.

TWENTY-EIGHT

Then

Cutter's Island was supposed to fix everything.

When Mom suggested we leave the town where we grew up and move to this glamorous island, I felt like maybe, just maybe, I would finally get a chance at happiness. Of course, I didn't realize how much work having a baby was going to be.

Mom is still passed out on the sofa from the night before.

"*Wake up!*" I shout at her.

Sylvie is two months old and a literal monster. I don't know how Mom did it all those years ago taking care of two of us alone. Not that I give her much sympathy. I suppose the real reason she managed to take care of her daughters was by drinking herself half to death.

"What?" Mom wipes her eyes and sits up on the couch.

That's where she lives. She doesn't have a bedroom because when we moved out here, we couldn't exactly afford a nice place. We didn't have enough money to put down a deposit to secure an apartment. We ended up moving into the tiny basement apartment of some rich person's house in exchange for Mom being their housekeeper.

They were annoyed when they found out it was a package deal. Of course, it was a surprise to Mom too.

I knew I was pregnant with Tommy's baby before graduation. And I had a whole plan worked out. Since I didn't get into college, I figured I would move in with him, we could be a family. A perfect little family, like I always wanted.

But him dying was not part of my plan.

It was why I knew I couldn't take the fall for his death. I had a child to protect.

I remember coming out of the hospital with the infant carrier on my arm, my body wrecked from pushing out a nine-pound screaming pink person, and thankfully the rich owners of this huge house decided to take pity on us and let me stay. The conversation was tense. I remember them talking with Mom, "This wasn't part of our agreement."

And Mom pleading, "I promise I will do extra work around the house. I'm great at gardening."

Mom had never planted a seed in her life, but it didn't matter to me.

All I cared about was having somewhere to go to sleep, and I did. I took up residence in the bedroom of that basement apartment, pushing Mom to the couch in the living room and wondering what I was going to do with the baby. *My baby*.

On top of it all, I could hardly cope with the guilt gnawing at me. I kept the baby a secret from Tommy's family. Am I supposed to get on my hands and knees, groveling for them to take pity on me? No way.

They hate me and my whole family. Hell, I hate them. They never even contacted me after Tommy died to ask if I'm okay.

His parents were only ever nice to me because I made

Tommy happy, and making Tommy happy was what they cared about because he was their kid.

I never was. I was the girlfriend and they had money, so buying me school supplies and taking me out to dinner wasn't some act of generosity. It was just what people did who were normal.

My life is distinctly not normal and increasingly not normal now that I have a baby.

A baby who doesn't stop crying. And a mom who doesn't stop drinking.

"If you don't get your shit together," I tell her now, "we're going to get kicked out of this place."

"If we get kicked out," she yawns, "it's going to be because *you* can't get your baby to be quiet."

"Don't blame it on me!" I shout. "I'm doing my best. *She's* the problem."

"Babies are demanding, end of story." Mom stands up and walks over to the fridge, pulling out an energy drink, popping open the can. "I got to get dressed. I have to go upstairs and do the laundry." She scowls. "Look, you're not carrying your load around here."

"I just had a baby," I laugh.

"*Two* months ago. I need help. Either you need to get a job and I can watch the baby, or I get a job and..."

"No, *I* will get a job," I tell Mom. "You can watch the baby and I will go work. Okay? I'm sick of this place."

I remember the way Mom looked at me as if I was missing something, but she didn't realize what was missing here is my happiness, independence and freedom.

Now I have Sylvie. My life is over.

"Just give me the baby," Mom says. "You go take a shower now, but I can't watch her while I'm cleaning. So you are in charge of her until my shift is up."

"Okay. Then I'll find a job tonight. I could work at a restaurant. The tips in a place like this are probably good."

"All right," Mom says. "But I am going to need you to get your mind around the fact that your life has changed," she tells me. "I feel like you're pretending you're still young and free, but the truth is, this baby needs you to survive."

"Fine," I seethe. "I can take care of her. You just go do your job."

"Hazel, that's not what I was saying. I was going to watch her so you could get showered and changed and..."

"No, whatever. It's fine." I abruptly end the conversation.

She always tries to make me feel bad about everything. Why should I feel bad? My boyfriend's the one who's dead.

Of course I ignore the thought that comes next, which is he's dead because of *me*.

Just like Meadow's in jail because of *me*, just like Vera is dead because of *me*. Just like Mom started drinking again because of *me*.

If I start thinking about those things too much, I don't know if I will survive.

If I can make it out of this mess alive.

Somehow two months becomes two years and two years becomes ten.

Time passes on Cutter's Island more quickly than I ever imagined. Mom is gone. After years of using drugs and alcohol to numb herself, one night she took too many pills, fell asleep and never woke up.

That's ancient history though, because now I live in the present, still in this mother-in-law apartment, and instead of Mom cleaning the house, that's what I do while Sylvie's in school. I became their housekeeper in exchange for rent. I work at a grocery store when I can get a shift.

Right after Mom died, I thought about moving back to Bellport, finding Tommy's parents, finding Meadow and trying to make things right, but by then it was too late.

I told Sylvie I didn't know who her father was, and Meadow never looked for me, as far as I knew.

Now, of course, Sylvie's a teenager. Sixteen years old and going to Cutter's Island High.

But she didn't end up getting the life that my mom imagined for her.

She hates me. Not that I've ever done anything wrong. She resents that we are the poor people in town, living in the tiny apartment of these rich people's house.

Ever since Sylvie was born, my life has been a struggle. Not like it was when I was back in high school, when I was with Tommy and free, feeling on top of the world.

Do I live with regret? Sure, but what was I supposed to do all those years ago?

I was eighteen years old without any options. I know some people might think I'm being a victim here, but those people don't understand how hard it was to grow up the way I did.

It's not my fault that Meadow went MIA. I did my best by Sylvie, and even if she hates me right now, it's because she doesn't understand how hard I've had it.

She'll grow up and realize I'm a good mother.

That I did it all for her.

TWENTY-NINE
SYLVIE

Three weeks earlier

I'm sprawled out on my bed, the lamp light casting long shadows across my room. Mom's been on edge ever since we found out we are being kicked out of the apartment. We've lived in their basement apartment all my life but now they want us out, so we have no choice. We have to go.

We don't even know where we are going to live next. Mom says she has enough money for a motel for a few weeks. But what am I going to do after that? I go to school here. Have my whole life here.

Mom doesn't care about how this affects me. She is usually drunk, hungover or angry that she isn't.

But we have to move out in a few weeks, which means I have to sort through things to pack. I don't want to move but I don't have a choice.

As I pack, I come across a box of Grandma's stuff. She died when I was little, so I hardly remember her. Now, going through all her things is giving me a glimpse into a person I barely knew.

I pull out one of Grandma's journals from the box and start

flipping through the pages. The ink feels like a secret, waiting to be uncovered.

Lots of entries are boring. She was sober for a while, which is funny because I only remember her drinking, the same way Mom does now. Then she must have gone back on the bottle, because the pages are blank for a while.

But after flipping through random pages, I find something interesting.

Shocking, really.

July 10

Today was hell. Meadow was charged, and I can't wrap my head around it. How could she be so reckless, so careless?

The anger inside me is boiling over. I wish I could turn back time, and make things right, but I'm trapped in this nightmare. All I can do is grit my teeth and keep pushing through, hoping for some rainbow. I have failed Meadow. And I feel like I failed Hazel too.

If I can do anything to fix things for Hazel, I will. She is all I have left.

I frown, looking at the journal entry. Meadow was *charged* with something, but Grandma doesn't say what. No one has ever mentioned this. My heart pounds.

Meadow was my mother's younger sister, but I only remember her name from Grandma. Mom refuses to talk about her. She always says Meadow is as good as dead and we shouldn't think about her. Every time I brought her name up, Mom would shut down, so eventually I stopped.

Now I can't tear my eyes away from the page. Grandma's words are like breadcrumbs, leading me deeper into a mystery. But I'm afraid of what I might find at the end. And I'm even more afraid of what Mom might be hiding from me.

With a trembling hand, I turn the page and keep reading.

August 6

Hazel told me the truth today. The truth I feared but was too scared to say out loud. She's pregnant.

My heart is shattered. How could she do something so stupid after all we've been through?

I know now that I've failed her. And deep down, I'm terrified. Terrified of what might happen to her and this baby. Terrified of losing her forever. But we have a plan—we are moving in together and will raise this child together. Somehow we will make it work. We have to.

The realization hits me hard. *I'm* the child that Hazel—my mom—was pregnant with when Grandma wrote this.

I swallow the lump in my throat, realizing I am getting a crash course in my family history. And that I was never wanted.

It's impossible to put the journal away and go back to packing. I need to know more. Now I've started, I need to know everything.

November 22

We moved to Cutter's Island and Hazel had her baby. I never imagined her being a mom so young, and without a father for the child.

I do what I can to help. Hazel uses me the same way she used to use Meadow. Taking advantage until there is nothing left.

I feel like a monster to think that of my child... but Hazel was never a normal girl.

There has always been a look in her eyes... a look that I pray Sylvie doesn't inherit.

> *Sylvie is a sweet baby though, and I will do what I can to make sure she has a good and normal life. I just need to stop drinking first. Then I will be a good grandma.*

I choke back a laugh at that. I'm sixteen and haven't had much in the way of good or normal. Mom has always been a house cleaner for the rich and famous on Cutter's Island. And I've always been the scholarship kid with out-of-style clothes and a homemade haircut.

Nothing has ever been *good*.

December 20

> *I went to the detention center to see Meadow today, but she wouldn't talk to me. A wall between us I don't know how to crawl over. I couldn't bring myself to tell her about Hazel's baby, I didn't want her to feel we were moving on with our lives without her. Especially as this child will never have a father.*
>
> *I've failed many times as a mother. And now she is locked away. Will I ever be able to make my wrongs right?*
>
> *She's lost to me, like I never knew her at all. My heart ached as I sat there, desperate for even a glimmer of recognition in her eyes. But she just stared blankly ahead, as if I were a stranger.*
>
> *Tears filled my eyes as I realized that the daughter I once knew was slipping away, replaced by this distant, unrecognizable figure.*
>
> *Did I ever know my daughters? Or was I just fooling myself all along, living in a fantasy of love and connection that never truly existed? The uncertainty left me feeling lost and alone in the sterile visitation room.*

As I read, I can't help but wonder what Meadow did to get

locked up. I need to know who Meadow really was... what she became. My need to know keeps me turning the pages of Grandma's journals. More than a year passes before she makes another entry.

June 10

Meadow was released from juvie today. I got to the center late, and they told me she had already left. I yelled at them for letting her go. She is just a child. I am her guardian.

But of course, Meadow is eighteen now. She was free to go without me.

So she left. Left us. Left me. Forever.

It is partly my fault, of course. After we moved to Cutter's Island, I stopped coming to visit. She was so withdrawn and didn't want to talk to me anyway, so I never told her about my move, about Hazel's baby, or who the father was. I couldn't bear to say the name out loud, not to Meadow, not after everything.

How could she just disappear like that? I am her mother. Doesn't she care about me at all?

I'm lying on my bed, the journal open in front of me. My hands tremble as I reread the entries.

All my life I have wanted to know who my father was. And to think, all this time he could have been in my life.

Maybe it isn't too late.

THIRTY
SYLVIE

Three weeks earlier

I know enough about my mother to know that if I want to know the truth, I shouldn't go asking her for it.

She's never been exactly forthright about her past. And what I read in Grandma's journals just confirms everything I already believed: Mom has secrets. Grandma had secrets. Now I will have secrets too. I'm done being on the outs. I didn't do anything to anybody. I deserve the truth about my father.

At school, I go to the library during lunch. I didn't want to risk Mom seeing what I was looking at on my laptop, the one the school checks out to every student at the beginning of the year. Not that most kids at Cutter's Island High need loaned laptops. Everyone here has so much money. I've never fit in. I tried, especially when I was younger.

I remember begging Mom to get me a pair of sneakers everyone else had in second grade. They were all glittery and gold, with laces up your calf. They looked like shoes someone in a movie would wear. Every other girl in my second-grade class had them except for me. I had sneakers Mom got at a secondhand shop. And even though I cleaned them up real nice, it didn't make a difference. They didn't sparkle.

And some moms maybe would've bought some glitter and glued it on themselves, but not my mom. She's never been that sort of mother. She's always been distant and cold, as if I was a burden, a bother, like me being in her life at all was ruining it.

It's been fine, for the most part. I do my thing, and she does hers. And I'm grateful she's kept a job and a roof over our heads, honestly. I'm not trying to sound ungrateful. I appreciate her. I love her even, I think.

But now as I sit down in the library, pulling out my laptop, wanting to search the things that I'm trying to understand, I wonder if I've ever really known my mom at all.

I wish Grandma were still alive. I could have talked to her, asked her about those journal entries and understood. But instead, I'm sitting alone in a library at lunchtime hating everything about sophomore year, wishing for a do-over.

It's easy to fantasize, of course. If I knew who my father was, maybe he could have taken me away from this hellhole, or at least sent Mom some money so I could fit in. If she knew who my dad was, why didn't she reach out and make him pay child support? Maybe then my whole life wouldn't have been such a struggle.

Living on Cutter's Island just seemed to make it all that more obvious how different Mom and I were. Besides being a single mother, she was a house cleaner my whole life. And I don't care about all that, but I always wondered why she didn't just move to a town where we would've fit in better.

Move us to a big city, where we could have lived in an apartment like everybody else? But she said it's not as easy as that when you're an adult and have to worry about things like first and last month's rent. When I was younger, I didn't quite understand, but now I do. It's hard enough for Mom to pay for my school supplies, let alone get together enough money to sign a lease for a new place.

Look at us now. About to be on the street. That is why I need to find my dad. He has to help us. He owes us that at least.

I check to see the Wi-Fi is on and I pull open a search engine, trying to think about how exactly I am supposed to find the truth. I never considered the piece of the puzzle of my life that my Aunt Meadow might have taken, the piece that could click everything together.

I pull on my long black hair, my eyes darting around the library. The librarian, Ms. Bloom, is behind the desk checking books out for some students I don't recognize.

I press my lips together, focusing. I only have twenty minutes before our lunch period ends. I type *Meadow Carlisle* into the search engine, doubting anything will come up, but strangely, it does. It's not hard once I click on the first article to realize the way my life went to crap. Why it was all my aunt's fault.

My heart pounds as I read the article, taking in the truth of it.

No. This can't be true.

But it is.

I read article after article.

Mom grew up in Bellport, and the local paper there has a whole tragedy from sixteen years ago, the year Mom graduated high school.

A boy in town—Tommy Donahue—was killed on graduation night.

It was a car crash. In the other car, the driver was...

Meadow Carlisle.

I swallow.

My Aunt Meadow killed this boy.

I pull the journal out from my bag, rereading the entries, understanding why Grandma was so insistent on that night being the night that everything changed, graduation night. Later, my mom told her that she was pregnant, and Grandma went on about how Meadow was part of all of it.

I click on Tommy Donahue. His name is linked to several articles in the paper about his high school football career. He had gotten a scholarship to Washington State University. A full ride, so he must have been super smart. I freeze when I look at that boy's face. I run my fingertips over my cheek. My skin's always been darker than mom's or grandma's. My hair is darker too. Mom's hair is brown and mine is silky black, my eyebrows firm lines.

I knew that Grandma had two daughters, Meadow and my mom, Hazel, and they had different dads. And neither of them knew who their dads were, so maybe mom just wanted to keep that storyline going, generational trauma and all, telling me she didn't know who my father was either.

And I had bought it.

I guess it made sense. Like mother, like daughter.

Except it was a lie. I see that now when I look at Tommy's face. I know the way I look in the mirror, and it matches his reflection.

Meadow killed my father.

Anger rises up in me, tears slipping down my cheeks. I brush them away. I type in Tommy Donahue's name in the search bar. There's no social media for him, which makes sense, he's been dead for sixteen years. The car crash was fatal. It took his life. All his hopes and dreams were gone in a heartbeat.

Why was all this kept from me? Grandma's journals plainly say she knew who my dad was. If she knew, Mom did too. But she's always lied to me, pretended she didn't know how to answer when asked. She had all the answers I wanted.

More tears come then, hot and angry, and I feel so utterly alone.

I force myself to keep reading the article on the laptop,

wishing the words weren't true. Wishing they didn't keep getting worse and worse. But somehow, they do...

I find accounts for his older brothers. I see a social media page for his mom. They all... look like me. Panicked, I scroll back all through the years, deeper and deeper, trying to find answers, trying to see where my story went all wrong.

The account's been active forever, and I'm able to scroll back far enough to see Tommy's mom talking about his death, about the person who killed him, Meadow Carlisle. She doesn't beat around the bush. She doesn't hide the fact it was a teenager who took her son's life. And where the newspaper was tactful, Ms. Donahue is blunt. She updates her status:

I hope she's tried as an adult. I hope she goes to jail for life. I hope she spends her life behind bars.

Later, she's angry because Meadow was tried as a child, a minor. "Two years in juvenile detention, until she's eighteen years old. That's when she'll be released," Tommy's mom said. "What a waste. I hope I never see her face again. I can't believe Meadow's sister was Tommy's girlfriend."

I swallow. Meadow never came back around, as far as I could tell. From Grandma's journal, it's clear that once Meadow left the detention center, she never looked for her family. It makes sense why. If my mom's sister killed her boyfriend, the father of her child, how could she show her face?

I swallow, horrified. I've always been so angry with my mother for not being more, for not having the ambition to get us out of a life where we just tried to make ends meet. But now I realize mom's probably been in mourning the last sixteen years because her own sister killed the father of her child.

I am horrified at what all this means.

Have I mislabeled Mom as a bad mother all this time, when in fact it's my own aunt who ruined our lives? And mom's never said a bad thing about her, not even once. Maybe my mom *is* a good mom.

When I type the name Meadow Carlisle into the search engine again, nothing comes up after the articles of Tommy's death. I wonder if she changed her name altogether and started a new life. I would if I were a murderer.

I feel stuck, looking at the homepage of the search engine, trying to find a clue when I see a news article just posted that makes me click. It is national coverage on Cutter's Island. My home.

The headline reads, *Cutter's Island Billionaire Family.*

When I click on the link, it sends me to *American Journal*, a magazine. The article just came out today. The online edition of the magazine shows a family, all fancy in some photo shoot with perfect parents, a perfect son, a girl holding a stupid dog, and a woman I recognize from the photos I just looked at online in the articles about Tommy's death.

I frown, not thinking it's possible. Could that be my Aunt Meadow?

I shake my head knowing that's ridiculous, isn't it?

I zoom in. Freckles across her face. She's holding a cute red-haired baby. Amelia Sterling is the name that's listed on the photo. But this is not some lady named Amelia. This is Aunt Meadow.

I saw photos of her in the stuff Grandma had, a red-haired teenager, with freckles on her face. *It is her.*

I type *Amelia Sterling* into the search engine, opening a new tab. There's nothing about her anywhere except for a wedding announcement in the *Tribune*. She and Timothy Sterling had married six months ago, but there is nothing more about her. No social media accounts, no job profile, nothing, like she just arrived out of thin air.

Of course she did. She'd been running, hiding. She changed her name and her identity.

And look, now she's married to one of the richest families in the country, living right here, on Cutter's Island.

I've never been one who believes in coincidences or fate, but this feels like destiny. It feels like I finally have the answers my heart has longed for all my life.

I close my laptop, shoving it into my backpack, and the journal too. My heart pounds as I absorb the truth of it.

My aunt killed my father.

Now it's time to make her pay.

THIRTY-ONE

SYLVIE

Two weeks earlier

Once I figure out where my aunt lives, I want her to suffer. Afterall, she has put Mom and me through hell. I start by dropping a letter off in her mailbox that very afternoon.

But then I become obsessed. I want to know everything I possibly can about the woman, but it's hard to find out much. She has a screaming baby and rarely leaves her house. I've never had experience being a stalker, but I quickly learn how I can get under her skin. The letters rattle her, I can tell.

I watch from the bushes, skipping school way too many days. I watch her read a letter after she pulled it out of the box, her eyes darting around the road looking for someone, anyone.

She never sees me. I park a block away, and I wear a hoodie. I'm just a teenage girl and it's easy to be invisible, especially when I've spent most of my life doing my best to go unnoticed. She never sees me coming, not once, and so I watch her reading my letters. I sense the fright in her eyes, and I feel a pang of guilt for just one moment, mostly because she has a baby.

I don't have anything against babies, even though I don't

even feel particularly connected to this one. Although, I suppose it's my cousin. But mostly I just feel jealous of it.

That baby has a perfect life, money and a fancy house and a perfect family. The baby has everything, even though she deserves nothing, with no idea what her mother's done. She killed my father and never even came back into my life to say, *I'm sorry*, to make things easier for my mom. Nope, she just ruined my mother's life and then went on living the perfect fantasy.

Every time I watch her reading a letter, my anger for her rises to a whole new level.

I reach for Grandma's journal, and press it to my chest, feeling connected to something, to someone beyond me. I want to scream. I want to tell Mom. I want to fight, but I can't.

I can't talk about it to anyone, so the anger just keeps growing inside of me until it feels unbearable. I try to write it down, and put into words how I feel, but what I mostly feel is jealousy for everything that the Sterlings represent. For everything that Meadow has made for herself, a life that is so far removed from my pitiful experience. I want her to suffer for it.

The letters are working. I can see the way she grips that stroller of hers, the way she panics as she walks down the street to her friend's house. When they go on walks, it is harder to follow, and they quickly make their way into either the coffee shop or back to their own homes, making it difficult for me to trail behind.

When they do talk, I hardly get any useful information.

I want to know something that can *hurt* her, something that can do more damage than those letters. But I can't figure anything out, so I kept writing them, all saying pretty much the same thing: *I'm going to make you pay*—because that's what I want. I want her to pay for what she's done, for what she's taken. It isn't fair.

My poor mom, working hard at crappy jobs all her life

when I could have had a whole extended family. Tommy's family seems perfect. I've been watching them on social media now, putting pieces together of who my uncle is, who my grandmother is, who my grandpa is, none of them in my life because they don't even know I exist. All they know is that their son was taken by my aunt.

My poor mom. How did she get through it all? Of course she has been drinking to cope.

What matters now is finding a way to make my aunt pay because I feel like I've suffered enough. Maybe I can get her to give me money, pay for my college? I don't know. Maybe that's stupid. Maybe I don't want her money anyway. What I really want is for her to *understand* what she's taken, and why it's not fair.

Now, I watch as she walks down the street with her friend, the only person I've ever seen her with, pushing a stroller. Her friend has her baby on her chest. I can't follow them. It'd be too obvious. So instead, I try to go inside her house. I know it's risky. I don't know about their alarm system or cameras, but I'm hoping there's nothing that's going to incriminate me. I just want to see more of her, to understand her.

The back door is unlocked, but I can't work up the nerve to open it. How rich do you have to be to not even care if you lock your door? How secure in your lot in life to not worry about a thing?

Being here, so close to her perfect life, causes a rage to boil within me. It isn't fair. How much I have suffered, how much my mom has suffered.

I want my aunt to pay. And when she does, I'll let my mom know everything I've done for her.

Because what I want is revenge.

THIRTY-TWO

SYLVIE

Present

All night, I toss and turn. I'm haunted by my aunt's voice calling after me.

Hazel. She called me *Hazel.*

She thought I was my mother. I can still hear her voice echoing in the darkness, and it's tormenting me, gnawing at the raw edges of my anger.

She thought I was my mom. She didn't see who I really was, just a shadow of the woman she ruined. But I wasn't ready for it. I wasn't ready for her to look at me like I was someone she knew.

Now, lying here, I don't know what to do next. The letters I sent were supposed to make her scared, rattled. I wanted her to feel like her world was falling apart. But after yesterday... it feels like *I'm* the one crumbling.

The morning sun barely peeks over the horizon as I slip out of bed. School doesn't matter today. Nothing matters but this. I need to see her again. I need to feel that moment of power, of control—when she looked at me and *knew.*

I grab my mom's car keys, slipping out the door quietly. She is passed out on the couch, a half-empty bottle of something strong on the floor beside her. The same as always.

I drive back to Amelia's house. Her perfect, pristine house. When I arrive, I park down the street where I won't be seen. My heart pounds in my chest as I walk the rest of the way, my feet sinking into the wet February soil, the air damp and cold, biting at my skin. It feels like the kind of chill that lingers in your bones, and it only fuels my anger.

I crouch behind the apple trees at the edge of their property, just out of sight. From here, I can see everything—the sprawling house, meticulously restored to look like one of those Pinterest-perfect farmhouses you see in glossy magazines. The kind with crisp white paint, dark shutters and a wraparound porch that probably gets decked out for every season. A fairy-tale life, right here on Cutter's Island.

The landscaping is so immaculate it makes me sick. The grass is perfectly trimmed, not a weed in sight. Even the flowers by the front steps, winter pansies or something, seem to thrive despite the biting cold. It's a house where everything has its place, every detail carefully curated to reflect a life of ease, of wealth, of happiness. A life that's been handed to her, and stolen from me.

Next door looms the Sterling estate—massive, towering over the property like some kind of castle. The mansion is secluded, tucked away behind iron gates and towering trees, but I know it's there. The whole island knows who the Sterlings are.

I want to scream. I want to run up to that perfect porch, pound on the door and make her face the truth. She doesn't deserve this. She doesn't deserve any of it.

But then, the front door creaks open, and I freeze.

There she is.

Meadow steps onto the porch, holding Clover. The sight of her cradling that baby so gently, so lovingly, makes my chest tighten with rage. Her red hair catches the morning light, falling in soft waves over her shoulders. She looks tired, worn, but there's something about her as she holds her daughter. Something I can't stand.

Her perfect life should be mine.

My throat burns as I watch her sway back and forth, humming softly to the baby. The perfect mother in her perfect house. I feel the bile rising in my throat, choking me. My hands clench into fists at my sides, nails digging into my palms. She ruined my life, took everything from my mother and me, and yet here she is, living this fantasy like she deserves it.

Clover stirs in her arms, and Amelia smiles down at her, brushing a strand of hair away from the baby's forehead. I want to tear that smile off her face.

A movement across the street catches my eye. My heart leaps into my throat as I spot the neighbor, peering out from behind her curtains, her eyes scanning the yard.

Shit.

I duck lower behind the trees, pressing myself against the damp earth, my heart hammering in my chest. I can't get caught. Not now. I glance back at the house, at Amelia still cooing to her baby, oblivious to the eyes watching her. To *me* watching her.

I wait, barely breathing, until the neighbor disappears behind the curtain. My pulse pounds in my ears, and for a moment, I feel lightheaded, the adrenaline pumping through me, making everything feel too sharp, too real.

Meadow walks back inside, and I stay hidden, watching her until the door closes. My anger builds inside me, pressing down on my chest like a boulder.

I need to *do* something.

This isn't enough anymore. The letters, the threats—they aren't enough. I need more. I need to take something from her. Something that matters. I glance back at the window, where

Clover's tiny face had been, and an idea starts to form. I could let her husband in on the truth I discovered.

I shift on my feet, feeling the dampness of the grass soak through my shoes, and as I stare at the house, something else chews at me.

What if her husband already knows her secrets? What if Meadow told him everything and they're living their perfect little life with their perfect little secret?

Sure, he married her and built this life with her. But maybe they've both been hiding behind this facade, keeping my mother and me out, knowing we'd never have a chance. Maybe I'm the fool, thinking I had any power in this.

What if he already knows she's not Amelia Sterling at all? What if he knows she's Meadow Carlisle? The thought makes me want to scream. I've spent weeks trying to break her, and what if they're both sitting in that perfect house laughing behind my back?

She took my father from me. She ruined my mother's life. Now, I'm going to ruin hers.

It's time for her to feel the pain I've felt my whole life—the pain *she* caused.

THIRTY-THREE
AMELIA

It's darker now, the evening stretching longer than usual, or maybe it just feels that way. I move through the house in a daze, every creak of the floorboards, every distant sound outside the window sets my nerves on fire. The word I read on my computer screen still flashes in my mind.

Mom.

I've read it over and over. Hazel has a daughter. I can barely wrap my head around the fact that the girl outside, the one I mistook for Hazel, wasn't her at all, but her daughter.

My niece.

I can't breathe.

The house feels wrong, too big and too empty all at once, like it's closing in on me. My skin prickles with the sensation of being watched, even though I know I'm alone. Clover's tiny sighs from the nursery are the only thing anchoring me, the only proof that I haven't completely lost my mind.

But I have lost something—control. And my promise.

She blamed me for our sister's death, said I was reckless, that I couldn't be trusted. And I believed her. I believed every word. I thought I could atone for what happened to Vera by never becoming a mother. We made a sister pact, vowing to never have children.

I agreed because I thought Hazel was right, and I never deserved to be a mother.

But here I am, holding Clover in my arms. When Clover came, it felt like fate, like something I couldn't run from, even though I tried.

But Hazel didn't keep her word either. She broke the vow, same as me.

What would Hazel think of me now?

But even more terrifying, what does her daughter think of me?

Clearly she hates me for killing her father.

I can see it now.

She's been tormenting me, sending those letters, threatening me from the shadows. And I can't even blame her. I would hate me too. And she may not even know the other secret I've kept buried—that I killed Vera—the child who would have grown up to be her aunt.

I stand at the kitchen sink, staring out into the blackness of the night, gripping the edge of the counter. The reflection in the window is pale and hollow. I barely recognize myself anymore. I'm not Amelia Sterling. I'm Meadow Carlisle. *A liar. A murderer.*

And now, a mother, the one thing I promised I'd never become.

My phone buzzes on the counter, the sound sharp in the silence. Timothy's name flashes on the screen, and my stomach twists. I haven't heard from him since the afternoon. But with the erosion of everything we built our life on, and his knowledge of my relationship with Jack, I can't help but wonder... Has Timothy known all along who I really am?

I don't answer the call. My hand hovers over the phone as it buzzes again, then falls silent. Timothy will be home soon. He'll walk through the door with that practiced smile, but tonight I can't stand the thought of looking into his eyes and pretending everything is normal. Nothing is normal anymore.

The front door opens just as I'm settling into the rocking chair in Clover's nursery, her tiny body curled up against mine. I hold my breath, listening to the footsteps moving through the house. Timothy is home. My heart pounds in my chest, my mind racing with thoughts I can't control.

Did he know about Hazel? Does he know about Sylvie? About everything?

I hear his footsteps stop just outside the nursery, the door squeaking as he pushes it open. His shadow fills the doorway, and for a moment, I freeze, clutching Clover tighter. His eyes flicker to her, then to me, and I see it—the darkness, the tension—simmering beneath his calm facade.

"You didn't answer my call," Timothy rebukes, his voice low. There's something sharp in his tone that sets off warning bells in my head.

"I was... putting Clover to bed," I manage, my voice shaky, as I stand, slowly placing her in the crib. I can feel his eyes on me, watching, waiting for something. I follow him back down the stairs to the kitchen.

"You've been avoiding me." His voice is still low but carries an undercurrent of something I can't quite place.

"No, I just—"

"You're *lying*," he cuts in sharply, stepping closer. His eyes narrow, and my heart skips a beat. "You haven't been the same since Clover was born, Amelia. And now Jack's canceled the article without any explanation. I heard it from my mother, and believe me, she's *furious*. You could have told me sooner. I deserve to know what is happening within my own family."

I swallow hard, the load of everything too hard to bear. "I didn't know until she came here and told me herself."

Timothy's gaze darkens. "You expect me to believe that?"

"I didn't ask him to cancel the article," I blurt out, my voice shaky. "Maybe he didn't like the way your family was treating me—"

Timothy's eyes flash with anger. "Treating *you*? Is that the story you're going with? Jack cancels out of nowhere, and it's *our* fault? Your past with him has nothing to do with it, does it?"

I stumble over my words, feeling the ground beneath me shift. "It's not like that. I didn't ask him—"

"Then why didn't you tell me about your history with him, Amelia? You're hiding things, and I'm starting to wonder what else you've kept from me." His voice tightens, frustration building with every word.

I can't breathe. I can't think. The walls are closing in around me, and I feel myself spiraling. Timothy steps closer. His presence is overwhelming and his anger palpable. "What else are you hiding, Amelia? Is there more to this than just Jack?"

I shake my head, my voice barely a whisper. "I'm not hiding anything."

But the lie sits on my tongue, bitter and unyielding. Timothy doesn't believe me. I can see it in his eyes. He lets out a harsh, bitter laugh, shaking his head. "Maybe you're not the woman I thought you were."

His words cut deep, and I feel myself collapsing inside of myself, my secrets crashing down around me.

"I need some air," Timothy mutters, turning on his heel and storming toward the door.

I watch him go, my heart in my throat, my legs trembling beneath me. *Don't go.* I want to scream the words, but they won't come out. I'm paralyzed, unable to move as Timothy pulls open the door and steps outside.

A few moments later, I hear the car engine start. And then, headlights flash across the window as his car pulls out of the driveway.

I rush to the living room window, barely processing what

I'm seeing, but as Timothy's car disappears down the street, I catch sight of another vehicle pulling out of the driveway across from us.

Celeste.

I freeze, my mind spinning. She's leaving at the same time as Timothy, again. My stomach churns, the realization hitting me like a freight train. They're together.

It's not a coincidence. It can't be.

My breath comes in shallow gasps as I watch Celeste's car follow Timothy's down the road. He's with her. All this time, it's been her.

I collapse onto the couch, clutching a pillow to my chest, staring blankly ahead. He's having an affair. I know it in my gut. The way he's been acting, the way he stormed out just now—it all makes sense.

Clover stirs in the nursery, her tiny cry pulling me back to reality. I push myself up, my legs weak, and walk to her crib, scooping her into my arms. She's so small, so fragile, and I don't know how I'm supposed to protect her when everything around me is deteriorating.

As I rock her gently, my mind races, the facts of the situation wrapping their cold fingers around my heart. Timothy's gone. My world is slipping away, and I don't know how to stop it.

And as I hold Clover tighter, I wonder if we need to run before it's too late.

THIRTY-FOUR
AMELIA

I wake with a jolt, heart pounding, sweat slicking my skin.

I don't know what's woken me, but my heart is racing. I'm tangled in the sheets, the room pitch-black except for the faint glow from the baby monitor beside me. I reach out, my hand searching for Timothy in the bed, but his side is cold. Empty.

A knot tightens in my stomach. "Timothy?" I call softly into the dark, but there's no response. My voice echoes back in the silence, and a chill creeps down my spine. *Where is he?* With dread, I remember him leaving, Celeste following in her car. Clearly, he never came back. Despite everything, my heart fractures at the thought.

The baby monitor flickers beside me, the grainy black-and-white image of the nursery glowing on the small screen. I reach for it, my fingers trembling, but something feels wrong—Clover isn't there.

I stare harder, willing the shape of my baby to appear. But the crib is empty.

My chest tightens as panic slams into me. This can't be happening. She has to be there. I blink rapidly, my vision blurring as I stare at the screen.

I throw the covers off and stumble out of bed, nearly tripping over myself in the process. My throat constricts as I rush down the hallway toward Clover's nursery, my legs shaking beneath me. She has to be there.

The door is slightly ajar when I reach it. The room is dark except for the soft glow of the nightlight in the corner. I shove the door open, gasping.

The crib is empty.

For a second, my body goes completely numb, the air sucked from my lungs. *No.* I rush toward the crib, there are no blankets to throw back, the crib is empty. I look around the room in a desperate attempt to make sense of what I'm seeing. But she's gone.

Clover. My baby is gone.

I stumble back, my vision swimming, and a scream of panic escapes me. This can't be real. My breath comes in ragged blows, my chest burning as I try to think—try to piece together what's happening. Where is she?

I back up, my hands trembling, and that's when I notice the smell. *Smoke.*

Thick and acrid, it clings to the air, curling around me like a warning. I turn toward the hallway, my mind spinning, my body moving before I can even think. The house is on fire.

I bolt down the stairs, the smoke growing denser with every step. The heat hits me as soon as I reach the bottom—a wave of it, thick and relentless. Flames flicker at the edge of the living room, climbing up the walls, spreading faster than I can process.

My eyes sting, my lungs burn as I cough, stumbling backward. The fire is everywhere.

I reel, choking on the smoke. But *Clover. I have to find her. I have to find my baby.*

The flames creep closer, licking at the walls, consuming everything in their path. The house—the perfect life I built to replace the horrors of the past—is turning to ashes right before my eyes. My perfect nursery. My perfect family. All of it is going up in flames.

I stumble toward the front door, my heart racing, but the heat is unbearable now. The fire spreads too fast. I can't breathe. I have to get out. I have to find her...

My vision swimming in front of me, I push open the front door and stagger outside, gasping for air. The cool night hits me like a slap, and for a moment, everything feels too quiet—too still. But then I collapse in the wet grass, my knees sinking into the damp earth as the world spins around me.

I look up, the house blazing in the darkness, the flames lighting up the sky.

Tears stream down my face, mixing with the smoke and the ash, as I choke back a sob. *Where is Clover?* The question is on repeat in my head, a deafening echo I can't escape.

The sirens are faint in the distance, growing louder with each passing second. Flashing red and blue lights reflect off the windows of the houses in the neighborhood, the flames engulfing my house dancing in the night sky, but I can barely focus.

It's already too late.

THIRTY-FIVE

SYLVIE

The cold night air bites at my cheeks as I hurry down the dark street, Clover cradled against my chest, her tiny body swaddled in blankets. I can't stop my hands from shaking as I strap her into the infant car seat I stole from Amelia's entryway. My heart races and my thoughts spin wildly.

My aunt deserves this.

Doesn't she?

I force myself to move quickly, but quietly, glancing around the empty neighborhood. The island is always quiet at this hour, but I know it won't be long before someone realizes Clover is gone. I've planned this moment, fueled by the need for revenge. Amelia deserves to suffer.

But now, as I buckle the car seat into my mom's old sedan, panic claws at me. My hands tremble as I reach for the door handle. My breath is shallow and ragged.

Clover stirs in the back seat, but she doesn't cry. Her eyelids grow heavy as she falls back into sleep. She's too innocent to understand the storm of emotions swirling around her, too oblivious to the chaos.

I sit in the driver's seat, staring at my shaking hands on the steering wheel. It wasn't supposed to feel like this. I was supposed to feel *vindicated*—powerful. But all I feel is fear. Fear that I'll be caught. Fear that I've made a mistake.

I can still see Amelia's face in my mind, the way she looked at me outside her house, mistaking me for my mom. She killed my father, and then left my mom to rot and raise me in poverty, while she built herself a perfect life on lies.

Now, it's my turn. My turn to make her feel that loss. To take something precious from her the way she took my father from me.

I look back at Clover, my mind racing, and I realize it's not enough. It's not enough to just take her baby. Amelia deserves to lose more than that. She deserves to lose it *all*.

My pulse pounds in my ears, and before I can stop myself, I climb out of the car, leaving Clover tucked safely in the back seat. I keep my head down, moving quickly as I slip through the shadows and head back toward Amelia's house.

I make sure no one's watching as I creep around to the back. The door I used to sneak in earlier is still unlocked. I push it open and step into the dark house, my heart thundering in my chest. The air smells faintly of lavender—the kind of scent rich people use to make their perfect little homes feel cozy.

I *hate* it.

I look around the immaculate kitchen. Everything in this house is designed to make her life easy, to erase the horrors of her past. To replace the life she destroyed. *Mine.*

My fingers tremble as I reach for the lighter I stashed in my coat pocket earlier. I had it just in case. I didn't know if I'd use it. But now, standing here in the middle of this pristine kitchen, the pressure of everything crashes over me like a wave.

I flick the lighter and hold it close to the curtains, watching as the flame catches. My pulse races as the fire grows, consuming the fabric. It spreads quickly, licking at the wood of the window frame. The heat pushes me back, and for a second, I freeze.

What have I done?

But there's no turning back now.

I run out the back door, heart pounding as I race down the street toward the car. My chest feels tight, every breath a struggle.

I climb into the car and slam the door shut, my whole body shaking as I turn the key in the ignition. I twist around, checking to see that the baby is still here. She is sleeping in her car seat, unaware. The car roars to life, and I accelerate down the road, trying to escape the panic clawing at my chest.

I drive like I'm being chased, though no one's coming after me. By the time anyone notices Clover is missing, it'll be too late.

Tears blur my vision as I speed through the dark streets, guilt and fear tangling inside me until I can't tell one from the other.

When I pull up to the house where Mom and I live, I can see the kitchen light glowing dimly from the basement apartment. She'll be home, probably on her second or third drink by now.

I cut the engine and sit there for a moment. As I stare at the steering wheel, I try to calm my racing heart. I glance in the rearview mirror at Clover, still peacefully asleep.

What the hell have I done?

I grab the car seat and carry it toward the door. The moment I step inside, the warm air hits me, and I hear the TV blaring. Mom is sprawled on the couch, a glass of whiskey in her hand, her eyes half-lidded.

"Sylvie?" she mutters, her voice slurred. "What the hell are you doing out this late? And—" Her eyes narrow as she focuses on the car seat. "Whose baby is that?"

I don't answer at first. My mouth is dry, and my legs feel like they're going to give out beneath me. I set the car seat down on the floor, trying to catch my breath.

"It's Clover," I finally whisper.

Mom stares at me blankly. "Clover? Who's Clover?"

I clench my fists, my throat tight. "Meadow's baby."

Mom's glass clinks against the coffee table as she sets it down, her face blanching. "Meadow? My *sister*?"

I nod, my voice shaking. "She's been living here on Cutter's Island for a few months. She changed her name. She's been pretending to be someone else—Amelia Sterling. I know the truth. I read about it all in Grandma's journals. Your sister killed Dad, and she's been living this perfect rich person life like nothing ever happened."

Mom's eyes widen, the color draining from her face. "Wait... what are you talking about?"

I can't stand it anymore. I sink to the floor, the sheer force of everything pulling me down. "She killed Tommy, Mom, my father. She built a new life, and we were stuck with nothing."

Mom's face pales, and for a moment, she doesn't say anything. She just stares at me, like she's trying to piece something together. Then, suddenly, she shakes her head, her voice hoarse.

"Sylvie, no," she chokes out. "You've got it all wrong. It wasn't Meadow driving that night..."

I blink at her, my stomach twisting in knots. "What?"

Mom's hands are shaking now as she clutches the arm of the couch, her eyes filling with tears. "It wasn't her. It was *me*."

THIRTY-SIX
SYLVIE

I feel like the ground is falling out from under me. "What do you mean? You... you said—"

"I *lied!*" Mom sobs, her voice cracking.

The words hit me like a sledgehammer, knocking the air from my lungs. I can't breathe. I can't think.

I look at Clover, her tiny chest rising and falling with each breath.

I've made the biggest mistake of my life.

THIRTY-SEVEN

Then

After the moment of impact, it is as if my worst fears are realized.

I press a hand all over my body, wanting to ensure that nothing has been punctured, but somehow I am completely intact.

The only blood on me is my brow, where my forehead hit the steering wheel. Across from me though, I see that Tommy's car flipped from the collision. My heart pounds in fear.

Is he dead?

There's been only one other time in my life I was this afraid. It was the day Vera died.

"Meadow!" I scream, "Meadow!" I reach for her hand. I shake her. Maybe it's the wrong thing to do. I don't know anything about car crashes and concussions, but Meadow's head just rolls forward, unmoving.

It's dark outside. The only light flooding through the windshield is from the lights of Tommy's overturned truck.

"Meadow," I repeat. "Can you hear me?" There's blood

pouring out of her ear. I reach for her shoulder, shaking her. "Wake up!"

"I didn't see it coming. It came out of nowhere," I tell her, wanting her to wake up and hear me. Believe me.

"I was driving us home. I was trying to get us home safely," I tell her, even though she is unresponsive. I swallow, thinking through everything at hyper-speed.

Me, in the driver's seat.

Me, the reason for the accident.

If Tommy is dead, really dead, what might that mean for me, for my future?

I press a hand to my belly, sick with fear.

"You have to do something for me," I demand of Meadow who doesn't register my words. I do the calculations quickly. I am eighteen. I'm an adult. Meadow is barely sixteen.

"I need you to climb into my seat," I stress. "I need you to climb into the driver's seat now."

But she doesn't hear me, she is either dead or on her way out. I just know I cannot be driving the car. I need my sister behind the wheel. As the driver.

"When the police come," I explain to her, even though she doesn't respond, "*you* need to say you were the one driving."

I tip her head up, wanting her eyes to open, for her to hear me. For her eyes to tell me this is all going to be okay.

But she is unresponsive. I wonder if there are more injuries than I can see. I press my hand to her chest, wondering if any of her clothes are saturated in blood, if there's a puncture wound that I'm not aware of.

I press my hand to her chest—feeling the beating of her heart. My sister is alive, but unconscious. It's a relief knowing she is still breathing—but I must focus on what I need in this moment. I need to be exonerated.

"Just do it," I hiss. "You *need* to do it. *Now*." I begin to pull at her, pushing her against me. I unbuckle her seat belt and do the same with mine. "I need you over here," I force. "We need to trade places."

I begin moving, moving her, even though I know she doesn't understand what I'm saying. We are lucky we're alive. This Buick of Mom's is one solid piece of steel, impenetrable. Across from me though, Tommy's tiny car has been completely crushed, and now I see flames from the engine. No one is getting out of the car.

Tommy has got to be seriously injured, if not dead. I can't be responsible for this. Not when I have a whole life spread out before me, when I have so many things I am going to do, even if they're all built on deceit. No one needs to know that. Not now, not ever. What needs to happen right now is for my sister to listen to me.

I tug at her shoulders. "Come on," I urge her body.

"Change places with me." I crawl up out of my seat, scooting toward her, shoving her as I move, maneuvering awkwardly, but it's working. Soon enough she is in the driver's seat, falling forward against the steering wheel.

I have just saved myself. And in doing so, I have destroyed my sister's life.

THIRTY-EIGHT
AMELIA

I wake to the sterile smell of antiseptic and the rhythmic beeping of machines. The soft murmur of voices nearby causes me to lift my head, but it falls back again. My body feels pulled down by exhaustion, by pain. There's an ache in my chest, a soreness in my throat and something else—panic, raw and unyielding.

Clover.

My eyes flutter open, but the room spins. The ceiling is white, too white, and my vision blurs at the edges. I try to sit up, but the effort sends pain shooting through my ribs. My heart pounds as I fight to make sense of where I am, what's happened.

The fire.

Flashes of memory come back in bursts—the flames licking at the walls, the smoke curling up the stairs, choking me. The heat, the crackling of wood as everything I'd built, everything I'd tried to protect, went up in smoke. And Clover—my baby—gone from her crib.

"*Clover!*" I rasp, my voice barely above a whisper. I try to sit up again, but my body won't cooperate. My limbs feel like lead, weak and useless. Panic grips me tighter.

"She's not here," a voice says softly from the corner of the room, and I turn my head, squinting against the bright lights. A nurse approaches, her movements gentle. "You've been in and out of consciousness, but you're safe now."

Safe? The word barely registers. Nothing feels safe. I need to know where Clover is. I need to hold her, to see her with my own eyes. "*My baby...*" I choke out, my throat aching with each word.

The nurse places a cool hand on my forehead, her expression filled with pity. "You need to rest."

But rest is impossible. My mind spins, memories crashing into the present. The flames, the panic, the empty crib. Clover gone. *Why is Clover gone?* The question claws at me, even as the nurse's calming voice fades into the background.

I close my eyes, but the darkness brings no comfort—only the past, seeping in, taking hold.

The doors of the juvenile detention center slammed behind me, the sound reverberating in my chest. I had walked out into the world, free but shackled by everything I left behind. *Meadow Carlisle, murderer.* The words echo in my mind, chasing me through the streets of Seattle, and into the shadows of my new life.

I hadn't wanted to see Hazel again, hadn't wanted to be reminded of what had happened to land me behind bars in the first place. The life Hazel wanted—a life with Tommy—was taken from her in the blink of an eye. I have carried the ache of that monstrosity since I was sixteen years old. I was behind the wheel, I was responsible. She was a part of the life I was trying to outrun, a tether pulling me back to Bellport.

But I couldn't forget what had happened. And I couldn't let go of the promise I had made to her—never to have a child, never to be a mother. Not after Vera.

Vera.

Her name is a knife twisting in my gut, her face a permanent fixture in my nightmares. I see her toddling toward the open door, her chubby little legs carrying her to the top of the stairs. I see her falling, her tiny body crumpling at the bottom.

I tried to move on after I left juvie. I tried to become someone else—someone better. *Amelia,* a woman with a new name, a new life, free from the past.

But it was never really gone...

I jolt awake, my heart racing as I come back to the hospital room. The machines beep in sync with the erratic thudding in my chest. I can feel the sweat on my skin, slick and cold.

"Clover," I murmur again, struggling against the haze of sleep that keeps pulling me under. My hands clutch at the sheets, desperate for something to hold on to.

The nurse is gone now, and I am alone with the memories I've tried so hard to forget.

I had found the bakery in Seattle, a place that didn't ask questions, didn't demand answers. My boss, Cal, didn't care about my past. We worked in silence most days, the smell of bread and sugar filling the air. It was there, in that flour-dusted kitchen, that I became Amelia for real. I convinced myself I could be someone new.

But at night, in the quiet, when the world settled into stillness, I lay in my apartment and thought of the life I had left behind. Of Vera. Of Tommy. Of Hazel.

I should have known better. I should have known the past would catch up to me.

. . .

The beeping of the machines grows louder in my ears, a frantic rhythm that matches the terror in my heart. I gasp for air, my lungs fighting to help. It's too much—everything is too much.

The fire, the smoke, the panic. *Clover gone.* My body trembles with the knowledge that I can't protect her, that I never could.

I try to sit up again, to tear the IV from my arm, to run to wherever she is, but my body won't let me. It's too weak, too broken.

Tears spill down my cheeks, hot and fast, as I lay back against the pillow. I'm helpless. I've always been helpless. I can't escape my past. I never could.

The hospital room fades in and out of focus, the sound of footsteps in the hallway are distant, like a dream.

I reach for Timothy, but the bed is cold.

I reach for Clover, but she's not here.

THIRTY-NINE
AMELIA

I wake slowly, my mind swimming up from some dark, tangled place. The light in the room feels too bright, pressing against my eyelids. My body is weighed down by exhaustion and fear. For a moment, I don't know where I am.

Then it hits me.

I'm in the hospital.

The beeping of a monitor is the only sound in the room, rhythmic and detached. It is a far cry from the panic I feel swelling in my chest. I blink, and my eyes land on a bouquet of lilies sitting on the table beside me. Their scent is too fragrantly sweet in the sterile air. Next to them is a small card.

Amelia,

It's gonna be okay. Clover needs you to stay strong.

Love, Tabitha

I gasp. The panic tightens around my throat like a vise. *Clover.*

I try to sit up, but my body protests, my muscles tight with pain. My throat is dry and scratchy from the smoke I inhaled. "*Clover*," I croak, barely able to form the word.

Before I can press the call button, the door opens and a nurse steps in. Her face is soft and full of sympathy, but it does nothing to calm the storm raging inside me.

"Where's my daughter?" I manage to ask, my voice trembling. "Where is Clover?"

The nurse moves closer to me, her voice gentle. "Your daughter is safe, Mrs. Sterling. She's being checked over by the medical team right now. You'll be able to see her very soon."

Safe. The word should bring relief, but all I feel is dread. I need to see her. I need to hold her, to know that she is really okay. The nurse steps aside, and two police officers walk into the room. They look somber, their expressions serious.

"Mrs. Sterling," one of them says gently. "We need to speak with you about what happened."

I swallow hard, nodding, my eyes still filled with tears. "Where's my daughter? Is she okay?"

"She's fine," the officer assures me. "We found her unharmed. But we need to tell you how it happened."

The other officer clears his throat. "Your niece, Sylvie Carlisle, took Clover. We identified her on neighborhood security cameras."

Sylvie. My mind spins. My *niece*. I can barely process the words.

"She was seen near your home late last night," the officer continues. "She took Clover, but we've recovered your daughter safely. We're still investigating what led to the fire at your house, but we believe it is connected to Sylvie."

I shake my head, disbelief coursing through me. "Sylvie? She... she *took* Clover?"

"Yes," the officer says, his voice steady. "She was angry, Mrs. Sterling. It seems she blames you for something from the past."

Tears blur my vision again. The past. My past. The one I have tried to hide. "Where... where is she now?"

"She's in police custody," the officer replies.

A painful silence settles in the room as I wrap my mind around the reality. Sylvie—Hazel's daughter. My niece. The child I didn't even know existed, must want me to pay for the death of her father.

"Thank you," I whisper, though my voice feels hollow, far away.

The officers nod and turn to leave, their presence lingering like a shadow in the room. As soon as they're gone, the door opens again. This time, it's Timothy.

The air in the room changes instantly, a coldness descending. His face is hard. He appears colder than I've ever seen him. There's no warmth in his eyes as he steps closer to my bed.

"Timothy," I say. My voice cracks with exhaustion. "Where were you?"

He just stares at me for a moment, his expression unreadable. "Where was *I*?" he repeats, his voice low and sharp. "That's what you want to know?"

My stomach twists with dread. Something in his tone and in the way he's looking at me, sends a chill down my spine. "Yes." My voice is barely audible. "Why weren't you there at the house?"

His bitter laugh echoes in the small room, harsh and cruel. "I wasn't there because I've been cleaning up the messes *you* created."

Confusion swirls in my mind. "What are you talking about?"

Timothy steps closer, his eyes cold as ice. "You don't understand." His voice rises, venomous. "My mother hired a private investigator when you were so opposed to having your photograph taken for *American Journal*. It is why she knew to get Jack to write the article, why we know the truth about the lies you told. I should've done it ages ago. When I met you, I thought I'd found some naive woman to play the part of my wife. God, how wrong I was. You are even stupider than I thought."

My blood runs cold. "A... a private investigator?"

He nods, his lips curling into a cruel smile. "Yes, Amelia. Or should I say *Meadow?*"

I can't breathe. The world spins around me. He knows. He knows everything.

"Timothy," I whisper, tears spilling from my eyes. "I didn't mean to lie. I didn't mean for any of this to happen."

He steps closer, his face inches from mine now. "Oh, but you did. You lied about everything—who you are, where you come from, all of it."

Tears fall freely now, my heart shattering with every word. "It wasn't like that," I plead. "I was just trying to survive."

"Survive?" He sneers, his voice dripping with disdain. "You're a liar, Amelia. And worse than that, you're a *killer*. You killed a young man, who had the whole world before him."

"I served my time. I did my best to make my wrongs right."

He laughs, the sound filled with contempt. "You've played me for a fool. Me, a *Sterling*. Do you think I can be associated with someone like *you?*"

"I didn't want to hurt you," I sob. "I love you."

Timothy's eyes narrow, his fury bubbling over. "Love? You don't even know what love is. You loved the life I gave you—the money, the power, the security."

My heart breaks, splintering into a thousand pieces. "No, Timothy. That's not true. I wanted a family. I wanted love, unconditional love, like I never had before."

"You're a *criminal*," he spits at me, his eyes blazing. "You've been hiding your true self for so long, you don't even know who you are. But you're certainly no longer my wife."

I shake my head, sobbing. "Please, Timothy. Please, I'm begging you—don't do this."

But he doesn't stop. He steps back, his face twisted in disgust. "You want to know something? That ring on your finger—it wasn't even meant for you."

My heart skips a beat. "What are you talking about?"

"That ring," he says, his voice sharp as a blade. "It was always meant for Celeste. You getting pregnant just put a pause on that. But after Clover was born it was clear I couldn't stay with you. You are too unpredictable. A liability. And honestly, you're a bad mother."

The words hit me like a punch to the gut, the air knocked from my lungs. The one thing I had clung to for so long was being taken away. "No," I whisper, shaking my head. "That's not true."

"It is," he says, his voice cold. "Celeste and I have been seeing each other for months. I know what I want, and it isn't you."

My world collapses around me, his betrayal crushing everything I have left. "I trusted you," I sob. "I loved you."

Timothy's eyes gleam with satisfaction. "You never deserved any of it, Amelia. You're a liar. You're *nothing*."

FORTY

HAZEL

Now

The handcuffs snap around Sylvie's wrists with a sharp click, the sound reverberating through my bones.

My throat tightens as I watch as my daughter—my baby girl—is led away, her face contorted with rage and fear. The police guide her to the car, and she doesn't look back. Not once. It's better that way. If she had looked, I'm not sure I would've been able to keep standing.

This wasn't how it was supposed to end.

I feel like I'm floating, detached from my body as I stand there, frozen on the steps of the house. My vision blurs as I see the patrol car drive Sylvie away. My legs tremble beneath me, and it's all I can do to stay upright. I clutch the doorframe for support, the reality of everything closing in like a vise.

Sylvie. Arrested. Handcuffed, just like Meadow had been. I never thought it would come to this.

I should have stopped it. I should have told her the truth before it got this far. My mind races back to the mistakes I made all those years ago.

When Meadow was taken from us, I stood by and let her take the fall for something I did. And now, my daughter is paying the price for my silence, for the lies and the hurt I let fester. I glance back inside the apartment. My eyes catch on the scattered boxes, now remnants of our half-packed life. We were supposed to be leaving this place, moving on. But how can you move on when you're still trapped in the same web of secrets?

Sylvie didn't know the truth. And now, she's gone. A repeat of the past, of *my* past. It's a cruel mirror, reflecting the cycle of mistakes that has haunted our family.

The temptation to grab a drink, to drown out the guilt and regret that gnaw at me, is overwhelming. But I can't do that. The alcohol, the hiding—it's what's kept me in the dark all these years, what has poisoned me. But it won't fix this. It never has.

There's only one thing I can do now.

I stand frozen for what feels like an eternity, my thoughts racing, heart pounding. I know where I need to go, but everything in me screams to stay. It's easier to pretend, easier to hide and let someone else take the blame. But that's how I do everything.

With shaking hands, I grab my coat from the hook by the door and head to my car. Each step feels like I'm wading through thick murky water, my body taking steps toward the shore.

What if I've waited too long?

What if I can't fix this?

The thoughts linger as I drive to the hospital, my hands gripping the steering wheel so hard my knuckles turn white. I shouldn't be doing this. I should turn around, go back to my dark little corner of the world, and let Meadow live her life in peace. She's probably better off without me anyway. I wasn't there for her when she needed me most, and now... now I'm the last person she wants to see.

But I have to try.

When I finally arrive, I sit in the car for a long time, staring at the entrance. It looms in front of me like a barrier, a line I'm terrified to cross. But I have to. I need to. For Sylvie. For Meadow.

For myself.

I push open the door and step out into the cold evening air. My legs shake as I walk inside, the sterile scent of disinfectant hitting me as I approach the front desk.

"I'm here to see Amelia Sterling," I say, the name unfamiliar on my tongue. To me, she'll always be Meadow.

The nurse nods and directs me to her room. With each step down the long echoing hallway, my heart races faster. What will I say? How do you apologize for ruining someone's life?

When I reach her room, I hesitate at the door. My hand hovers over the handle. I almost turn back, but I can't. I've run from the truth for too long.

I take a deep breath and push the door open.

Meadow—Amelia—is lying in the hospital bed, her face pale and drawn, the toll of everything she's been through etched into her features. But in her arms, cradled so tenderly, is her baby girl. Clover, I think Sylvie said. So small, so innocent. A symbol of everything that's good, everything that could be saved.

Amelia looks up and her eyes lock onto mine. For a moment, neither of us speaks. The air between us is thick with unspoken words, with years of resentment. But there's something else there too. Something fragile, but soft.

"Hazel," she says softly, her voice barely above a whisper. "Why are you here?"

I have to force the words out. "I'm sorry, Meadow."

Meadow's eyes fill with tears, but she doesn't look away. She's waiting. Waiting for me to finally come clean.

"Tell me what you remember the night Tommy died," she says, shifting the conversation. She looks up at me now, her eyes meeting mine with a depth I haven't seen since we were children. Meadow was always kinder, sweeter, more understanding. She was always patient with Vera, with Mom, with me.

"Tell me what you remember," she presses. Her voice is calm, but insistent.

This is why I am here. Why I came even though it terrified me. To set the story straight. To make right all the things I have made wrong.

"The night Tommy died, it was me driving. Not you. You filled the gas tank up, but I was behind the wheel. After the crash, you were unconscious. I already knew I was pregnant. I was scared. I was stupid. I dragged you into the driver's seat. I knew you were alive," I say, the words spilling out. "I checked your pulse. I wasn't a monster..." I wipe the tears that fall from my eyes. "But I couldn't go to jail. I was eighteen, you were a minor... I thought... I had to protect myself."

Her face doesn't change—there's no shock, no disbelief. Only a deep, tired sadness.

It hits me then.

A truth I never saw coming, never even imagined.

And now, I see, she has always been too good for this world.

She knew. She's known all along, and she's been carrying my burden anyway.

"You knew?" I ask, my voice trembling.

A tear slips down Amelia's cheek as she looks at Clover in her arms. She brushes a hand over the baby's soft red hair. When she finally speaks, her voice trembles, but it is steady.

"I knew what you were doing, Hazel, when you moved me to the driver's seat." She whispers. "But I wanted to take the fall because there was no way for me to be punished for Vera's death once it was declared... an *accident*." Her shoulders shake as she continues to speak, the pain written on her face. The pain she has carried. "I wanted to be punished because I was already a *murderer*."

There's a beat of silence. And I know it's now or never.

"But you weren't. You didn't cause Vera's accident. I did."

She shakes her head, as if in disbelief, staring at me with her mouth open.

"I let you think it was your fault, that she opened the door herself, that you neglected her. But you didn't..."

Tears fall down her cheeks, and she looks down at the baby in her arms. She runs a finger over Clover's cheek.

"I always thought it was my fault," she whispers. "That's why... that's why I..." Her words trail off, her eyes glassy and far away. "You made me promise to never have a baby." She sobs quietly. "You told me I could never be a good mother..."

I press a hand to cover my face, shame overwhelming me. "I should never have scared you like that, never have made you make a promise like that. You were a child."

She wipes her eyes. "I never held it against you for blaming me for Tommy's death if that's what you're worried about, if that is why you're here."

The relief in her words washes over me, but it doesn't take away the guilt. It just shifts it, makes it slightly more bearable.

I nod, unable to stop the tears now. "I can't do this anymore, Meadow. I can't keep being this person. I'm going to rehab," I tell her, my voice breaking. "I need help. I don't want to end up like Mom, drinking away the pain, hiding from everything. I don't want to ruin Sylvie's life the way I've ruined yours. I have to stop this."

Amelia looks at me, *really* looks at me. I see something in her eyes that I haven't seen in years—hope. Maybe not forgiveness, not yet, but the possibility of it. And that's enough.

We sit there in silence for a while, Clover's soft breathing filling the room.

"I'll make it right," I whisper. "For Sylvie. For you. For all of us."

Amelia nods, holding Clover a little tighter.

In that moment, as we sit there together, I realize that maybe, just maybe, we can break the cycle. Maybe we can finally stop the lies, the abuse and the pain that has haunted our family for so long.

For the first time in years, I feel like there's a chance.

FORTY-ONE
AMELIA

One week later

I stand on the sidewalk, Clover nestled in a sling against my chest, her tiny body warm and close.

The air is crisp, but the sky is a bright cloudless blue. Sunlight filters through the bare branches of the apple trees, casting long shadows on the ground. It's a beautiful day—so different from the chaos that has surrounded me for so long.

The house in front of me is nothing more than a ruin, the charred remnants and shattered windows stark in the cold morning air. The walls that once held my secrets are blackened and broken, crumbling into themselves. What's left is a hollow shell of the life I built with so many lies.

But standing here now, I don't feel defeated. I feel... light.

Clover stirs gently, and I press my hand to her back, feeling the rise and fall of her breathing. For the first time since she was born, I don't feel panicked that I'm doing everything wrong. I don't feel the voices—Hazel's voice, my own voice—telling me I wasn't meant to be a mother. That I'm too broken, too damaged, to raise this child.

The sun hits my face, warm against the chill in the air. I breathe deeply, letting it settle into my bones. This island, with all its dark memories and smothering secrets, will no longer be my home. The claustrophobic pull of Cutter's Island loosens its grip on me with every step I take.

I'm something else now. I'm stronger. And I can be a good mother.

I think of Tabitha and Keith, of the struggles they've been facing. They have choices to make about their lives, and so do I. We all do. But now, standing here, I realize that I've already made mine.

My choice is to be free, to step into the light and leave the shadows behind.

As I walk down the paved sidewalk toward Main Street, I pass by Eleanor Salsberg's house. Her perfectly manicured lawn, her grand front porch—it's all as pristine as ever. I used to admire homes like this, with their carefully curated lives behind closed doors. But now, the sight of it only makes me feel more certain. I don't need that life. I don't want it.

Timothy and Celeste may have each other, may even build a life together behind these very walls, but that life isn't mine anymore. And for the first time, I feel thankful for that. I'm glad it's not me locked in those gilded chains, living a lie.

As I walk past the Sterling estate, I glance up. Lydia, my sister-in-law, has completely ghosted me, just like the rest of the family. I used to think maybe Lydia and I could be something like sisters, that we could forge a bond despite everything. But now, I know better.

Lydia will have to choose for herself if being a Sterling is worth the price. It wasn't for me.

I pause, looking at the grand house one last time, and I feel nothing. No anger, no regret, no sadness. Just a quiet acceptance. Isabelle and Alexander don't control me anymore.

Timothy doesn't control me. The lies that once tied me to this place are nothing but ashes now, scattered in the wind.

I kiss Clover's head, her soft curls brushing against my cheek, and I feel a warmth spread through me—a strength I've never felt before. I think of Hazel, of the apology she whispered in the hospital, of the tears we shed together for the life we lost and the future we still might build. The cycle of lies, of pain and silence, ends with us.

I adjust Clover in her sling, feeling her settle against me as I take a deep breath, the cool air filling my lungs. This is it—our new beginning. A life free from secrets, free from fear. It's not going to be easy, but nothing worth having ever is.

My phone buzzes in my pocket. I pull it out and see Jack's name flash across the screen; he is waiting for me at the coffee shop. I just wanted to see the neighborhood one last time, on my own.

Jack: *Are you okay?*

I pause, my thumb hovering over the keys. Then I type back a simple response.

Amelia: *I'm headed back now.*

I don't explain further, and I don't need to. Jack knows me, maybe better than I realized. And somehow, after everything, I feel a strange sense of calm knowing he's there, waiting for me.

I slip the phone back into my pocket and look up at the Sterling estate. I see a figure, a woman, standing in the open curtain. I stop, staring straight at the person so intent on hurting me. Isabelle Sterling. She never saw me as an equal, and while her respect meant something at one point, now I know better. Now I know self-respect is something no one else can ever give me. I can only choose to walk bravely ahead, offering it as a gift to myself.

Isabelle draws the curtain, but I know she is still standing there, lurking. Hiding. Watching.

Let them watch.

With one final glance, I turn and walk away. The burden of the past lifting with each breath. The sunlight filters through the trees, casting golden patches on the ground. The future stretches out before me—open, wide and full of possibility.

Clover lets out a little sigh in her sleep, and I smile, pressing her closer. We are going to be okay. I know it now, deep in my bones.

I am a good mother.

EPILOGUE
AMELIA

Nine months later

Clover was born December 10, which means now, at her first birthday, there is a Christmas tree twinkling with lights in the cozy living room and two stockings hung. One for me, one for her.

It's crazy how fast your life can change.

A year ago, my whole world was buried in secrets and fear. Impending motherhood was my greatest worry. And I had so many other worries buried beneath that one.

I didn't think I could do it, didn't know *how* I would do it, and every bit of it felt like I was walking toward a collision course of my own making.

But now, I'm celebrating my daughter Clover's first birthday with the people who mean the most to us in the world.

Jack finds me in the kitchen, where I am frosting the cake. "It looks just perfect," he tells me with a grin.

"Thank you. I didn't know if the buttercream was going to set properly, but it's so pretty, right?"

"It's beautiful. I'm so glad you've been baking again."

"Me too," I say, smiling up at him. I'm wearing a linen apron around my waist, my hair in a long braid down my back. I finally feel like myself again. Those frazzled early months of motherhood where I was just barely hanging on by a thread, wracked with impending dread that I was going to do the wrong thing, have vanished and been replaced with more steady steps.

Sure, I don't know what this next year is going to entail. Clover has just started walking. A few teeth have come in. She likes to bang her fists on the high-chair table. And while she doesn't wake up in the middle of the night anymore, her 5 a.m. alarm clock is consistently getting me up earlier than I like.

However, we're figuring it out together.

Clover toddles toward Jack, reaching for him, a smile on her face. She wears a pair of ballet flats and stomps her feet on the floor, her fingers now tightly gripping around his hand.

"Mama," she says, and we laugh. It's her only word, and I admit that I will never get sick of hearing it.

"When is everyone getting here?" he asks. He leads Clover into the corner of the living room where her toys are. She sits down, reaching for a stack of blocks, and they begin building a tower. Instantly, Clover happily knocks it all over.

The apartment is a blessing. Seattle should have been out of my price range, but Cal, my former boss, has taken pity on me. I am living in the attic apartment above his garage. It is one bedroom with a cute kitchen and living room, more than enough for what we need.

"I think any minute," I say as I finish the last edge of piping on the cake. The food is ready, the table set.

Earlier today Jack came over to help me make a pot of black bean soup and cornbread, a simple but comforting meal for a winter day. It's an intimate birthday party, with the people we are closest to. I know some people like to go over the top for things like this, but I want a happy celebration in my own home with the people Clover and I love most.

On that note, there is a knock on the door, and I walk from the kitchen to answer it. It's Tabitha and Johnny and her husband, Keith.

"Oh my gosh. I'm so glad you guys were able to make it!" I exclaim. "Was the drive full of traffic?"

"It wasn't bad at all," Keith tells me.

Tabitha gives me a big hug. "Look at you," I say, taking her in. While Keith and Tabitha weren't sure about what they were going to do in terms of staying on Cutter's Island or not, last year, when Johnny was only four months old, Tabitha told Keith under no uncertain terms she was not going back to work anytime soon. She was pregnant again. It was unexpected, but maybe the biggest blessing that could've ever happened to them.

Keith, though reluctant to sell their home on Cutter's Island, decided it was the best thing for their family, and they moved off the island to a small town about an hour away, not too far from where I grew up in Bellport, actually.

They were able to get a larger home with a big plot of land, and Tabitha's able to stay at home with Johnny, which was her unexpected dream. Now, she is very pregnant, and they all seem like they're at peace. Keith still works from home, and they live closer to his family. And while it's not what they imagined their life would be before Johnny was born, it seems like they're in the right place for them.

I miss her, of course. Our early-morning coffee walks and those afternoons when we got takeout and could binge-watch reality TV. But we still make time for them every so often. It can be hard with my shifts at the bakery—especially since it is mostly Cal and Jack who help with Clover. But it does make our time more intentional.

Now, I give her a big squeeze. "You're glowing," I say.

She laughs. "Okay, we can call it that, but I think I'm just sweaty and tired. It was a long trek."

Keith sets Johnny down on the ground. He starts crawling down the hall as if he can sense where Clover is.

I hear Jack in the other room excitedly say his name. "Johnny," he says. "You're here. Look at you, big guy."

"So, how are things with Jack?" Tabitha asks as Keith takes her coat and hangs it on the wall rack by the door.

"Me and Jack?" I laugh. "We are great *friends*," I emphasize. I am not in a place to date—I am still healing from the loss of so much. Right now, I am focused on being a healthy mom for Clover.

Before the conversation with Tabitha and Keith can continue, there is another knock at the door and Cal is here, with gifts and bottles of wine to share. I give him a big hug, grateful for the family I have found. For the people who have stuck by me when I was at my lowest, with nothing to my name besides my precious daughter. The Sterlings never fought for Clover—turns out they want to pretend we were a short blip that is erased from their family history.

Later, when we gather around the kitchen table in this house I've made a home, we light the candles and sing happy birthday to Clover, who has no idea why she's getting all of this attention.

But it feels like every one of my dreams has come true. I have a family. I have nothing to hide, and I'm loved for who I am, not for who someone might want me to be. Not loved because of the way I could be used by someone else.

When we finish singing the birthday song, someone calls out, "Make a wish."

And of course, Clover doesn't understand that either, but I do.

I close my eyes and I hold my breath, and I make a wish for my little girl.

I wish to be a good mother.

A LETTER FROM ANYA

Thank you so much for reading *Good Bad Mother*. I love writing books about mothers championing their children and doing anything in their power to protect them. As a mom of six children, I have spent plenty of time wondering if I am a good mother or a bad one. I hope for more good days than bad!

While the challenges I have faced are not as extraordinary as Amelia's, I do my best to put my heart and life experience into my characters. If the story resonates with you, please click the following link. Now you will always be up to date on my new releases!

www.bookouture.com/anya-mora

Don't hesitate to leave a review for *Good Bad Mother*—your support means the world!

With gratitude,

Anya Mora

anyamora.com

instagram.com/anya_mora_
facebook.com/AnyaMoraThrillerAuthor

PUBLISHING TEAM

Turning a manuscript into a book requires the efforts of many people. The publishing team at Bookouture would like to acknowledge everyone who contributed to this publication.

Audio
Alba Proko
Melissa Tran
Sinead O'Connor

Commercial
Lauren Morrissette
Hannah Richmond
Imogen Allport

Cover design
The Brewster Project

Data and analysis
Mark Alder
Mohamed Bussuri

Editorial
Jess Whitlum-Cooper
Imogen Allport

Copyeditor
Ian Hodder

Proofreader
Nicky Gyopari

Marketing
Alex Crow
Melanie Price
Occy Carr
Cíara Rosney
Martyna Młynarska

Operations and distribution
Marina Valles
Stephanie Straub
Joe Morris

Production
Hannah Snetsinger
Mandy Kullar
Jen Shannon
Ria Clare

Publicity
Kim Nash
Noelle Holten
Jess Readett
Sarah Hardy

Rights and contracts
Peta Nightingale
Richard King
Saidah Graham

Made in the USA
Columbia, SC
28 February 2025